What the critics are saying

"I loved this book! Three incredible stories by three talented authors. Overrunning with spicy sex scenes and hot bondage, this book is a must buy for erotic and bondage lovers alike. You'll enjoy what each story contributes and will leave you wanting more from the talented trio of authors. If you love your stories intense and the sex hot, pick up Party Favors." – *Angel Brewer, The Romance Studio*

"Party Favors has three very talented writers pulling their talent together to make this an unforgettable anthology. Each story can stand on its own merits. I couldn't find a favorite as I loved them all. There is some bondage and the sex sizzles. This book will make any erotic reader happy. Don't pass it up!" – *Patricia McGrew, Sensual Romance Reviews*

PARTY FAVORS
An Ellora's Cave publication, 2003

Ellora's Cave Publishing, Inc.
PO Box 787
Hudson, OH 44236-0787

ISBN # 1843606542

ISBN MS Reader (LIT) ISBN # 1-84360-649-6
Other available formats (no ISBNs are assigned):
Adobe (PDF), Rocketbook (RB), Mobipocket (PRC) & HTML

DANCING IN THE DARK edited by Martha Punches.
TRICK OR TREAT edited by Sheri Ross Carucci.
LOUISANA HEAT edited by Kari Berton.
Cover art by Darrell King.

PARTY FAVORS

Dancing In the Dark

by Jennifer Dunne

Trick or Treat

by Madeleine Oh

Louisiana Heat

by Dominique Adair

DANCING IN THE DARK

Jennifer Dunne

CHAPTER ONE

Keri Montero clicked on the television remote and sat down on the couch to leaf through her mail while she waited for tonight's rerun of *Charmed* to begin. It was one of the episodes with Cole.

The darkly powerful demon transformed by love made her weak in the knees. Even though she had every episode from his three seasons on tape, she still watched the reruns. Knowing that women across the country were sighing and swooning over the same man at the same time made her feel less alone in the empty apartment. And she was still trying to place the accent of Julian McMahon, the Australian actor who played Cole. It changed throughout his three years on the show, from a strangely delivered but undeniably American accent to something indefinable yet incredibly sexy. The closest she'd come to identifying it was that it sounded vaguely French Canadian.

A black envelope with gold lettering drew her attention away from thoughts of hunky half-demons. It was the size of a greeting card, made of heavy, high-quality paper. Wherever it was from, it hadn't come from Hallmark.

There was no name on the return address, just an address, somewhere in the newly renovated arts plaza. She volunteered as an usher at the theatre once or twice a month, allowing her to attend operas and concerts for free. Maybe it was something connected with that?

Slowly, she slid her finger beneath the loosely glued flap and pried the envelope open, prolonging the suspense. Nothing unusual ever happened in her neat and orderly life, and she was strangely reluctant to end the mystery. But finally, the envelope parted, and she pulled out the invitation tucked inside.

"I'm invited to a Halloween costume party to benefit the opera? They must have confused the names of the volunteers with the names of the donors." She glanced at the price tag for the evening. $100 per person. These definitely hadn't been meant for the volunteers.

She watched the good-natured squabbling of the sisters on the television, but their witty dialogue no longer captivated her. Instead, her thoughts turned to the invitation. Should she go?

Cost wasn't an issue. She could afford the ticket. She volunteered as an usher because it was the most efficient solution, helping the theatre and other theatre patrons at the same time as it allowed her to see the performances.

A car salesman shouted from the screen, bragging about the huge discounts his stores offered. First commercial break. Unthinkingly, Keri stood up and walked into the kitchen to put a frozen dinner in the microwave.

She stopped, staring at the box in her hand. "What am I doing?"

Her nights all fell into the same routine, if she wasn't volunteering or working on an urgent project she'd brought home from the office. Read the mail while watching *Charmed*. At the first commercial break, heat up a dinner. Eat dinner and watch the rest of the show, cleaning up at the second commercial break. At the third commercial break, write checks for any bills that came in the mail, discard junk mail, and otherwise handle all incoming papers. When the show was over, turn off the TV and head to her craft room to work on her latest quilt. Efficient. Predictable. Boring.

She tossed the box in the microwave and gave it three minutes on high, while she retrieved silverware and a plate. Regardless of her sudden dissatisfaction, she still needed to eat.

As she settled back down in front of the television, her mind continued to worry at the problem of the opera party. Normally, she avoided parties. She'd never Mastered the polite chitchat and small talk required for social mingling. It all seemed so pointless. No one really cared about the weather, or the traffic, or any of the other things people discussed at these events. Why, then, did they spend so much time and effort conversing on these subjects? It was one of those things she'd just never understood.

She wasn't shy, and she was perfectly capable of holding her own in a discussion on any number of a wide variety of topics, from the latest in network security protocols to the intricacies of creating a double wedding ring quilt. As the team leader for her group of consultants, she'd led plenty of meetings over the years, both internally and with customers. Efficient, well-run meetings that accomplished more than any of her peers, which was reflected in her high contract closure rate.

The problem was that she just couldn't grasp the subtleties of the social roles. They'd moved frequently when she was growing up, following her father from job to job. As a freelance efficiency expert, he never spent more than two years in the same place. No sooner had she learned the complex rules governing social interactions at one school, than she was thrust into another school where those rules didn't apply at all. The other children ostracized her for her missteps, until she gave up trying to fit in with them, and focused on the student-teacher interaction that remained essentially the same from place to place.

Her parents approved of her good grades, which were high enough to get her a full scholarship to college. And she wasn't a complete loner. She had friends, gregarious people, who made the first move and approached her.

She'd even had a boyfriend at college, who'd been determined to thaw her ice princess reputation. The reputation mystified her. She wasn't frigid. She just didn't like wasting her time. Brian seemed to understand her feelings, because he hadn't wasted any time before getting her into bed. They were together for three years, but both knew it would end when they graduated.

With her grades, she easily found a job as a well-paid computer consultant, where the analytical skills she'd learned at her father's knee were highly prized. She understood her role. She fit in. So why the sudden feeling of discontent?

She reread the invitation. "Live a legend. Come dressed as your favorite character from any opera."

If she went to a party as a character from an opera, she didn't have to make pointless chitchat or wonder what the correct social niceties were. It wouldn't be her attending the party, it would be the character.

Keri smiled, picturing herself as the Merry Widow throwing one of her famous masquerades. Or perhaps Carmen, enticing all the soldiers present. They had well-defined, thoroughly understood roles. She could follow their social rules for an evening, and enjoy herself with no risk.

But which was her favorite? What part did she want to play?

She cleaned up her dinner according to schedule, reviewing all the parts she knew. She quickly discarded the ingenues. They simply looked beautiful and waited for someone to rescue them. They'd be no fun at a party.

Someone like Carmen, on the other hand, would be tons of fun at a party. Perhaps too much fun. Did she really want to spend an entire evening doing nothing but teasing and flirting? She'd be exhausted by the time the party ended.

No, what she needed was a role that was similar to her own personality. Something that would allow her to be herself, yet give her the security of an external endorsement of her behavior.

That was harder. They didn't write operas about computer consultants.

She needed to think outside the box. Not the lead roles, but supporting characters, ones who were similar to her. She laughed. The stereotypical spear-carrier, that was her. Marching straightforwardly from one side of the stage to the other, in the most efficient and expedient manner, speaking to the leads only when spoken to.

Spear-carriers tended to be male, though. Keri vaguely recalled an opera with Amazon women warriors—maybe Aida? But she didn't want to be an Amazon. She wanted to be soft and feminine. Like…Images of opera scenes flipped through her mind's eye, one after another, too quickly for her to get more than a quick impression. She could almost sense the unifying thread. Almost.

The common character burst into her awareness. A slave girl.

Perfect! A warm glow of contentment settled in her stomach, as if she'd just eaten a big bowl of cinnamon-sugar oatmeal. As a slave, she couldn't possibly make any social errors. She'd just be doing what she'd been told to do. Complete freedom.

Ignoring her usual habit, Keri didn't wait for the show to end before unpacking her laptop and connecting to the Internet. She needed to find a costume, and order it to arrive before Halloween.

She quickly disregarded the usual Halloween slave girl costumes. They'd be fine for a house party, but not if she was planning on donating it to the opera after the event, as the invitation discreetly suggested. She needed an authentic stage costume.

Finally, she found one. There was no picture, but the description sounded promising. "Authentic female slave costume. Silver colored chains, belt, and halter. Pale blue harem pants/skirt of washable gauze."

She blinked at the price. The costume cost more than the ticket. But that made her realize it must be authentic. She knew that stage costumes were terribly expensive, which is why they were designed to be easily altered to fit a wide variety of sizes. And why the always-short-on-money opera company was hoping to pick up some free costumes from this party.

She clicked the appropriate buttons to purchase the costume and typed in her credit card information. An entire evening of partying with the A-list of the city, without having to worry about any of the rules of social mingling. It was worth the money.

* * * * *

Keri's heavy laptop case swung in front of her body, getting in the way as she struggled to pull the stack of mail out of her box. She hitched the strap firmly over her shoulder, twisting her upper body so that the padded case thumped into her back. From experience, she knew she'd have about fifteen seconds to finish retrieving the mail before the awkward case overbalanced in some other direction.

The piece of yellow card stock that had wedged itself into one of the box's metal seams finally ripped free, and Keri staggered backward, bumping into the mailboxes lining the opposite wall of the vestibule.

"Ow." She slammed her mailbox closed with more vehemence than was necessary. Then she realized what she was holding. She had a package.

Finally! The Halloween party was tomorrow night, and her costume had yet to arrive. She'd worried that she wouldn't be able to go to the party after all. There was no point in attending if she couldn't dress as a slave girl. Her normal social shyness would keep her hidden in a corner, and fumbling for words on the few occasions she ventured out into the crowd. And she refused to wear some cheap nylon and spandex Halloween costume from the nearest party store, not to a party where some of the guests would be wearing outfits that cost thousands of dollars.

She unlocked the inner door and turned to the supervisor's apartment. One of his duties was accepting all packages for building residents. A trim, energetic man in his mid-40's, he traded his maintenance skills for a rent-free apartment and workshop, spending his off-hours on the scale reconstructions of steam trains that he crafted and sold. Instead of aftershave or cologne, he always smelled of metal filings and solder.

Dave answered his doorbell immediately, still stuffing the rag he'd wiped his hands on back into his jeans.

"Keri. I was expecting you. I've got your package."

A standard shipping box sat on his kitchen table, surrounded by tiny pieces of cast metal, delicate rasps, and a large magnifying glass on a stand. He waved her inside the apartment as he got the box for her.

It was smaller than she expected, not much larger than the box her Nikes had come in. But when she took it from him, the box was reassuringly heavy.

"Thanks, Dave. I was waiting for this."

"Costume supply, huh? Going to a Halloween party this year?"

Keri smiled, thinking of her plans. "Yes. At the Opera."

The supervisor raised an eyebrow. "Mingling with the jet-set, now? What, did you win the lottery and forget to give me my share of the winnings?"

She laughed. "Just my reward for being an unpaid usher the rest of the year."

"Well you have fun, kiddo. You deserve it."

Her smile faltered. The conversation was heading into personal territory not defined by the tenant/supervisor dynamic she understood. As if realizing his comment had made her uneasy, Dave broke the tension with his normal affability. "Smuggle some hors d'oeuvres out in your napkin for me, okay? I can't sit through hours of people yowling in some language I don't understand, but they always put on a great spread."

Keri blinked. "You've been to the opera? I never saw you."

"You couldn't have missed us. Twenty old guys wearing engineer's caps."

She laughed, remembering her fellow ushers' horror at the group of men who'd worn *baseball caps* to the *opera*. "I wasn't volunteering that night. But why'd the train society go to the opera?"

"It was a mix-up. We were supposed to be seeing a traveling production of Starlight Express." He hesitated, then obviously feeling he should say something nice about the opera that she donated so much of her time to, he added, "The show wasn't bad, for something that had no trains in it."

"And the food was great, right?"

"Right! Remember, bring me back some hors d'oeuvres."

"I don't think the costume has pockets."

"Too bad. Eat some for me, then."

Still chuckling, Keri headed up to her apartment to open the package. But when she slit open the shipping tape and looked inside, her eyes widened with horror. This was no stage costume.

A printed flyer lay on top of a pile of folded blue gauze. It featured three eye-popping photos illustrating how the outfit could be worn.

"Authentic slave costume," she read. "Designed to cater to all styles of slaves, whether your desires are for submission, bondage, or discipline."

The first photograph showed a woman wearing blue gauze harem pants with a calf-length gauze overskirt, also in blue. The interlocking rings of a chain mail bikini glinted beneath the overlapping layers of gauze, and the metal disks covering her nipples were clearly visible beneath her halter top of twisted blue gauze. Her head was bent subserviently, and her arms were extended in supplication. Bold red letters beneath the photo proclaimed "Submission".

The second photo, labeled "Bondage", showed the same woman, standing on tiptoe with her arms stretched above her head. The gauze had been wrapped tightly around her legs and chest until she looked like a mummy, but from her expression, she clearly enjoyed being rolled up like a carpet. Keri's nipples tightened in sympathy.

Almost afraid to see what the final picture showed, she turned her attention to the image labeled "Discipline." The woman knelt on her hands and knees on the floor, at an angle to the camera. She wore no overskirt or halter top. The gauze panels that formed her harem pants were bunched at her hips, exposing the pale skin of her ass, bisected by the thin silver chain of her thong. A reddened handprint was clearly visible on one ass cheek. Her breasts hung down, a second chain connecting the disks clipped to her nipples. Just visible in the picture, a man's hand tugged lightly on the chain. The woman's head was thrown back, an expression of wild ecstasy transforming her features.

Keri's breath came quickly, embarrassment heating her cheeks and flooding over her tingling breasts to pool in her stomach. No, below her stomach. And it wasn't embarrassment.

Desire pulsed between her legs. Oh, God. These pictures were turning her on. She wanted to be that woman. She wanted to be the slave girl whose nipples were tugged upon until her breasts were hot and swollen. She wanted her ass slapped until her Master pushed apart the tender flesh and thrust his cock inside her, making her subjugation complete.

She opened the flyer, eagerly reading the instructions for how to assemble and wear the costume. She could wear the Submission design to the Halloween party at the opera. It covered enough to be considered acceptable, if somewhat daring, clothing. If she wore a mask, so that no one recognized her, she could have a fantastic time playing the part of a slave girl for the evening.

But tonight, she wanted to wear the Discipline costume. She had no Master to whip her into a frenzy, but she could pretend.

She emptied the contents of the box onto the table. The two panels of blue gauze, four feet long by three feet wide, with an open hem on one narrow side, looked like nothing so much as sheer curtains. A second set of shorter panels were only three feet long. The final gauze panel was only two feet wide, but was five feet long. In addition to the fabric, there were lengths of fine gauge steel chain, the serpentined metal broken by half-inch loops at odd intervals. Some of the chains ended in sturdy lobster-claw clasps, which no doubt attached to the loops in patterns that the instruction manual would describe. She recognized the piece of steel mesh in the shape of a thin rectangle coming to a point at the end as the front of the panty visible beneath the Submissive model's harem pants.

The final item had appeared in none of the photos that she could see. It consisted of two six-inch bars joined by five toggle closures. She flipped it over to check the reverse side, and saw a series of thin metal rods running the length of the bars. The central rod slid from left to right, with a small switch to lock it in position.

She frowned, wondering what it could be, and puzzled by a nagging sense of familiarity. Glancing at the instructions, she ran her finger down the list of contents until she reached the name, "Halter clasp." Suddenly she recognized the familiar positioning of the rods. She had adjustable belts like this, whose buckle could be repositioned anywhere along their length simply by releasing the tension rods, passing a loop of the belt through, then locking the tension rods in the new location. The ends of the long, narrow strip of gauze must run through the bars, then get locked in place when it was at the right length.

Flipping the pages in the instruction booklet, she found the Discipline instructions, and assembled the pieces she needed. The six-foot chain with the ring a third of the way down its length, three six-inch chains, and one two-foot chain. Apparently, she had a choice for the medium length chain between a smooth one and a heavier one with an additional ring part way down its length.

She checked the notes below the instructions, hoping for guidance. "The crotch chain comes in two varieties—a narrow gauge for maximum penetration, and one designed to hold a dildo fully inserted during play."

A rush of heat pooled between her legs, and her mouth went dry. Oh, God. A dildo. She'd never owned one, but suddenly she wanted one. She imagined it shoved all the way, deep into her vagina, held tight by the chains as her muscles contracted around it, every slap of her Master's hand on her ass driving her against it.

She moaned softly. And what if it wasn't her Master's hand, but his cock, pounding into her ass, while she was already filled with the hard length of the dildo? How good would that feel?

She was definitely going to buy a dildo. But for now, she'd use the fine-gauge chain.

"Maximum penetration," she whispered. The words alone made her hot. When she imagined the chain sawing against her clit, sliding between her folds and pressing deeply, she shivered with anticipation.

The long panels of gauze were threaded onto the waist chain, one on either side of the ring, with plenty of chain left over. The lobster clasp on the crotch chain snapped onto the ring, hanging down between the panels. It was starting to look like the picture. Keri's ass tightened, eager to feel the weight of the chains.

She stripped off her work clothes, standing naked in her living room, and picked up the costume. Centering the ring on the back of her waist, the crotch chain hung down the cleft of her ass. It was cold, and heavy, and completely alien. Her vision swam with the delicious sensation, knowing it was just the beginning of the erotic invasion of her body.

The waist chain crossed in front of her then the long end wrapped completely around her waist a second time. The instructions implied the two ends of the chain could be attached at either the front or back, depending on the waistline of the slave, and which of the small rings you affixed the lobster clasp to. A sizable length of chain could be left over, if desired, and used during play.

Keri wondered how. Would the Master beat the slave with it? Tow the slave around on a leash? Run it up to the chain hanging between the breasts and keep a constant pressure on them?

She groaned, imagining that. Now her nipples ached, begging to be tugged and squeezed, while the hot flesh between her legs pulsed in needy demand.

Clipping the ends of the waist chain in front of her, she let the weight settle on her hips. She adjusted the gauze panels so that the ends met beneath her belly button, then gathered the panels so that they clustered over her hips, exposing her ass and her pubic hair.

She reached between her legs and grabbed the dangling end of the crotch chain. Slowly, she pulled it up until it touched her skin. Reaching one hand between her legs, she spread her labia, her fingers sliding over the slick flesh, and pulled the crotch chain until it slipped between the spread folds.

A pulse of pleasure throbbed through her, and she moaned, tightening the chain. She felt the pressure on her hips as it pulled down on the waist chain, taking the little bit of slack she'd left. The waist chain pulled taut, and still she tightened the crotch chain. It dug into the cleft of her ass, pressing against her anus. Her muscles tightened in instinctive response, forcing the chain to bite deeper. She thought she was going to come right then from the pleasure.

Barely able to see what she was doing, she passed the end of the crotch chain around the strands of the waist chain in front of her and clipped it in place.

Experimenting, she bent down in a squat and stood again. The chain stroked her deeply, slick with lubrication and tantalizingly cool. She whimpered. Unable to stop herself, she bent and straightened again and again, until the chain burned her sensitive flesh and she wanted to beg for release. But there was no one to beg. No one was forcing her to endure this relentless torture, and no one could free her from the teasing strokes by plunging deeply inside her.

Grabbing the edge of her counter, she stood completely still, panting for control, until the frenzied need faded.

"What's next?" she whispered.

The loose panels became harem pants by rolling the bottom edge around a short length of chain until they were the right length, then clipping the chain closed around her ankle. She very carefully lowered herself to the floor to do this, gasping when the crotch chain rasped across her swollen clitoris. But soon the "pants" were tied around her ankles.

Now she needed to attach the clips to her breasts. The backs of the silver disks were hinged, hiding a keyhole-shaped piece of brass wire.

The wires slid around her nipples, the narrow sections pinching the nipples and making them erect so that the rounded sections would cling to them. The slight pressure was just enough to keep her nipples tight.

Closing the hinges, she gasped as the disks tweaked the tips of her nipples. The small chain clipped on brass rings soldered to the back of the disks. The added weight tugged on her nipples, a flash of fire that connected straight to the smoldering crotch chain.

She walked—slowly, as each step rubbed the crotch chain between her labia and over her clitoris—into her bedroom, and faced the full-length mirror. She didn't recognize herself.

The woman in the mirror radiated sex, from her high, pointed breasts swaying as she moved, to the visibly swollen labia showing deep pink between her widespread legs. Her face was flushed with passion, her eyes glazed and somewhat wild, and her deep red lips parted to let harsh breaths escape.

Keri tugged lightly on the chain connecting her breasts. Fire blazed across her nipples. She tipped her head back and moaned, tugging the chain again, then again.

Her world faded in a red haze. Somehow, she staggered back onto the bed, falling upon it in an ungainly sprawl. She drew her legs up, spreading her knees and thighs wide, and flexed her hips in time to her tugs. The lace of her comforter chafed her ass while the crotch chain rasped up and down over her throbbing clit. She pumped harder, imagining the stroke of her Master's hands.

Sliding one hand down the slippery chain, she slipped her fingers past the teasing metal, deep into her vagina. Her muscles contracted around her fingers, and she yanked the breast chain. The climax overwhelmed her, arching her body up off the bed in a trembling bow for what felt like hours of agony as she teetered on the precipice. Then she fell.

A hoarse scream of triumph ripped from her throat. She collapsed onto the bed, too weak to move, glowing aftershocks pulsing through her body. One thought kept playing over and over in her head. If it was this good when she was alone, how much better would it be if she had a partner?

CHAPTER TWO

The next evening, Keri flicked on the television as soon as she got home. She needed the reassurance of her *Charmed* fix after the day she'd had.

They'd finished the bid for the Uninational account, and were going over presentation strategies for the Monday meeting, when she got the news that the lead on the competition's bid team had changed. They'd put Andy Thibodeau in charge.

Her team had immediately gone into scramble mode. Thibodeau was a shark, infamous for his ability to destroy his competition's bid proposals with a few well-placed questions. Their bid proposal had already been solid. But with Thibodeau across the table from them, they needed to make their case airtight.

She'd assigned two of her team to scrutinize the competition's initial bid, searching for weaknesses Thibodeau's team might not have solved in their final bid, or areas where their solution used back-level technology compared to her team's solution. Meanwhile, she'd reviewed all of their competitor's proposed efficiencies.

The first time she'd suggested the strategy of analyzing efficiencies, as a junior consultant working her first bid proposal, the team leader had thought she was crazy. He couldn't imagine why she'd want to highlight the opposition's benefits. She'd run the analysis anyway, doing it on overtime so it wouldn't impact the work her team leader had assigned. When her analysis tipped the scales during the presentation meeting, she'd instantly won a convert.

Other consultants had tried to copy her strategy of spiking the opponent's efficiencies, but they'd never equaled her success. It wasn't surprising. She had an innate understanding of efficiency analysis that they could never grasp.

As a child, she'd fallen asleep to her father reading aloud from his efficiency reports. Combining his quality time with his daughter and the overtime reading he needed to do for work was, of course, the most efficient solution. But one of the truisms she'd quickly learned was that efficiency did not exist in a vacuum. Efficiencies, whether of time, money, or resources, were gained by sacrificing something else. It might be individual power and control, process flexibility, or something as simple as never learning any fairy tales until you were in junior high school. The trick was to give up something you didn't particularly care about, to increase the efficiencies in an area you did care about.

When she reviewed competitors' bids, Keri found that the underlying compromises of the efficiencies jumped out at her. She could tell at a glance what they'd be sacrificing in order to implement their proposed savings. Using the value charts her team drew up for their own proposal, she could make a grid of all the ways that their solution enhanced values that the competitors' solution compromised in the name of "efficiency."

With a little careful questioning during the presentations, she could find out which of those values meant the most to the customer, then play up how their competitor's solution would sacrifice those very things the customer valued most. Invariably, the customer asked the competitor if their solution could be modified so those values wouldn't be sacrificed, at which point the competitor would have to admit to the loss of efficiency. If they didn't admit to it, Keri would ask clarifying questions until it was obvious to the customer.

She was rapidly developing as feared a reputation as Thibodeau's, and she'd looked forward to someday matching her skills against his. But she'd hoped to have more than one day of warning before she was called upon to do so!

Realizing she was working herself into a totally unproductive tizzy, she sat on the couch and breathed deeply, allowing Julian McMahon's resonant voice to wash over her as Cole lectured Phoebe on the dedication needed to fight demons.

Oh, that man looked good shirtless and sweaty. Keri swallowed, her eyes tracking his broad chest and skintight black pants. She wouldn't mind a little hand-to-hand training from a dark demon like him.

Her thoughts skipped to the costume waiting for her in the bedroom, the costume she'd be wearing to the opera party in a little over an hour. Her imagination was a little vague on exactly what other sorts of training a slave might receive, but her blood hummed with the possibility.

Unable to sit still in front of the television, Keri abandoned any attempt to pay attention to the episode, now filled with "Crouching Tiger, Hidden Dragon" style martial arts fighting, and hurried into the bedroom to dress for her party.

The Submission outfit started out similarly to the Discipline outfit, with the gauze panels on either side, but they stayed spread out, their edges meeting at the front and back. The two shorter panels were then threaded on to the long section of the waist chain, with their edges meeting at the sides, so that none of her skin was exposed. She rolled up the bottoms of the longer panels around the small chains which she fastened around her ankles, and studied the effect in the mirror.

To the casual observer, she was wearing harem pants, with a slit skirt over them. No one would know that the "pants" left her inner thighs and crotch bare, but every step she took would remind her of her secret nudity.

The crotch chain was attached similarly to how she'd attached it last night, but looser. Instead of sliding between her vulva and pressing against her clit, it hung just below her skin, teasing her with swaying metal caresses as she moved. After all, the party was supposed to run for at least three hours. She'd never make it if her clothing got her so hot she started climaxing in the first fifteen minutes.

A new addition was the chain-link modesty panel that covered the crotch chain in front. A tiny hook at the tip linked it to the crotch chain and the wider part simply folded over one of the inner loops of the waist chain. The weight of the mesh kept it in place.

Keri moaned softly when she attached the nipple clips. The firm embrace of the wire tightened her nipples into hard nubs, aching to be tugged and squeezed. The Submission outfit called for a gauze halter to be wrapped over her breasts, allowing the silvery disks covering her nipples to peak through. But she wanted more than just the occasional brush of gauze to arouse her sensitive breasts.

Opening the box her costume had come in, she found the short chain from the Discipline style, and clipped it to the disks. The added weight tugged gently at her swollen nipples. Keri groaned softly and tugged the chain twice, sending flames leaping from the tip of her breasts to her clit.

She pulled her hand away, torturing herself by not continuing the exquisite torment. Instead, she pleated the remaining gauze panel and threaded the ends through the bar clasp, locking it in place when the panel had been shortened to the correct length. She wrapped the halter around her neck, crossed the gauze between her breasts with a twist, then pulled it behind her. After a moment of awkward fumbling, she managed to link the two sides of the clasp together.

It felt like she had a bar of metal soldered to her spine, it was pressed so tightly. The gauze hugged her breasts, and pushed against the metal disks covering her nipples. She undulated, in a faux belly dance, and moaned with the pleasure. It felt like a lover cupped her breasts in his hands, kneading them gently as she moved.

She should probably avoid the dance floor at the party.

The last part of her costume was an addition she'd picked up on her way home from work. A large white, beaded domino mask covered most of her face. It allowed her to wear her slave costume in public without worrying about who would recognize her, and how she'd react the next time she saw them, back in her normal role.

Tonight, she was a slave girl. Keri had even thought up a story for her slave persona. Her Master had instructed her to go to the party, and treat it as an auction block, displaying her wares so that he could sell her to a new Master. This assured that she would mingle with the maximum number of men, without worrying about how to act. If any of the men rebuffed her, it only meant they were not in the market for a slave, and she should simply move on to the next.

Checking her appearance one last time in the mirror, she reassured herself that no one who knew her would recognize her. She barely recognized herself.

She slipped on a thin pair of ballet slippers, then pulled on a beige full-length raincoat. It was nothing distinctive, nothing that other guests at the party might recognize as hers. Fortunately the nights were still warm enough that she did not need to wear her wool coat—the brilliant eggplant would give her away to the other ushers immediately.

Knowing she wouldn't be able to carry a purse once she arrived at the party, she dumped out her pocketbook and removed her apartment key and cab fare. They went in the coat's concealed inner pocket, where they'd be safe until the party was over. She retrieved her invitation from the magnets that had held it to her refrigerator door and slid it deep into the coat's side pocket, then checked to make sure it couldn't accidentally fall out.

Ready at last, she hesitated in front of the television, remote in hand. Was she really doing the right thing? Maybe she should be reviewing the proposal again, before facing Thibodeau on Monday, rather than wasting her time at a party.

Her eyes focused on the screen, watching Cole tease Phoebe by pretending to mistake her kiss for her sister's. As if echoing Keri's thoughts, Phoebe asked what element of their training they were going to work on next. He answered that he wanted to take her on a picnic, instead.

"That's right," Keri said. "You can't work all the time. You need to take breaks to rest and recuperate, or you lose your efficiency. Thanks for the reminder, Julian."

She clicked off the television and tossed the remote onto the coffee table. Belting her coat securely, she took a deep breath then left her apartment.

* * * * *

Keri accepted the claim check for her coat, sliding it into her halter-top. She felt the coat check attendant's eyes following her motion, his gaze riveted on the glittering silver disks just visible beneath the folds of blue gauze.

A proper slave, she undulated, shifting her breasts to "make certain the ticket wouldn't fall out." Her disks flashed and he sucked in a quick breath.

"Careful, ma'am. You don't want to come out of your costume."

She laughed breathily. "Yes I do. But not until after the party's over."

His gulp was clearly audible as she turned in a flurry of gauze and headed into the main hall. Swirling colors and fantastic shapes surrounded her. Many of the guests had chosen to wear traditional masquerade costumes that could be used for any opera's masquerade scenes. Headdresses in the shape of animals abounded. She spotted two horses, a swan, a peacock, and a glorious red and orange bird that was either a phoenix or a firebird. Other guests wore opulent robes, the diplomatic costumes for imaginary imperial courts, or military costumes full of glitter and brocade that had never been worn in any army. While most of the guests wore more than Keri, some wore less. A tall, toned woman carrying a rubber spear was strikingly dressed in an extremely revealing Amazon costume.

A tuxedoed waiter swept by with a silver tray containing three crystal champagne flutes. "Champagne, ma'am?" he offered.

"Yes, thank you." She took one of the flutes and sipped the sparkling vintage. It was deep and mellow with just a touch of sweetness, not the overly tart drink familiar to countless wedding attendees.

Turning in place, she allowed her gaze to sweep the party, searching for the first man to whom she would display her wares. A young officer dressed in blue and red stood near the wall, tripping himself on his cavalry sword whenever he moved. Keri smiled brilliantly and sashayed over to him.

"Greetings, sir," she purred, pulling back her shoulders to thrust her breasts at him. She swayed lightly from side to side, causing the chain links of her modesty panels to clink and rattle. The man's eyes widened as his gaze dropped first to her breasts, then to her crotch. He inhaled sharply.

"Good evening." He licked his lips, visibly struggling for composure. "I'm Don José, the soldier from Carmen. Who are you?"

"I am Adina, the slave girl." She winked conspiratorially. "I appear in many operas. I'm a very *popular* character."

"Yes, I can see why." He flushed, then blurted out, "So, are you having fun at the party?"

Keri hesitated a fraction of a second, then decided to stay in character. That was the whole point of dressing as a slave.

"Not as much fun as I could have," she answered.

The conversation stuttered through a few more awkward exchanges, but it was quickly clear to Keri that the young soldier would have no idea what to do with a slave, unlike the real Don José, who had known exactly what to do with Carmen. She needed to move on to her next prospect.

"It was lovely to meet you," she said. "I'll look you up if I'm ever in Carmen. But I'm on a mission from my Master, and must leave now."

Her next prospect was an older man in a gold- and jewel-encrusted purple turban, swathed in layers of purple, blue, and green robes. No sooner had Keri begun speaking to him than a woman wearing a matching outfit in shades of pink, red, and violet, appeared at the man's side, possessively laying her left hand on his shoulder. Keri couldn't miss the flash of light on the 3-carat diamond.

She dipped a curtsey to the woman, smiled at the man, and turned to find another prospect in the milling crowd.

Four prospects later, she was beginning to tire of the game. The teasing brushes of the crotch chain were making it difficult to concentrate, and she longed to find someone who would know how to treat a slave properly. But so far, none had been willing to play the role of her Master.

She smiled brilliantly at the man before her, laced into the skintight breeches and cutaway coat of a Victorian lord, and introduced herself again.

"Sir Edgar, from Lucia of Livermoor," he responded.

Keri nodded, and dipped a slight curtsey, flushing as the crotch chain stroked her. "A pleasure to meet you, my lord."

"So I see." He chuckled. "But that's nothing to the pleasure of getting to know me better."

"My lord?" She held her breath, hoping.

"Nothing's happening at this party. Why don't we slip away, and you can show me your dance of the seven veils in private."

She hesitated. It was all just pretend. But how far should she go in character?

"Come on," he urged, speaking to her chest instead of her face. "Once I'm out of this frog suit, I can show you a few moves of my own."

She was sure he could. But his eagerness to get her alone and out of her costume did not excite her. She felt vaguely panicked, and quickly reassured herself that there were plenty of people around to prevent him from getting violent when she refused.

"I've been ordered by my Master to stay at the party, and that is what I must do," she said, backing up half a step.

"Your Master, huh? How'd you like a new Master, genie? Let me rub your bottle, and you'll be happy to serve me."

Keri inched back another half step, bumping into someone who'd come up behind her. She spun around, half afraid that Sir Edgar had a partner who had moved to block her retreat.

The man facing her was tall, made even taller by a radiant sun mask of gold-colored metal, covering his entire head except for a cutaway block at the bottom exposing his mouth and chin. He'd coated the visible part of his face and throat with shimmering gold body paint, even his lips, so that he seemed made entirely of metal.

He put out his arm to steady her, parting his orange and gold robes and revealing a yellow silk shirt and pants that clung lovingly to his body. Keri's mouth went dry at the sheer masculine appeal of him.

His hand, even encased in a gilded leather glove, burned like the sun of his costume where it rested against her arm. She glanced up at his eyes, hidden behind slits in the mask, and mouthed, "Play along. Please."

She curled her fingers around the silk-clad iron of his biceps, and turned to look back at Sir Edgar. "I already have a Master who pleases me."

Sir Edgar glanced up and down the length of the sun god, measuring him, then snorted in disgust. "Tell your girlfriend not to be such a tease."

He turned and stalked into the crowd, aiming for one of the circulating waiters and another glass of champagne.

Keri smiled up at her savior and reluctantly released his arm. "Thanks. I'm Adina, the slave girl."

The sun god's golden lips twisted in a wry smile, and he lifted his hand to brush her cheek with the warm leather of his gloved finger. "I don't recall any operas where the slave wears a mask."

His voice was deep and resonant, with a hint of an accent in his vowels and the cadence of his words. Something melodic. Possibly French, or Spanish, or Gaelic.

Keri couldn't help herself. She closed her eyes and leaned into his touch, like a flower seeking the sunlight.

She felt his warmth along the length of her body, and knew he'd stepped closer. His thumb gently stroked her cheek, then traced the shape of her lips. Her lips opened on a soft sigh.

His other hand brushed her hip, his fingertips caressing her side and back as he followed the line of the waist chain. He ran his index finger down the length of her spine, dipping below the edge of the chain. Then he hooked his finger in the ring and tugged, pulling the crotch chain up between her legs.

She gasped, her eyes flying wide open. "What are you — ?"

He released and tightened his hold on the ring, tapping her clit and labia with the chain. Her words dissolved into a moan. "Would you like to dance?"

She blinked, fighting her way out of the sensual haze he'd surrounded her in. "What?"

"In case it's slipped your notice, we're at a very public party. Dancing is the only socially acceptable reason for me to put my arms around you." He gave another light tug on her chain. "And I very much want to have my arms around you."

"Me too."

He guided her to the wooden floor tiles laid down over the marble to make a dance floor. A string quartet in the corner played a graceful waltz, drowning out the babble of conversation from the rest of the milling and mingling guests.

He clasped her hand in a warm grip, and rested his other hand at the small of her back, where he could toy with her chain at his leisure. Gently, he pressed her body forward, until their hips brushed. She could feel the tip of his erection, hard and hot beneath the thin silk of his pants, brush her stomach, but the chain mesh of her modesty panel shielded her from his more intimate touch. Her free hand clutched his shoulder, bunching the silken layers of his cloak in her fingers as she tried to find a stable point of reference. Her senses were whirling out of control, and she feared she would collapse unless she hung on tightly.

Slowly, they began to move, swaying in time with the music. Pressed against him, she found her feet echoing his movements, circling the dance floor in a flawless box step.

A wave of heat washed over her cheeks, and she knew she must be blushing furiously. She ignored it. "I already told you, I'm Adina, the slave girl. Who are you?"

"I'm the sun god, Apollo. A Mozart creation, for either a lavishly costumed Apollo and Hyacinth, or from the masquerade in *Cosi Fan Tuite.*"

"You put quite a lot of thought into your costume."

"I put quite a lot of thought into everything I do."

"I'll bet. Your costume suits you."

"As does yours." His golden head bent closer, although he was careful to avoid hitting her with any of the wavy rays extending from the mask. "I've been watching you since you entered the party," he confessed.

"Really?" The thought sent a warm glow through her, that this godlike being had sought her out.

"Yes. But I was trying to figure out who your Master was. I hadn't realized you were unattached, or I'd have approached you much sooner."

"Why?" Her conversational skills were not at their best right now, since all she could think about was the man pressed against her, the heat of his body, the caress of his gloved hands, and the pulsing need flaring to life beneath his skilled touch.

"It's bad form for one Master to approach another Master's slave without permission."

That got through, startling her so that her dance steps faltered. She quickly recovered, once again matching her movements to his.

"You're a Master? A real one?"

"Yes. Aren't you a real slave?"

"No. I never…that is, I'd like to, but I didn't know how."

"It's easy. All you have to do is follow your Master's every instruction, and let him guide you to fulfilling your sensual potential."

"I could do that. If you were the Master."

"It just so happens, I'm in the market for a new slave."

"What happened to your old one? If you don't mind my asking." Keri blurted the apology out, realizing that her question could be considered prying, and not knowing what was allowed within the context of a Master/slave relationship.

"You must never fear asking a question," her new Master told her. "I may answer or not, as I wish, but I will never chastise you for asking."

He tugged rapidly on her chain, stroking her deeply with the crotch chain and rubbing it back and forth across her clit. Keri closed her eyes and sighed with pleasure. She wanted more, much more.

"You were right to ask my permission, though. A good slave always asks her Master for permission. And you see how good slaves are rewarded."

"Oh, yes, Master. I do. I want to be a very good slave."

"Then take your hand off my shoulder and slide it beneath my cloak. Let me feel your fingers caressing my back."

"As you will it, Master." Keri followed his orders, smoothing her palm over the silk, warmed from his body heat, that encased his muscled back. Her fingers played up and down his spine in long strokes, then feathered out over his shoulder blades.

"Nice," he whispered, pulling her chain in time to her leisurely caresses. "Very nice."

She lost all awareness of the string quartet, and of the other dancers surrounding them. Her world narrowed to the man before her, the heat of his body blazing forth, his muscled back bunching and relaxing beneath her touch, and the teasing chain stroking her labia and brushing her clit. And still they danced.

Warm liquid trickled down the inside of her thigh, and she gasped. "Master!"

"What is it?"

"I'm so ready for you, I'm leaking."

"And, of course, you're not wearing any panties."

"No."

"Well, then, we'll just have to take you somewhere that this won't be a problem."

"Where?" The swollen flesh of her labia pulsed with every beat of her heart, and she wriggled against the taut chain, trying to find relief. Her movement flexed her breasts against their constraining wrap, pressing the disks onto her nipples. Fire blazed through her, and she moaned.

"And when, Master? Soon? Please?"

He pulled away from her, releasing her hand so that he could turn and lead her from the dance floor. "We'll get our coats now. My apartment is only a short drive away."

She gave him her coat check ticket, and he claimed both their coats, dropping a five-dollar bill into the bowl for tips. He helped her into her beige raincoat, then tossed back his cloak to free his arms and shrugged into his camel-colored wool coat. The muted gold of the wool made it seem as if he had diffused the splendor of his costume, but been unable to completely conceal it.

They waited while one of the parking attendants retrieved his Magma Red Mercedes glass-topped convertible from Valet Parking. Without his teasing pulls on the chains of her costume, the arousal that had been building in her started to disperse. Instead of burning fire between her legs, an all-over restless itching consumed her.

Keri reached up and pulled off her mask, shaking her hair free then rubbing her eyes.

"Now that I'm respectably clothed, I don't mind who recognizes me."

Her sun god turned to respond, then froze in place. She wondered instantly if she'd done something wrong, if he found her looks less than pleasing.

When he finally spoke, his voice was barely more than a whisper. "You have lifted your first veil to reveal great beauty. I hope it is only the first of many enjoyable revelations tonight."

Keri blushed at his extravagant compliment. But it was too smooth and polished, as if it was a line he'd spoken many times before. Whatever had stopped him in his tracks, it hadn't been her great beauty.

His earlier admonition to ask any question she wanted gave her the courage to ask, "What about you? When are you removing your mask?"

"The seats and mirrors of my car are already adjusted, since I drove here in costume. I'd prefer not to waste time resetting them. And haven't you always dreamed of making love to a god?"

He reached over and stroked her cheek with his gloved fingers, caressing the faint line where her mask had rested. Her skin turned to molten flame beneath his soft touch, lava flowing through her veins to burn her face, her neck, her breasts.

Her head tilted back, offering herself to his onslaught. His ornate mask blocked out the bright lights from the marquee under which they waited, reflected lights sparkling from the gold plating on his wavy brilliants, but leaving his face in shadow. Then his gilded lips closed over hers, soft and warm as a kiss of sunshine.

His hand stroked gently from her cheek to her jaw line, then down the column of her throat. Then lower still. His fingers slipped inside the collar of her raincoat, gliding down her chest until the twisted gauze of her halter-top stopped them.

"I will be your god," he whispered. "And you will worship me."

He nipped her lower lip, just hard enough to startle her without hurting, at the same time as he tugged on the chain linking her breasts.

Her climax took her completely by surprise, bursting over her in a fireball of light and heat. He swallowed her startled cry, and wrapped one strong arm around her to steady her until she regained control of her body. She realized she was clutching the lapels of his coat, crushing the fine wool, while he continued nibbling and tasting her lips.

Sensing her return to awareness, he lifted his head and allowed air to invade the space between their bodies. The gold body paint on his lips and chin was smeared, with patches of dark red lip showing through.

"Yes, Master," she whispered. "I will."

CHAPTER THREE

The short ride to his apartment in the artists' section of the city passed in a haze. He ordered her to open her raincoat and spread her legs, and reached over to stroke the damp skin of her inner thigh or tug on her crotch chain whenever he didn't need two hands for driving. With her head tilted back, Keri could look out the glass roof up at the distant stars as her sun god fondled her.

She was moaning and writhing in her leather seat, paying attention only to his teasing caresses and the burning need that followed his touch, when the car suddenly became surrounded by darkness.

She blinked, shocked into awareness. "Where are we?"

"Private garage."

He opened his door, the Mercedes illuminating the doorsill for him. It was enough light for her to see that they were in the center stall of an old wooden carriage house, with room for three vehicles. Once he'd carefully maneuvered his large mask out of the car, he moved quickly, coming around to her side and opening the door for her.

Grateful for his steadying hand, she exited the car on trembling legs. Her body hummed with hot anticipation, so that she could hardly think of anything but getting their clothes off and feeling him inside her at last.

He stepped behind her to close the car door, then wrapped her in a tight embrace, the heat of his erection cradled in the cleft of her ass and one of his hands cupping the chain mail mesh of her mock panty. He lifted the gauze panel at the back of her costume, pushing aside the other panels to expose her ass. His cock slid up her cleft, only the thin crotch chain preventing her from completely engulfing his hot length.

His free arm encircled her chest, his fingers resting on the chain connecting her breasts.

"I want you," he whispered, the gloved fingers of his other hand slipping past her slack crotch chain to slide between her wet folds.

She moaned, closing her eyes and leaning back against him, her knees flexing to lower her further onto his sweet caress. He moved with her, rubbing his cock against the chain on her ass, then forcing his way past it to stroke his cock against her bare skin.

They groaned in unison.

"I want to take you now, spread you on the hood of my car and feast on your delights until we're both ready to die from the pleasure."

His fingers stroked deep within her, burning her with a fire that brought shivering ecstasy in its wake. She whimpered, writhing against his hand, feeling his cock hot and solid behind her. It was good, so good, but it could be so much better.

"Yes, Master. Whatever you want."

"My sweet slave. You deserve better for your first time."

He took a deep breath, and gave her one last deep caress, then withdrew his fingers. A moment later, he stepped away from her, depriving her of his warmth. She staggered, and nearly fell.

His arm came around her again, holding her steady without a hint of sexuality. "Come on. My apartment is on the second floor."

She followed her sun god to an enclosed walk connecting the carriage house and the main building. He unlocked the outside door to the building, then entered a code in a surprisingly sophisticated burglar alarm to confirm that he truly belonged in the building. It was a far cry from her building's antique dual-lock system.

"Isn't that an unusual amount of protection in this part of town?" she asked.

"The first floor is an art gallery, with some extremely pricey artwork. The owner doesn't want to take any chances."

They climbed the stairs at the back of the building, then he unlocked the door on the second floor landing. His apartment wasn't just *on* the second floor, it *was* the second floor.

A long hallway stretched the length of the building, hung with black and white photos and brilliantly colored paintings. He hung his keys on the wall beside the door, and flicked on the lights. Recessed spots illuminated the paintings, making the yellows and reds seem to burst into flame.

He steered her toward the second door on the right. It was a bedroom, but a bedroom like none she'd ever seen.

The walls were painted a flat, matte black. A full-size four-poster of wrought iron claimed pride of place in the middle of the room, covered with a black and gold comforter. Heavy black drapes covered the window opposite the door, gold tassels hanging useless beside them. A strange contraption of black leather and wood vaguely resembling a hammock chair hung suspended from the ceiling in one corner of the room, with a padded black massage table underneath it. Artfully arranged on the wall, a collection of whips in all sizes, shapes and colors filled the next corner, providing a welcome splash of color. They ranged in size from a tiny blue one that looked like a nylon feather duster, to one that was easily three feet long, containing a dozen lashes of knotted red leather.

In the third corner, a small bureau of gleaming black lacquer displayed a forest of pristine white candles. The fourth corner contained a door — black, of course — and the room's only artwork, an ebony-framed painting of a blooming red rose under glass.

Her sun god waited patiently, letting her study the entire room. When she did not move, he said softly, "Welcome to my dungeon."

"What are all these things?"

"Suspension sling, whipping bench, whips, bed, bureau, and connecting bathroom," he answered.

"You use them all?" Her voice cracked on the last word.

He folded her reassuringly in his arms, holding her against the warmth of his body. "Not all at once. Certainly not for someone just learning the joys of slavery."

Keri relaxed into his embrace. "That's a relief."

"Ultimately, the decision to use or not use any equipment rests with you. You can stop anything I'm doing just by saying 'red light.' And start it again by saying 'green light.'"

"It's my choice?" She turned, instinctively trying to see his expression, but his golden sun mask merely reflected her own wide-eyed fears at her. "But I don't know…"

"Shh." He placed one gloved finger on her lips, silencing her. "I will tell you what to do, and how and when to do it. I will push your body past the boundaries of what you thought you wanted, into realms you've never dared dream of. That journey may be scary, but trust that I always have your safety and pleasure in mind. If anything I do causes you pain due to an awkward position or incites unwarranted fear, stop me. I can fix your position, and we can discuss your fears."

She shivered, his deep, accented voice stroking her soul the way his touch stroked her body. Keri nodded. "Okay. What do we do first?"

Gently, he opened her overcoat and lifted it off her shoulders.

"First, you dress like a proper slave. Let me see those sweet breasts and honeyed lips."

He turned her to face him, his shielded gaze lowering so that she'd understand he wasn't talking about her mouth.

Keri trembled, filled with excitement and just a hint of fear. She breathed deeply, thrusting out her chest, kicked off her ballet slippers and spread her legs in a wide stance, her hands on her hips.

"Should I remove the chain mesh, Master?"

"Yes."

She pulled the modesty panel free, sighing as the weight was lifted from the chains around her waist. Her sun god scooped up the slippers, then reached out and took the chain mesh from her, deposited them with her coat onto the whipping table.

He walked around her, studying her, then announced, "I still can't see how you hunger for me. Open your pants."

Keri swallowed, remembering how good the Discipline outfit had felt last night. Her eager fingers fumbled on the waist chains, finding and releasing the lobster clasp. Quickly, she pulled the two shorter gauze panels off of the chain, then refastened the clasp. Again, her sun god was there to take the panels out of her hands, adding them to the pile on the table.

She parted the gauze in the back, exposing her ass. Then she opened the front, exposing her damp pubic hair. Her sun god's golden lips turned in a satisfied smile.

"Yes, that's better. Now to transform you into Snow White, with snow white skin and lips as red as blood."

She trembled again at his words, not knowing what to expect. It sounded dark and sinister, something worthy of a powerful demon rather than a sun god. She could hardly wait to find out what he planned to do to her.

He crossed to the bed, and swept aside the covers. There were no sheets on the bed, only a glossy black covering.

"On the bed, slave. On your back, with your legs spread."

Keri eagerly climbed onto the bed, stretching herself spread-eagled across the cool rubber sheet. He strolled slowly to her side, then leisurely reached between her legs and slid one gloved finger beneath her slack crotch chain. His finger stroked over her pubis, then back, the tip caressing the inner folds of her labia, then brushing her clit. She tilted her hips up, and his finger slipped further still, until it circled the entrance of her vagina. She moaned, eager for him to enter her further. Instead, he took his hand away.

"Your lips are honeyed, but they're not yet red as blood. We'll have to fix that."

"How…?" she breathed, following his gaze to the whips hung on the wall. "You're going to whip me? There?"

"Yes. With the softest whip I own. It will feel like a hundred silk threads sliding over your flesh, the teasing caress of a waterfall pounding against you, demanding entrance to your hidden mysteries."

Warm liquid dribbled down the crack of her ass as her body reacted to his words. "Oh yes, Master. Please."

"Turn sideways on the bed, so that I can reach you. And tuck up your knees."

She did as he instructed, bending her knees so that she could fit crosswise on the bed, her eager pussy inches from the edge. She spread her arms wide in a gesture of offering.

While she repositioned herself, he walked over to the wall of whips and lifted down the tiny blue whip, then took the two heavy golden tassels from the drapes. He looped each tassel around a bedpost, and placed the ends in her hands.

"Hold onto the tassels. If you let go, I'll stop whipping. Do you understand?"

"Yes, Master."

He unclipped the crotch chain, letting it slither across her sensitive flesh until it pooled on the bed between her legs. Keri tightened her grasp on the tassels, eager yet afraid at the same time.

Softly, slowly, he stroked the tips of the whip's many lashes across her primed flesh. It felt like hundreds of delicate butterfly caresses. She sighed with pleasure and closed her eyes, the better to devote her attention to the sensations with which he was blessing her.

He flicked the whip sharply, slapping her pussy with the side of it. Keri gasped in shock, but her flesh pulsed and warm liquid trickled over the lip of her vagina. He slapped her again, but when her body tensed for a third blow, he surprised her with another teasing caress, drawing the tips of the lashes from her ass all the way up to her pubis.

Then he feathered more caresses down the insides of her thighs, for all the world feeling as if he was painting her legs with a thick, soft brush. Keri relaxed, her thighs falling further apart, as she opened herself to his gentle touch.

The whip-slap against her pussy shocked her into half-rising from the bed, her fists clenching the golden tassels and her chest and shoulders lifting up. The lashes continued to flick against her swollen labia, short, sharp taps that teased her wet lips to open for him, pulsing in time to his strikes.

Half-sitting as she was, Keri could see her pussy spread before him, gleaming with the lubricant he'd called from her eager body. The wet red lips of her labia pulsed and clenched with every kiss of his whip. Soon she was rocking her hips, leaning into his strokes, gasping and groaning with each hit.

He whipped her one last time, the nylon lashes of the whip curling deep within the gaping crevice of her exposed pussy, and she came in a powerful rush, screaming in wordless ecstasy.

Shuddering and trembling with the aftershocks, she clutched the golden tassels with aching fingers, knowing only that she could not let go, or this wonderful, blissful feeling might end. His gloved fingers stroked her pulsing flesh, fondling her clit and probing into her vagina. She moaned, unable to form words to beg him to continue touching her that way.

"Now your lips are sweet with honey, and red as blood," he told her. "Time for the kiss from the prince who will awaken the sleeping Snow White."

She heard his robes rustling, then felt the heavy, hot tip of his cock sliding down the path his fingers had just traveled. Keri whimpered, needing him inside her, filling her. She was wide open, hot and wet, and his cock slid smoothly into her in one long thrust.

He grabbed the chains around her waist, pulling her hips closer.

"Lock your legs around my waist," he ordered.

She obeyed instantly, pulling him tight so that his balls brushed her ass, and his thick pubic hair teased her swollen clit.

She expected him to move inside her, thrusting in and out, using his cock like a whip. Instead, he held completely still, sheathed deep inside her. Slowly, he glided one gloved hand up her quivering stomach, over her gauze-covered breasts, to the chain hanging between them.

He tugged the chain. Sharp pain blossomed on her nipples, then flowed in a wave to her center, where his cock was still sheathed tight inside her. Her muscles clenched around him, hot, and hard and oh so good, and she moaned.

"Oh yes, Master. Again. Please. Again and again and again."

Carefully, he pulled the gauze of her halter top up, freeing her breasts. He tapped lightly on each disk, sending waves of fire through her. Each time, her muscles clenched, tightening around his rigid cock.

Instead of building her to a blazing climax, he smoothed his gloved hands over the curves of her breasts, stroking the sides and swirling around the base where they rose from her rib cage. Keri's eyes drifted closed, her breathing slowing to match his caresses as she sprawled bonelessly on the bed.

Then he tugged on the chain.

She bolted half upright with a gasp, fists clenched around the drapery tassels and shoulder muscles straining to lift her from the bed. Sheets of fire cascaded from her nipples to her core, and she tightened around his cock, the unyielding iron sending spasms of pleasure through her as her muscles clenched and released, again and again. She panted for air, unable to breathe in the sudden heat consuming her.

Then his hands were stroking and gentling her, once again soothing her body until she relaxed. Her shoulders sagged, and she collapsed back onto the bed. Her breathing slowed, but she did not truly relax. Every time his caresses shifted position, she held her breath and tensed her body, wondering if this time, he'd bathe her in a wave of fire that would completely destroy her.

Eventually, even though his hands remained soothing and gentle, the anticipation coursing through her sparked its own restless fire. She panted for breath, fearing that he would not give her the release she desired until she was calm and placid. The fear fed the hunger, and she trembled with need. Her deep muscles quivered, gripping and releasing his hard cock.

"Who's your sun god?" he asked, his accented voice harsh with strain.

"You are," she moaned.

"Who do you worship?"

"You."

"How do you worship me?"

"However you say."

"I am the sun god. Worship me with *fire!*"

On the last word, he yanked on the nipple chain. The pain exploded over her in a ball of fire, lifting her body in a glorious arch between her head, suspended between the taut drapery cords, and her hips, locked to his. He grabbed the chains wrapping her waist and held her tight as he thrust even deeper.

They cried out together, his wordless shout of triumph cutting through her screams of "Yes! Yes! Yes!"

The dim corner of her brain still capable of rational thought noticed the lack of his seed spurting into her, and realized he must have put on a condom at some point. Then the aftershocks claimed her. As she gasped and shivered beneath him, he reached out and squeezed her breasts in time with the flames coursing through her. Instead of subsiding, they built, quickly flaring out of control. Once more, he tugged on her nipple chain.

She went supernova, and the starburst swept her consciousness into a deep black hole, leaving nothing but pleasure.

* * * * *

Keri blinked her eyes and groaned. She was sore all over, worse than the hardest workout in the gym, and she just wanted to snuggled deep into the soft cloud surrounding her and go back to sleep. But the light was shining directly into her eyes.

She turned her head, pulling the comforter up to her ears, trying to evade the unwelcome reminder of morning. But it had roused her enough for her other senses to kick in. An unfamiliar scent of spices rose from the too-soft pillow. Soft flannel sheets caressed her naked body, instead of crisp cotton sheets and a nightshirt washed until it was softer than the fuzzy fur of a kitten.

Where was she? Her window was at the foot of her bed. Yet the morning light was shining across her face.

She opened her eyes, blinking and trying to focus on the unfamiliar surroundings. She was in an unfamiliar bedroom, with olive walls, antique gold bedding, and burgundy curtains at the windows, held back with golden cords.

The sight of the cords brought back the memory of last night. She closed her eyes and let her head fall back onto the pillow, reliving the exquisite torment her Master had meted out to her. She'd never dreamed that slavery could be so liberating.

Her Master must have carried her into his bedroom after that last glorious orgasm that had shattered her world. He'd also stripped off the remnants of her costume and put her to bed. But where was he?

Keri smiled, anticipation warming her blood. Last night, she had been a slave girl and he had been a sun god. Today, she'd see who had been behind that mask. She tried to imagine what he looked like, but her mind's eye could only picture the demonic Cole from *Charmed*. After all, her mystery lover had a sexy accent that grew stronger when his passions were aroused, just like Julian McMahon's character.

She threw off the covers and swung her legs out of bed, wincing as the movement pulled muscles in her groin that she'd overexerted last night. Tentatively, she reached between her legs and pressed on the sensitive flesh. It was sore, but it didn't hurt enough to be bruised. Just strained.

A straight-backed leather and chrome chair had been pulled over next to the bed, and her clothes were piled neatly on top of it. A folded piece of paper, inscribed "Adina" rested on the pile.

She opened the note. Strong black handwriting filled the page beneath a monogram of the letter A chiseled in stone.

Thank you for a wonderful night. I hope you enjoyed yourself as much as I did. I regret that I had a previous engagement, and had to leave before you awoke. The bathroom is well stocked for guests—help yourself to whatever toiletries you need. I put out a T-shirt and pair of sweat pants you can wear home, if you'd rather not wear your costume. You may keep them if you're having second thoughts about what we did last night. However, if you would like to continue your training with me, bring them with you when you come back tonight at 8pm. Buzz twice at the door and I will let you in. Here is your first order, if you choose to be my slave: Do not investigate the rest of the apartment. All rooms but the bathroom and bedroom are off limits to you, and as soon as you're ready, leave by the back door. It locks automatically. I will know if you've disobeyed me. Sincerely, Master Alex

Keri stared at the note, rereading it a second and then third time. He wasn't here. He'd given her the most phenomenal sex of her life, and then left without speaking to her, just leaving a note. Did it mean so little to him?

She shook her head. No. He said right there at the beginning of the note that he thought it was wonderful. And he wanted her to come back again tonight. So then why did he leave? He must've known she'd want to see him this morning. The excuse of a prior engagement seemed flimsy at best.

Puzzling over his strange behavior, she recalled his words when she'd first entered his dungeon. Ultimately, the choice was hers. By making himself scarce, he was giving her the opportunity to choose, with no pressure from him.

She nodded, certain she understood his purpose. After the night they'd shared, if he'd been beside her when she woke, she'd have eagerly begged him to take her back to his dungeon. Her body came to life under his skilled hands, leaving no room for thought.

But she needed to think about her actions. Did she really want to give a man that much power over her? A niggling voice of strident feminism insisted she was betraying her sisters by embracing inequality, by allowing a man to dictate how, when, and where she would feel pleasure. And there was the disturbing insight into her personality that she'd had the strongest orgasm she'd ever experienced when a man was beating her. Did that mean if she continued to see him, she'd turn into one of those women who welcomed abuse from their lover, until one day he hit her hard enough to send her to the hospital, or kill her?

She had a lot to think about. She was glad he'd given her the opportunity to think about it on her own, and take all day before making her decision.

But first things first. She needed to use the bathroom, and take a shower. Her hair was a mess, and her skin itched from dried sweat.

The bathroom was vaguely art deco, with frosted wall sconces and fluid lines to the fixtures. Black and white tiles formed an abstract mosaic on the floor, a theme carried over in the stylized geometric motif on the shower curtain. The room's only color was provided by two sets of towels—red and gold ones that were still slightly damp hanging on the rod, and a dry set in orange and yellow sitting on the counter that he must have put out for her.

A bamboo basket on the back of the toilet contained soaps, shampoos, conditioners, and lotions from a wide range of hotels, as well as a selection of travel sized toothpastes and deodorants. A small plastic comb of the five-for-a-dollar variety and a plastic-wrapped toothbrush embossed with the name of a dentist completed the array of toiletries available. She lingered over the possible choices, finally selecting a glycerin soap and citrus scented shampoo and conditioner.

The showerhead was a six-position shower-massage. Keri let the warm water pound her scalp and her back, finding the tension in her shoulders and kneading it away. She lathered her chest, washing away the salty remains of last night's exertions. When she turned to face the spray, the water pummeled her tender breasts, making her wince and jump back. She reset the showerhead to a gentle fall of rain, and carefully rinsed the soapsuds away.

She stayed longer than necessary in the shower, enjoying the warm water on all of its settings. It was an uncharacteristic waste of both water and time, but her uncertainty about how to proceed kept her in the known environs of the shower. When her skin began to wrinkle, she finally admitted that she'd been in there long enough, turned off the water, and toweled off.

Wrapped sarong-style in the largest of the towels, she combed out her hair while she returned to the bedroom. Her first decision was a simple one. Alex's apartment was much further from her apartment than the opera, and she hadn't brought enough money to take a cab that distance. No way was she riding the train wearing her slave costume! So she'd have to wear the sweat pants and T-shirt Alex had offered. But he'd made it clear they were a no-strings-attached gift. Taking them didn't mean she was accepting anything else from him.

She picked up her pile of clothes from the chair, and found Alex's underneath her folded raincoat. The sweat pants were navy blue 100% cotton that had obviously shrunk in the wash. She pulled them on. A little loose, but better than the alternative.

The T-shirt was red with white lettering, advertising a marathon. Keri considered what that meant. Had Alex competed in the marathon? He'd certainly seemed fit last night. Was his hobby jogging?

She shook her head. She didn't know. She didn't know anything about him. If he hadn't signed his note, she wouldn't even know his name. In fact, he'd never learned hers. His note was addressed to Adina, the character name she'd given him last night. He'd put the name in quotes, showing he knew it wasn't her real name, but at the same time making it obvious he didn't know anything else to call her.

Keri dropped the T-shirt on the rumpled bed, and found her halter-top from last night. Alex had folded it neatly, but hadn't disassembled it. The clasp was still attached to the gauze panel. She put it on as a makeshift bra, then pulled Alex's T-shirt on over it. The T-shirt hung to her hips.

She wouldn't win any fashion awards, but that didn't matter. She only cared about getting home.

She shrugged into her raincoat, belting it securely around her waist, and stuffed her feet into her ballet slippers. Then she unfolded one of the gauze panels of her costume and rolled the rest of her outfit up in it like a giant blue burrito.

Tucking it under her arm, she followed Alex's instructions and left his apartment the same way she'd arrived, going down the back stairs to the service entrance of the art gallery. Instead of following the walkway to the carriage house, she followed a path that led between the house and its nearest neighbor, through a narrow wooden door that locked behind her, and out to the sidewalk.

People thronged the sidewalks, Saturday tourists visiting art galleries, trendy shops and cafes. Keri followed the crowd, looking for landmarks so she could find a subway stop. She didn't know how long Alex's "engagement" would keep him away from his apartment, and she wanted to be well and truly gone by the time he returned.

CHAPTER FOUR

Keri finished tying off her latest quilt, and put her needle and thread away in her sewing box with her scissors. Standing up, she spread the quilt over the back of her couch to study it. A log cabin quilt in over a dozen different blues and greens, it was restful and orderly without being boring. Perfect for the women's shelter she was donating it to.

She'd used the quiet time while sewing to think about her options, and had decided not to see Master Alex again. It wasn't that she thought their relationship would count as abusive. Once she'd considered it, she realized that his attitude toward her had been domineering, but never abusive. He'd placed her needs and desires above his own, which was opposite to the patterns of abuse.

No, the problem was that there was no future in the relationship. Eventually, she wanted a family, children, all the things any girl wants when she imagines where she'll be in twenty years. If she got involved with Master Alex, while she was with him, she wouldn't be looking for a potential life partner. Even though the sex was the best she'd ever had, sex wasn't enough. Sooner or later, passion died. What then? She'd be older, less desirable, and more jaded, so she'd be even less likely to find an acceptable partner.

No. She had to think of her future. She had to plan ahead. A life partner would have common goals and experiences, and would share more with her than just hot sex. It was best not to see Master Alex ever again.

She folded the quilt neatly and tucked it into a shopping bag to carry to the shelter, then placed it next to her computer case by the door where she would be able to grab them when she left for work Monday morning.

She looked at the case for a long moment, then picked it up and started unpacking her laptop. If she wasn't going to see Master Alex tonight, she might as well work. She might get some last brilliant inspiration of how to fight Thibodeau.

The first thing she did when she logged on was check her email. If there was any news about the proposal, she needed to know.

Nothing. Just her father's first of the month bulk mailing to friends and relatives. He found it more efficient to simply write one letter and send it to everyone. Keri hoped he hadn't put any embarrassingly personal messages in it this month.

Feeling much like a motorist driving past an accident scene, who knows she shouldn't look and yet is compelled to slow down and stare, she intended to open the proposal document, and instead found herself opening his letter.

Hello, all. Hope you had an enjoyable Halloween. We had forty-seven trick-or-treaters stop by the house. Molly counted as they came up the walk, even though we left the bowl filled with candy on the porch for them, rather than waste time and energy getting up to answer the door every time they rang. She said their costumes were even more inventive than last year.

In other news, Molly and I bought a new car. One of those new gas/electric hybrids that is so fuel efficient. Molly uses it to drive to her new volunteer job, as a social outreach worker to shut-ins at nursing homes. She enjoys helping others, and this allows her to visit all the area nursing homes, to see how the patients are really treated. That will be good information to have should either of us need assisted care living. We're not getting any younger, and we have to think of our future.

Bonnie, hope your no-good ex-husband is history, but if not, tell your father to teach you how to use those hunting rifles of his. You'll feel safer, and you can get some inexpensive venison for Thanksgiving dinner at the same time.

'Til next month, all.

Bob and Molly

Keri stared at the letter in horror. Dear God, she was turning into her parents.

"No way am I ending up like that, so busy planning for the future that I never live in the present."

She slammed the laptop closed, and quickly repacked it in its case. There was no time to waste. She had a date to get ready for.

* * * * *

At ten of eight, Keri found herself surreptitiously walking past the front entrance to Master Alex's building. Lights blazed from the gallery, which didn't close until eleven. A crowd had gathered inside for some sort of party. Many of the people held wine glasses or napkins full of cheese or fruit. Six men and women robed in white draperies, their costumes completed by white body makeup and powdered hair, circulated through the crowd, occasionally freezing in place like marble statues.

She peered through the window, wondering what the gallery contained that was so valuable. The usual sorts of paintings hung on the walls, some vivid splashes of color that looked like nothing so much as spilled paint to her, and some highly detailed works that could have come from a camera lens, except that their subjects never existed in the real world. Pedestals scattered through the room were picked out by track lighting positioned to highlight the sculpture, pottery, and jewelry upon them.

Suddenly recognizing the subject of the painting closest to the window, Keri choked back a snort of laughter. A menacing tower, ringed all around with briars, had a single window, from which descended a long blonde braid. Bits of cloth waved from the wickedly long spikes of the briars. At the edge of the briars was a somewhat tattered but triumphant bald-headed woman. Rapunzel had apparently tired of waiting for Prince Charming, and rescued herself.

The artist's style looked vaguely familiar. After a moment, she placed it. The same person had done the painting of the rose hanging in Master Alex's dungeon.

Keri smiled, wondering what fairy tale subversion lurked in the depths of Alex's painting. Given his obvious fondness for fairy tales, or at least the adult retellings of them, no wonder he'd found the artist's work appealing.

She glanced at her watch again. Time to go.

Hitching her tote bag more securely over her shoulder, she pushed open the glass door leading to the building's foyer. Instead of going through the second door to the gallery, she turned to the heavy wooden door in the back of the foyer, and pressed the second floor buzzer. Twice.

A moment later, the door buzzed loudly, indicating the lock was now disengaged. She shoved it open, and started up the winding steps. Halfway up the flight, a plaster statue stood in a niche. At first glance, it looked like a copy of Michelangelo's David. Except she'd never seen a David with a rampant hard-on and no fig leaf in sight.

She hesitated on the stairs, suddenly uncertain. What was she letting herself in for? True, the sex had been great. But was that really any basis for a relationship? She should go up there, return the sweat pants and T-shirt she had in her bag, then turn right around and go home where it was safe. And she could become her parents.

Stiffening her shoulders, she marched up the rest of the steps to the second floor landing. The door to Alex's apartment was open, and a note was taped to it.

Welcome back! Come inside and close the door, then follow the trail. You obeyed my instructions this morning, and deserve a reward. It's waiting for you at the end of the trail.

She ripped the note off the door and went inside, closing the door behind her. A trail of deep red rose petals began in a pile at the door, then led down the hall. The sight of them reminded her of the sight she'd had last night of her red and swollen labia, plump and aching for Alex's touch. She felt herself getting wet, and hurried down the trail to the dungeon.

When she entered the dungeon, she was surprised to find it candlelit and empty. The candles had been spread out around the room in addition to being on top of the bureau. Some stood on the whipping bench, some hung from brass sconces hooked over the whips and the picture frame, and the posts on the bed were topped by four more. All were lit, giving the room a dim, flickering light that was not enough to see any details.

"Master?" she called softly.

"Welcome to your second training session. Please kneel on the floor."

His voice came from the darkness somewhere to the right.

Keri dropped her bag on the floor, swept a spot clear of rose petals, and knelt on the hardwood floor. Images she'd seen during her online research into the world of BDSM earlier today flickered through her mind, of naked slaves kneeling with their arms tied behind them or stretched above them while their Masters flogged or beat them.

"Eyes forward," he ordered.

Keri stared at the bed in front of her. From this angle, she could see that the decorative iron scrollwork of the footboard and posts was actually designed as a series of links to which chains could be attached. She shivered, wondering when he planned to tie her to the bed, and what he'd do to her once she was unable to get free.

The bathroom door creaked slightly, then footsteps echoed across the wooden floor. She felt the warmth of his presence standing behind her, accompanied by a faint scent of spice, but obeyed his command and kept her eyes fixed firmly ahead.

"This is a pretty jacket," he said, his hands stroking her shoulders through the quilted blue satin. "You wore it for me?"

"Yes, Master." She'd taken great pains with her appearance for this date, not at all certain what to wear for someone who'd seen more of her naked than he had clothed. She'd settled at last on flaring black slacks that emphasized her hips and thighs, high-heeled black ankle boots, and a zip-fronted Chinese jacket in deep marine blue, decorated with tiny brass studs in the center of each quilted square.

He knelt behind her, his strong legs bracketing hers. Reaching in front of her, he slowly inched down the zipper. She could barely breathe as his hands glided down her front, following the zip.

Finally, the zipper slipped free, and he parted the front of her jacket. Reaching inside, he cupped her breasts. His thumbs skimmed the edge of her black lace bra.

"What pattern is the lace?" he asked.

"Roses," she whispered.

He breathed a sigh of deep contentment, bending his head and kissing the side of her neck as his fingers found her nipples and squeezed. Keri closed her eyes and let her head loll back, resting on his broad shoulder, while he continued to kiss her neck and fondle her breasts. The soft hair at his temple teased her cheek, and she sighed with pleasure. All of him was caressing her.

Gradually, he pushed the jacket off her shoulders and down her arms, until it landed in a pile on the back of her calves. His hands smoothed over her exposed stomach and ribs before releasing the hooks on her bra and sweeping that away as well.

Slowly, with no sense of urgency, he stroked and caressed all of her available skin. Flickering candlelight painted dancing vistas on the back of her eyelids as she swayed beneath his guiding touch.

"What do you think about making love in the dark like this?" he asked softly, whispering the question against the pulse point in her neck he was licking.

"Mmm. I like it. It heightens all my other senses, like touch."

He licked her neck again. "And taste."

"And taste," she answered. Would she taste him soon? If so, what would he have her taste? Would she taste the spice of his cologne clinging to his throat? Lick the salty sweat from his skin? Sample the dewy drops of cum from his cock?

He shifted position, reaching behind himself for something. A moment later, she felt a cloth draping across her face, and the dim flickering of the candles was extinguished. She was in total darkness.

She jerked upright. "What...?"

Alex's gentle hands stroked and soothed her, caressing her arms and breasts, but at the same time blocking her attempts to reach up and tear the cloth from her eyes.

"It's a blindfold," he told her. "Now you're completely in the dark. You'll be completely focused on what you feel."

"May I touch it?"

"Yes. But don't remove it, or the training session is over."

She nodded her understanding. Wearing the blindfold was tonight's golden tassels—her sign of consent. Delicately, careful not to dislodge it, she reached up and patted the edge of the mask covering her eyes. It was a soft, padded satin the same size and shape as her beaded domino mask, over rigid eye cups that allowed her to open her eyes beneath the mask and further blocked all light.

The mask had a thin elastic band to allow it to be positioned, but both sides also connected to a strong nylon belt. While she felt the front of the mask, Alex fastened the belt behind her head and tightened the slack. The blindfold settled flush against her skin, the eye-cups resting firmly against her face but not digging in.

"Can you see any light at all?" he asked.

"No, Master."

"Good."

The heat of his body vanished from behind her, and she strained her ears, trying to hear where he had gone. A drawer opened and closed in the far corner of the room. He'd gone to the bureau.

She felt the radiant heat of his presence even before he spoke, announcing his return to her side.

"Stand now. Do you need a hand?"

"No, Master." Carefully, Keri placed her hands flat on the polished wood floor, shifted to kneeling on one knee with one foot carefully positioned by her hand, then got the other foot beneath her and rose fluidly to her feet.

"Very graceful, almost as if you were dancing." He stepped behind her, leaning her body back against his so that her shoulders rested against his chest, and her head was pillowed on his shoulder. Holding her lightly around the waist, he swayed sinuously from side to side, brushing the bulging front of his slacks against the back of her hip huggers. Gradually, his movement ceased being side to side, and became a forward and back rocking, pressing his erection into the cleft of her ass.

Keri moaned softly, her buttocks clenching in a futile effort to draw his teasing pressure deeper. Why were they still wearing clothes? Clothes only got in the way of touching, and stroking, and thrusting, and…

"You'll dance with me, here in the dark, won't you?" Alex's deep, accented voice broke into her thoughts. "The two of us, linked together, making our own music."

"Oh yes, Master. Whenever you say."

"Then first, you must be dressed for dancing."

His hands slipped from her hips to the front of her pants, deftly unbuttoning them and lowering the zip. Hooking his thumbs inside the waistband of her panties, he slid pants and panties down, stroking and caressing her hips and thighs as he went. He knelt behind her, his soft hair rubbing against her hip, as he worked the clothing down to her ankles, then helped her out of her shoes.

When she was completely naked, he nudged her legs apart. Damp anticipation misted her lips as she wondered what he would do next. Kiss her? Stroke her? Lick her? Probe her with his fingers? Or simply thrust his cock into her?

The anticipation built as he seemed to ignore the temptation displayed before him, rubbing her calves and caressing her legs. But she was the one who was blindfolded, not him. She knew he could see her, spread in front of his face, her labia growing pinker and plumper the more she thought about his hard cock slipping between them. The short hairs glistening with the damp lubricant that overflowed her channel.

Alex turned his head, pressing a quick kiss high on her ass, then following it up with a sharp nip. Keri gasped, her knees trembling at the unexpected pain. A wave of pleasure washed over her, and hot fluid rolled down the inside of her thigh.

"Master," she moaned, pleading for something although she didn't know what.

He stood, stepping away briefly before his near presence warmed her back again.

"Put out your arms, away from your body," he instructed.

She did as ordered. He reached beneath her, and wrapped something around her chest. Her first thought was that he was using a gauze panel, like she'd seen illustrated in the Bondage picture for her costume. But it didn't feel soft like gauze. It was clingy and unyielding, wrapping tight around her breasts and ribcage.

A sharp ripping sounded from behind her. Then he passed a second layer of whatever it was around her lower ribs and stomach. Another ripping sound, and a third piece bound her hips and ass. He ripped and applied a fourth piece between her legs, tucking it into her crevices and pulling it tight. The brief caress of his fingers pressing inside her made her pulse with readiness, steaming inside the clinging covering.

"Plastic wrap?" she asked.

"Yes. You're all shrink-wrapped, perfect for preserving you in a state of hot, wet readiness." His fingers slid between her legs again, rubbing the plastic wrap over the skin too slick for it to adhere to.

She groaned, wishing he would punch through the seal and put his fingers deep inside her. Or better yet, his cock.

Instead, he put his hands on her hips and guided her forward half a dozen steps. "Do you know where you are?"

"In front of the bed?" she guessed.

He turned her around, so the bed was behind her, then pushed her slowly backward onto it. She landed on the familiar black rubber sheets.

The bed creaked slightly as Alex climbed onto it after her. He wrapped soft fur around her wrists, buckling the fur in place, then lifted her arms with a rattle of chains. The chains clipped onto the headboard posts with two sharp snaps, holding her arms away from her body at a comfortable angle.

He stroked two more lengths of fur down her thighs, then over her shins, to finally wrap tightly around her ankles. The chains pulled her legs further apart as he spread her ankles and fastened them to the footboard posts.

She quivered, hearing him moving and not knowing where he was or what he was doing. Finally, she felt a puff of hot air brush her cheek.

"You remember the candles decorating the room?" he asked, his voice low and promising the possibility of incredible ecstasy or excruciating torment.

"Yes, Master," she whispered. Was that what was heating the air near her face? She strained her ears, and thought she heard a faint sizzle of wax.

"They're having an artist's reception downstairs. But I'm going to turn you into my own personal work of art. Think of this as a wax casting."

She *did* hear wax sizzling. The heat of the candle was now down by her breasts, dangerously close to her left nipple. Plastic wrap was flammable. What if he lit her on fire? There was no way she could drop and roll, chained to the bed the way she was.

Keri flexed her arms and legs, testing the limits of the chains. She could straighten her arms, but only if she stretched them above her head. The chains prevented her from touching any part of her body, although she could snatch the mask from her eyes if she tilted her head while she reached.

She barely considered it. Alex would not hurt her—not in any way that didn't eventually lead to pleasure. It was just the path to that pleasure she wasn't sure about. Nervously, she began trembling and rolling from side to side.

"Careful!" Alex commanded. "You must lie completely still. You don't want me to accidentally burn you, do you?"

Keri froze, terrified of what might happen if she so much as breathed. A drop of hot wax dripped from the candle he held over her breast, splashing onto the sensitive skin.

She screamed, arching against the chains binding her to the bed frame. At the same time, she felt a rush of fluid between her legs, as her body could not tell the difference between intense arousal and intense fear. She fell back onto the sheets, panting, and completely confused.

The wax had shocked her, but it hadn't been hot enough to burn. Now it was cooling, solidifying against the curve of her breast like a warm caress.

Alex chuckled, no doubt reading her emotions on her face. "Surprise."

A second drop of wax fell, splashing the other breast. Again, her body arched from the shock, her brain screaming that she was burning, and her sex pulsing hot and wet with a fire of its own.

Alex drew his finger through the warm candle wax, spreading it in a thin layer across her breast. She heard a faint clink, as if he'd placed something on a dish, and then the burning heat was applied directly to her nipple.

She screamed, arching against her chains in a futile effort to escape that only pressed her skin deeper into the flame. Alex pulled the flame away, leaving her shaking and gasping for breath, thrashing in her bonds in a desperate bid to escape. But gradually rational thought conquered her unreasoning terror.

She stopped moving. "Why aren't I on fire?"

"The human nervous system processes both extremes of heat and extremes of cold the same way. That was an ice cube." He stroked her cheek gently with warm, slightly waxy fingertips, then brushed her tangled hair back from her face. "I promised I would not hurt you. But I will terrify you, to push your mind and body past the comfortable safety of what you know, into the liberating ecstasy of the darkness beyond."

In the darkness of her blindfold, unable to see his expression, she hung on his every syllable, wringing his softly accented words for each drop of meaning she could squeeze from them.

"That's right. You told me that last night. I forgot."

"No, you didn't. Or you'd have taken off the blindfold." He leaned down and pressed a kiss to her chilled nipple, inside its plastic wrap covering. "You wanted to be frightened."

Recalling her recent panicked frenzy, Keri's heart pounded, her pulse raced, and her breathing turned shallow and harsh, as if she was reliving the fear. But now she was also aware of the tingling in her breasts, straining against the confining plastic wrap, and the hot liquid pooling at her throbbing sex. She wanted him to rip the plastic away and ram his cock into her, to cover her body with scalding wax until she burned for him, and to torture her in ways she hadn't even begun to think of yet.

"Oh, God, yes," she whispered. "Take me. Terrify me. Make me scream."

"I will," he promised. "I will."

Keri lost all concept of time as he covered her wrapped body with molten wax and melting ice. She shivered and screamed and came in a shuddering rush, only to have him push her trembling body into another tense buildup and shattering release.

Alex prodded the plastic wrap between her legs — with his fingers, a candle stump, or his cock, she neither knew nor cared. She tilted her hips, begging him to press harder, further, ripping through the plastic so she could feel him inside her at last.

"I think you might be leaking," he said softly, stroking her swollen labia through the plastic. She moaned and writhed beneath his touch, rattling her chains. "We'll have to plug that leak."

"Plug me," she begged.

"With a wax seal," he answered.

The heat of a candle flame hovered above her open thighs, and a sudden panic gripped her. "No! Not there!"

She tried to close her legs, to move away from his candle, but the chains kept her spread, and rocking her hips only allowed one side of her to escape. The other side rose up, even closer to the blazing candle.

He tilted the candle, the soft hiss of molten wax hitting the flaring wick announcing his intentions. Keri whimpered, frozen with fear, no longer able to think clearly enough even to beg.

The wax dripped, a hot splash knifing through her open sex. Keri screamed, her body spasming uncontrollably, pain, pleasure, heat, and pressure swirling chaotically through her senses until she didn't know what touched her, or where. Then he thrust a blazing firebrand deep into the crevice of the plastic wrap. She screamed again, the muscles of her vagina clenching the fiery invader, trying to pull it deeper, even as she arched up from the bed, trying to escape the overwhelming sensation.

The combination was too much for her. She climaxed, then almost immediately climaxed again, shattering her last hold on rational thought and sending her spiraling into the darkness where the flames of thousands of suns lit her way.

The first thing she noticed when she regained her senses was that Alex was lying beside her, stroking her breast with a soft piece of fur. Her bare breast. The plastic and the wax had been removed while she was floating through the cosmos.

She turned toward him, and realized her arms and legs were no longer chained to the bed. He'd also removed her blindfold, although since he'd extinguished the candles as well, she couldn't see any more than she could when she'd been blindfolded.

"That was...I can't even describe it," she said softly. "What was that you put in me?"

"Another ice cube." Alex moved the fur, stroking her hip and ass, and placed his mouth to her breast. He licked, and kissed, and suckled her, slowly, in time to the gentle sweep of the fur against her skin.

She moaned softly, and buried her fingers deep in his hair to keep his talented mouth on her aching breast. Running her hands through the thickness of his hair, she discovered it had a slight wave, and was neatly trimmed just below his hairline.

Sudden realization froze her hands in mid-caress. She'd had no idea what his hair was like, picturing it like Julian McMahon's simply because he reminded her so strongly of Cole, the dark demon, and she had no real knowledge to supplant that mental picture. She had only the vaguest of notions of what he looked like at all, knowing his height and build, and what his chin and lips looked like when they were painted gold. Her questing fingertips found the edge of his ears, his jaw line, and then tried to construct an image of his cheeks and nose.

He pulled away from her breast. "What is it?"

"I just realized I don't know what you look like."

"Because I did not want you to know. You must promise me that you won't try to see my face."

Her fingertips had encountered no scars or deformities, just a slight stubble of beard shadow. He seemed well proportioned, with sweeping, arched brows, a straight, slender nose, full lips and a strong jaw.

"But—"

He placed his finger on her lips, silencing her protest. "Do not argue with me on this, or I will be unable to train you."

She hesitated, her natural curiosity warring with the fear of never making love with him again. But she trusted that he would do nothing to harm her. Whatever his reason for keeping his face hidden, it was nothing dangerous. She was certain that all would be revealed in time.

"As you will it, Master. I am your obedient slave."

His tense body relaxed, and he rolled her beneath him, his hard cock probing for entrance. "As a good Master, I must reward you for your obedience."

Keri sighed, completely forgetting about finding out what he looked like, caring only about the wonderful way that he made her feel.

CHAPTER FIVE

Keri came to her senses in darkness, aware of Alex's warm, toned body beside her, the weight of his arm draped across her, and his deep rhythmic breathing. She nuzzled his chest that had been serving as her pillow, finding and licking his flat nipple.

His breath hitched, and the nipple sprang to life beneath her lips. Another sign of his interest rose to life against her thigh.

"Are you awake?" she whispered.

"I am now."

"Can we make love again?"

"My dear Adina, you're insatiable."

Keri shook her head, brushing his chest with her hair. "My real name's Keri."

She heard the rustle of his hair against the rubber sheet as he shook his head in response. "No. That's your real name, for the real world. Here, in the magical world we create together, you need a magical name. You are Adina, ornament of pleasure."

She blinked in surprise. "Is that what the name means? I just thought it sounded exotic."

"Yes. I looked it up."

"And Alex? Is that your real name or is it just for use here?"

He hesitated, until she thought he wouldn't answer, then finally replied, "It's the name I was given, or part of it, anyway. But I only use it here."

But thinking of the real world reminded her of her job, and her responsibilities. "Is it morning yet?"

He turned away, reaching for something. A bright blue light flared in the darkness, casting strange shadows on the wall of whips, but at the wrong angle to illuminate his face. "No. It's about one o'clock."

The light faded as he released the IndiGlo button on his watch, then turned back toward her. His hand stroked over her ass and hip, then shifted her thigh so that his cock slipped between her legs.

"We have plenty of time," he whispered. "You won't have to wait until tonight for another session."

"I won't be able to see—I mean be with—you tonight. I have to get ready for a big presentation at work. We're planning—"

"Shh." His hissed order came out sharply, but the fingers he laid across her lips were gentle. "No talk of work. That belongs to the real world, out there."

Keri nibbled his fingers, feeling his leap of response between her legs. He growled softly, rolling onto his back and pulling her astride him.

"I obviously didn't tire you out enough earlier. I'll just have to make love to you again and again until you're too exhausted to move."

She shivered, feeling the heat building where he was pressed against her, and rubbed back and forth against his cock, seeking the angle that would put him inside her. "You're not at all tired, either."

He grabbed her by the waist and held her still. "I'm also not wearing a condom, so none of that. No, you're moving too much. That will be our next lesson."

The blood pooled in her sex, throbbing with eager anticipation. Her breathing turned shallow, her skin flushing first hot and then cold. "Will you chain me to the bed again?"

"No. It's the suspension sling for you. But first, I have to find the blindfold. I want you completely at my mercy."

He flipped her over, the tip of his cock stroking her as he moved away. She saw the blue flash of his watch again, out in the room, as he opened the bureau and searched through the drawers, his naked body highlighted in stark relief. A moment later he was back, placing the familiar blindfold over her eyes, then rolling her onto her stomach so that he could buckle it around her head.

She heard him moving about the room, and the click of a light switch, but she remained in complete darkness. He helped her out of the bed and across the floor to the corner of the room where she remembered the hammock-like contraption hung.

"Climb up onto the bench," he told her, his strong hands guiding and lifting her as she followed his instructions. "Now stand. Turn. Lean back as if you were going to sit down. That's it. A little further."

The feel of leather unexpectedly brushed the back of her thighs, and she toppled backwards, her feet flying out from under her. The sling caught her, swaying gently, the curved leather supporting her from her shoulders to her hips.

Alex fastened the familiar fur-lined cuffs around her wrists and ankles, then lifted her arms straight up and clicked the cuffs to the chains supporting the sling. She could move her hands and arms a little bit, and grab the chains to ease the weight on them, but she couldn't lower them.

A delicious thrill of fear tingled through her, making her heart race, and her sex wet. She was in his power now, and had no idea what he planned on doing to her.

He picked up one of her feet, and kissed the sole of it. She gasped at the unexpected touch. Then he lifted her leg straight up. Resting the outside of her thigh against the support chain, he bent her knee slightly so that the inside of her calf brushed the support chain, then clipped her ankle cuff to the heavy chain. A moment later, her other leg was similarly chained in the air, wrapped around the heavy support chain.

Hanging on her back with her arms and legs above her and her sex spread wide open, Keri felt incredibly vulnerable. She was completely exposed to him. Blindfolded, she couldn't see his reaction, or know what he had planned. She was literally in the dark.

Her fears rushed to the surface. He gave her no clues. She didn't know how to behave. She'd do something wrong and displease him, then he'd send her away. The same pattern had repeated throughout her school years, again and again. Who was she to think it would be any different now?

Then his mouth closed over her sex, his tongue sweeping between her folds, searching for her clit. She gasped, then moaned as he found it. His lips closed around the tiny bud, sucking and nibbling until it bloomed.

Keri clenched her fingers around the cold chains, seeking some point of reference as she swung in the darkness, waves of fire cascading over her from his skilled teeth and tongue. She lost all sense of direction, feeling as if she floated, or perhaps flew, and still his mouth plundered her wide-open sex, the rough stubble on his cheeks scraping the tender skin on the inside of her thighs as he feasted on her flesh.

She came in a crackling burst, like lightning flashing across her skin, quivering and jerking against the chains that contained her. Alex's tongue moved faster, lapping the fluid that flowed from her body, and she moaned, recognizing the buildup to a second orgasm. She wanted to move, to rock her hips in time with his tongue, to urge him on, but she had no leverage, no solid ground on which to brace herself. Only the chains, twisting and swaying, and his mouth, devouring her with single-minded intent.

He placed his mouth directly over her opening, his tongue plunging deep inside. She moaned and whimpered, shivering and twitching, clattering her chains and spinning the sling until she felt dizzy. Then he sucked on her, hard, and she burst again, flooding his mouth as she screamed in mindless passion.

She panted, suddenly bereft of his touch, feeling alone and exposed as her wet sex pulsed with heat. Then his cock slid into her, thrusting deep in a single motion. Her muscles clenched around him, but he pulled out as quickly as he'd entered.

"Please," she begged. "Please, Master."

"I will," he promised.

He thrust into her again, pulling the sling toward him as he did, so that he pierced deeper than before. With her legs chained up and out of the way, nothing interfered with his access to her, and he rocked her back and forth as he slid in and out, tipping her body so that the angle changed every time. Sometimes his cock thrust straight back, almost entering her womb, sometimes the head of it pressed along the walls of her vagina, stretching her to take him, and sometimes he ground his cock against the sensitive nerves at her entrance as he pushed inside her. She never knew what to expect. Soon she lost all sense of their bodies as separate entities, and felt only that they were joined together, stirring and churning to create an overwhelming ecstasy.

Buried deep within her, he swung her up and down and side to side on the chains, rocking her against him as she moaned and begged, tears pooling inside the eyecups of her blindfold. His breath was loud and ragged, harsh groans escaping from his lips with every brush of his balls against her, every time her muscles gripped his cock.

The rocking motion shifted, changing to short, sharp thrusts, as he crushed her against him, harder and faster, until he cried out and burst. He shuddered and shook with the force of his ejaculation, and she swayed and rocked with him.

"Oh please, Master. Please. Let me come, too."

He didn't answer, but his fingers slipped between their bodies and unerringly found her clit. He rubbed it, squeezed, then pinched, and her world burst into millions of brilliant stars, all floating and flying with her as she soared.

* * * * *

Keri finished her presentation to Mr. Carlisle, the President of Uninational, and returned to her seat on her team's side of the oval conference table. She'd felt Thibodeau staring at her the whole time, trying to rattle her, willing her to fail. But she'd kept her cool, and proceeded with a flawless delivery of her team's final proposal.

She preferred to deliver the pitch proposal, watching the client for subtle reactions that she could use to adjust how she stressed various items during the pitch. There were other team leaders, like Thibodeau, who preferred to have one of the team members deliver the pitch proposal, so that he could give his full attention to the client's reactions, and plan the rebuttals and negotiations accordingly. But she always felt it was easier to be the favored proposal going into final negotiations. That put the onus on the other team to refute your claims, rather than forcing you to refute theirs.

Carlisle shuffled the papers in front of him, glanced at his note pad, then turned toward Thibodeau. "The most obvious difference in your solutions is the help desk. You want twice as large a staff, and to use the Internet only to enter problems in lieu of calling. Won't that be more expensive?"

Thibodeau nodded. "If all you consider are the salaries, yes. The 'savings' created by putting more of the front-end solution on the people reporting the problems assumes that this work is in addition to their normal workload. But in four independent studies—the details are in Appendix B with the other supporting documentation— it was shown that what actually happens is that your key employees, the ones driving your sales and development, spend more time suffering from a problem and working unproductively before finally reporting it, take longer to get a problem resolved because of the time they waste trying to navigate the 'tool' supposed to assist them, and feel a greater level of frustration and impotence which leads to unhappiness with the work environment, and ultimately, the company they work for. By trying to save a few dollars on some low-level technical salaries, you risk losing your most productive, experienced people."

Carlisle had listened intently to Thibodeau's speech, nodding his head at the description of frustrated end-users. Thibodeau's polished delivery, his deep, rich voice sounding like a radio announcer or evening newscaster, enhanced the believability of his words.

Keri blessed the added research she'd done on Sunday, accessing the company Win/Loss database and looking up all the proposals they'd lost to Thibodeau for any insight into the strategies he might use. She'd actually hoped he'd take this tack, and had her rebuttal well in hand.

She turned to Carlisle. "Mr. Thibodeau's studies are correct. Our company reviewed the same material, two years ago when they were originally published. Instead of simply throwing up our hands and declaring automation a fool's choice, we put our programmers to work developing a better tool. The key problem with all of the self-help automation used in those studies is that they do text searches for key words. While technical support people may apply technical words to a given situation, the end-user will likely choose different words, reflecting the impact when using the product. So someone reporting an application that 'does not compute the sales ratios correctly' won't find a solution for a 'currency conversion error'. We solved that problem by the use of an innovative thought-mapping system, which allows the end-user to choose among groups of related concepts, rather than being forced to guess specific matching words, as well as by allowing contextual error reports. A sample session of a common problem report is in Appendix C."

Carlisle immediately flipped to Appendix C of her proposal. He hadn't investigated Thibodeau's Appendix B.

She fought back a smile. It wouldn't do to look too smug. But she knew she'd read Carlisle correctly. He considered himself an intelligent, competent man, and his inability to use his company's previous attempt at help desk automation had been a black mark against all future automation attempts. She'd reframed the problem as one of miscommunication, and offered a solution not to the automation problem, which he wasn't convinced needed to be solved, but to the communication problem, which he knew existed.

He nodded his head, flipping the pages to look at other examples. "This is good. Both the engineers and the sales reps could use this."

"And of course there are overrides," she continued, closing in for the deal. "People who have reported similar problems in the past or who are familiar with the system, such as desk side support technicians, can skip any or all of the prompts to speed their entry of problems."

The room was silent as Carlisle leafed through the remaining pages of the appendix.

"It's proprietary, I assume?"

"Of course." She favored him with a brilliant smile, finally allowing a pleased expression. "This is pre-announce information, which is why you hadn't heard of it yet. It will be officially launched at next month's industry trade show, but it's been going through real-world testing at two of our other clients. They're willing to serve as references. But the productivity studies we've done with them indicate end-users resolve their problems faster, and feel a much greater sense of ownership and accomplishment, enhancing their workplace morale."

He glanced at Thibodeau. "Any comment?"

Thibodeau shrugged, but Keri knew his mind must be racing, trying to find a counter-argument. "There's still the issue of trying to capture the information in this new format correctly, populating the database it uses with the knowledge from the support staff. You have a high initial cost of personnel resources that might not be recouped by slight future savings."

"And that is an issue, if you choose to build an initial comprehensive database," Keri admitted. "We propose that as our favored solution, because we feel it provides the best results in terms of end-user satisfaction and confidence in the new tool. But the option exists for situations to be entered as they are encountered, allowing the tool to be loaded with the most common problems first, and leaving less common situations until later or not at all. Optional solutions numbers three and four use this methodology, and the resultant cost savings are detailed in the solution breakdowns."

The meeting continued for another two hours, hammering out the details of Uninational's final solution. But both teams knew Thibodeau's company would be unable to meet Uninational's new criteria. As long as Keri's team didn't do anything to lose the account, the win was hers.

"That's it, then. I look forward to receiving your best and final offers next Monday." Carlisle shook hands all around, and left the room.

The two teams gathered their materials, packing up their laptops and calling their respective offices to get the urgent phonemails that had been left for them during the meeting. Thibodeau extended his hand across the table to Keri, in the manner of a tennis player reaching across the net after a match.

"Well done. That help desk tool wasn't in your initial proposal."

She shook his hand, surprised by how warm it was. She'd expected it to be cool, like him. But their handshake ended before she had a chance to analyze the sensation.

"A girl's got to keep her secrets," she answered, shrugging dismissively. He knew as well as she did that no one ever disclosed their big guns in the initial proposal.

His eyes darkened, and his gaze flitted down and up her quickly, as if searching for any other secrets she might be concealing. Her cheeks blazing, she lowered her head and turned away to continue stuffing her gear into her briefcase. He wasn't reacting the way she expected, and that always threw her. It didn't help that she really did have secrets, now. What would her teammates, or Heaven forbid, Thibodeau and his teammates, think if they knew how she'd spent Friday and Saturday night?

She was saved from further embarrassment by the interruption of one of his team who'd been checking phonemail. "Hey, Andy. Rosenberg moved the Thursday meeting up to Tuesday at ten. He wants to know if you can make it."

He muttered a curse under his breath and immediately went to attack his new problem, leaving Keri feeling curiously abandoned. She didn't question her good luck, and simply grabbed her briefcase and fled.

Her teammates caught up to her in the hall. Jimmy slapped her on the back. "Great job, Keri. You really nailed it."

She felt the heat resurfacing in her cheeks, her mind returning to the weekend, and the way she'd been nailed by Alex. Was there no word that didn't have a sexual connotation, now? She forced the images aside. But it was hard. The memories were so vivid, she fancied she could even smell the spicy scent of his cologne.

"It was a solid proposal. We all worked hard on it, to make it unassailable. The team deserves the credit."

"Yeah, but you uncovered the details of the studies they used to support their proposal. That really sold Carlisle, making their data seem out of date," Susan said.

"That's why they pay me the big bucks."

"We'll all be getting the big bucks for this one," Jimmy answered. "I smell a signing bonus. And I know just what I'm doing with mine. There's a sweet little sailboat down at the marina that's been calling my name."

They chatted casually about their plans for any bonus they received as they drove back to the office in Susan's SUV.

"I thought I might take a vacation," Keri said, after listening to Jimmy's plans for a bigger and better sailboat, and Susan's plans for redoing her kitchen.

"A vacation? This'll be a *big* bonus," Susan reminded her. "You'll have to take a pretty big vacation to use it all."

"Well, there's the vacation wardrobe to be considered."

Jimmy laughed. "Oh, this I've got to see. You? Buying clothes that can only be worn once? Watch your driving, Susan. Frogs are about to start falling from the sky."

Keri grinned at his good-natured teasing, and turned around in her seat to face him. "I never said they could only be worn once. Just that they could only be worn on vacation."

"Oh, so you're not planning one vacation," Susan said. "You're planning a whole string of them. Gallivanting around the world, while we hold down the fort for you back here."

"It was just an idea. I don't even know where I'd go."

But she knew who she wanted to go with. She imagined traveling someplace exotic, someplace that came alive at night, in the company of her mysterious Master Alex.

"Ooh, I know that look!" Susan squealed. "You're going with someone."

Keri's face heated again. It seemed to be a common condition for her today, no doubt related to how Alex had made her blood boil over the weekend.

"It's nothing definite," she mumbled. "Just an idea."

"So who is he? Do we know him?"

"Knock it off, Susan," Jimmy said. "She's practically ready to climb out the window to get away from your questions."

"Well, you'd tell us before you actually went anywhere, right?"

"Of course. Someone would have to cover my workload."

Susan pulled a face. "That wasn't what I meant."

"I know. So, Jimmy, tell me more about this sailboat of yours. How big did you say it was?"

Jimmy cheerfully filled the awkward silence with a loving description of his prospective boat. Keri smiled and nodded at all the right times, but her mind was a million miles away, thinking about Alex.

What could she tell Susan? After all, Keri had made love to him more intimately than she'd ever imagined was possible, and yet, she didn't even know what he looked like. She'd pictured him as looking like Julian McMahon, but she didn't expect that's what he really looked like. It was a sign of how badly Susan's questions had rattled her that she couldn't even do that much, without Andy Thibodeau's features getting tangled in her thoughts.

She stared out at the surrounding city scrolling by, a smile slowly spreading across her face. She'd faced down Andy Thibodeau, "The Shark," and she'd won. She'd dreamed of this day, the day she'd finally prove that she was the best of the best. And she was.

It wouldn't last, of course. There'd be other accounts she wouldn't win, simply because her team couldn't put together a cost-effective proposal that met all of the client's needs. Other cases where her competitors would have proprietary software or services that gave them the edge. But for today, at least, she was on top of the world.

And tonight, she would celebrate. Master Alex had been gone again when she woke Sunday morning, leaving her another dry note of apology, saying he didn't want to unduly tempt her. But he'd invited her to return again tonight at eight o'clock. Sunday night, alone in her bed, she'd ached to be with him. The day had crawled by, fueling her restless need to research, the research that had paid off so handsomely in today's meeting.

She had much to thank Master Alex for. And she would. However he wanted her to thank him.

Her body pulsed, heating with readiness for his touch, and she rolled down the window to get some air. The ride back to the office couldn't be quick enough. She needed to get away from Jimmy and Susan, and be alone with her thoughts of Alex.

CHAPTER SIX

Eight o'clock found Keri bounding up the stairs to Master Alex's apartment. Just the thought of soon being with him had her blood pumping, her nipples tight and tingling, and her sex hot and wet. She was so primed, she'd probably come just from hearing his voice.

Once again, the door was open. This time, a trail of aromatic cedar shavings led back to the dungeon. She inhaled deeply, thinking of secluded meetings in dark woods, of Alex tying her to a tree while he ravished her completely, of lashings with pine boughs whose tiny needles brought her to one shuddering, screaming climax after another.

Oh, God, she wanted him. She was trembling so hard she could hardly walk. There must be something wrong with her, to need Alex so badly. Yet she'd never felt as right as she did with him, as completely loved and cared for, and as certain of her place in the world.

She entered the dungeon, stopping just inside the doorway. Alex was not there, not that she'd expected to see him, but he'd arranged three of the whips artfully on the bed, their bright colors clearly visible on the black and gold comforter.

He'd curled the lashes to make the form of a woman. The handle of the red whip formed the head, with four of the knotted braids separated and spread out to form the woman's arms and sides. The final two lashes curled around to form breasts, the knotted ends rising up like erect nipples.

She imagined the heavy lashes of that whip beating her back, her arms, and her delicate breasts, and trembled with fear. It would be too much to bear. She knew she could never withstand it. But Alex would know that, too. He wasn't planning on using such a brutal whip on such delicate flesh. Was he?

The rest of the whip figure didn't reassure her. A beautifully ornate gold-handled whip with dozens of flat leather lashes of deep green leather was spread to form the woman's legs, bent at the knees, with the handle rising between them. The tiny blue whip nestled against the gold and green handle, mimicking the soft bush of the woman's pubic hair.

That was the whip Alex had used on her the first night. That was where he had used it.

Keri grabbed one of the wrought iron bed posts and held on, no longer certain her legs would support her.

Alex moved quietly, her only awareness of him when she felt the heat of his body behind her, and smelled the spicy scent of his cologne. She closed her eyes and leaned her head back, finding his shoulder.

"Master," she whispered.

He put his arms around her, holding her close, and let her draw strength from his hard, firm body. Slowly, as her shivers abated, he unzipped her quilted jacket and slid his hand inside, gently fondling her breast. She was soothed beneath his touch, and was soon arching into his cupped palm and moaning softly as his fingers tweaked and squeezed her nipples.

"Adina, my ornament," he murmured, kissing the side of her neck and under her jaw. "What troubles you?"

"The knotted whip. It's so...brutal looking. To have it hit *there*..."

She whimpered as she turned her face into his shoulder, nuzzling his neck with her eyes closed. Reaching up, she grabbed his arm to hold him tight, keeping his hand warm and reassuring over her heart.

Alex continued stroking and caressing her until her panic faded. He kissed her temple, her cheek, her ear, and her jaw with soft, feathery kisses that were like gentle caresses of his lips. Then his mouth closed over hers.

The kiss began softly, with a gentle brush of his lips against hers. He nibbled her lower lip, teasing it to fullness, as his fingers brushed and flitted over her nipple in time to his kiss. When he unexpectedly pinched her nipple, Keri gasped, and his tongue thrust into her open mouth.

Soon she was writhing in his arms, the sweep and thrust of his tongue keeping time with the pulls and tweaks of his fingers. She was burning, each touch stoking the fire to blaze hotter and higher. She rocked her hips, leaning back to fit her ass against the bulge of his erection, the friction maddening her with promise but leaving her pulsing core achingly empty.

Alex reached between her legs with his free hand, cupping her sex. She moaned into his mouth, and bucked her hips more urgently. Shifting his hold, he bent one finger so that the knuckle pushed against her clit. Her next pump of her hips drove her against the rigid lump, sparking a climax that had her muscles clenching and spasming in uncontrollable tension and release. He just held her, supporting her and comforting her, until the shaking stopped.

"Feel better now?" he asked.

"You know I do."

"Good. You know that I would never harm you."

"I know."

"The whip was another ice cube, another way to frighten you with possibilities. You're not ready for that whip yet, and would never be ready for it to hit your breasts. It's meant for lashing backs and asses, well-protected areas that can take that kind of punishment."

She shivered, her fear rapidly translating to arousal. Catching herself turning in his arms, she checked the motion before she could accidentally see his face. Instead, she bent her head to lick and nuzzle the pounding vein in his neck, while her hands rubbed and caressed his broad back through the fine cotton of his soft shirt.

"I promised myself that I would thank you, tonight, however I could. What can I do to thank you, Master?"

"Thank me for what?"

She hesitated, not sure how to explain without breaking his rule that she not discuss the real world while she was with him.

"I had a very successful day at work, today. And it was because I was so lonely for you yesterday, I threw myself into the preparations with more passion than usual."

A short laugh escaped him. "Then it seems my loss will be amply rewarded. Although I would have preferred to have you here with me yesterday."

"Me, too."

"I know the perfect way for you to thank me, then. Keep your eyes closed."

He moved away, and she heard the rustle of bedcovers, followed by the zip of his pants and the twin thumps of his shoes being kicked off. Taking her by the hands, he led her to the bed, then sat on the edge while she knelt between his legs. The soft weight of the comforter settled over her head, cocooning her in a dim tent with only his rampant cock for company.

Alex's fingers stroked through her hair. "Open your eyes, now."

She admired the sight of his cock, large and straight, thrusting up toward her face. The musky scent of him made her mouth water.

"Do you want me to take you in my mouth?" she asked. It would be a struggle to fit his entirety. The head of his cock would go all the way to the back of her throat, maybe even sliding down it a ways. She'd be choking on cock, endlessly swallowing until he found his release. The thought terrified her, at the same time as it made her wet with desire.

"Eventually," he answered, his words only slightly muffled by the comforter. The same gaps that allowed light and air to enter let her hear him clearly. "But before I put my cock down your throat, it needs to be lubricated. Lick it. All over. Until it's as wet as your sex."

Perversely, her mouth went dry at his provocative image. Her sex pulsed and steamed, wetting her panties with her readiness, while her tongue stuck to the roof of her mouth.

She bent her head, nuzzling his cock and balls and inhaling deeply of his scent. Heat rose from his balls, and blood pulsed loudly in the artery of his thigh.

Moisture flooded her mouth, and she began kissing and licking, working her way from the hairy base all the way up to the open and eager tip, already beading with desire. She lapped up the salty-sweet droplet, probing the cleft with her tongue.

He groaned, his fingers clenching in her hair. Then she scraped her teeth along the underside of the head. He cried out, his hips lifting from the bed, his hands tightening into painful fists.

Keri slid her hands beneath his raised hips, cupping his firm ass, and continued to kiss and lick his cock while her fingers found the cleft of his ass, probing inside for the sensitive entrance.

He cried out again, his ass muscles tightening around her questing finger, and his cock bobbed and waved with the trembling of his thighs.

"Too much," he gasped. "Too much. Back off."

She pulled her finger away and lifted her mouth from his swaying cock. Above her, he panted in ragged breaths, slowly regaining control. Finally, he was able to speak again.

"God, if you do that again, I won't be able to stop myself from coming. And I want this to last a lot longer than that."

"Yes, Master. Tell me what you want me to do."

He paused, and she suspected he really wanted to tell her to do exactly what she'd just done. But eventually he said, "Suck my balls."

"Yes, Master."

Obeying his order, she pushed her face between his thighs and took his left ball into her mouth. With her tongue, she stroked and caressed the soft skin, while she sucked it deeper into her mouth, pulling it gently. Alex's soft groans of pleasure guided her to discover what he enjoyed the most. Turning her attention to his right side, she repeated all of the things that most pleased the left.

"Now the cock," he whispered, his heavily accented voice hoarse with strain. "Lick it again, then suck it."

She complied, bathing his cock with long strokes of her tongue until it glistened. Then she opened her lips and let the heavy weight of it slide into her mouth. She swept her tongue around the head, teasing the cleft and the tender underside of the head, while Alex groaned and moaned in agonized ecstasy.

Slowly, she swallowed him, one precious quarter of an inch at a time, rejoicing in the slippery slide of his head along the roof of her mouth, and the hard sides of his cock against the inner walls of her cheeks. As he moved further into her mouth, she sucked, pulling him even deeper, drawing reluctant beads of cum from the open head. The first drop hit the back of her throat, and she swallowed convulsively.

Then she had to keep her throat loose and relaxed as he pushed his way to the back, filling her mouth and throat with cock just as she'd imagined. His cock trembled, her head rising and falling with the shaking of his thighs, but always keeping him sealed tightly in her mouth.

His hands found her skull, and guided her mouth to slide up and down his wet cock. Every slick thrust elicited a harsh grunt from him, and every slow release pulled forth a shuddering sigh.

Soon he was gasping for breath, thundering in and out of her mouth while she gripped his ass and struggled to hold on to his writhing, bucking body.

"Now!" he gasped. "Now!"

There was no way she could ask what he meant, not with her mouth full of cock, and she knew better than to interrupt his rhythm for something as trivial as words. Realizing she needed further guidance, he released her head, trusting her to maintain the driving rhythm he'd established, and gripped her wrists.

Oh! She slid her fingers over the taut and straining muscles of his ass, slipping on the sweaty skin, until she found his cleft.

"Yes!" he rasped. "Now!"

His hands once more held her skull, urging her to take his cock faster, deeper, and harder. Meanwhile, she struggled to keep her grip on his sweaty, straining ass, while her fingers probed for the elusive entrance. Finally, she found it, thrusting her finger against his tight bundle of nerves.

Alex screamed his release, flooding her mouth and throat as he spasmed and twitched, his muscles convulsing around her finger. He kept coming and coming, longer than any release he'd ever had with her before, while she swallowed again and again, taking all that he had to give.

Finally, he subsided, his muscles quivering, and his cock slid out of her mouth to lie limp and spent, glistening wetly between his legs. His hands stroked and petted her hair, the only embrace their positions would allow.

"Oh, God," he whispered. "Oh, God. That was... Oh, God."

Keri smiled, thrilled beyond words that she had pleased him so thoroughly. Her heart glowed with gentle radiance as she lay her head in his lap, closing her eyes and resting her cheek upon his still quivering thigh.

"I'm happy that I pleased you, Master."

"Oh, you did." He hesitated. "Are your eyes closed?"

She fought the instinctive urge to open them at his question. "Yes, Master."

"Keep them closed."

He pushed the comforter away, freeing her from the dusky warmth that had contained her, and pulled her up onto the bed with him. Drawing her close, he lay with her in a full embrace, him still wearing his shirt and her fully clothed but with her jacket undone.

As he clung to her, his face buried against her neck and his arms wrapped tight around her, she realized this was not part of their elaborate Master/slave play. This was Alex, needing to hold her close because the gift she'd given him had so stunned him, he couldn't bear to part from her. This was real, true emotion, beyond fleeting passion and great sex, even though it had been the sex that created it.

Softly, gently, unfurling like the tender green shoots of a flower stretching toward the sun in the Springtime, a previously unknown emotion took hold and grew inside her. Her arms settled around him, returning his embrace and holding him close as they breathed in tandem. And she realized that somehow, in the blazing inferno of their lovemaking, passion had been transmuted into love.

They held each other, neither saying a word, just breathing together, for nearly an hour, before Alex finally spoke.

"That wasn't what I had planned for the evening, but I certainly approved of the change. What about you?"

Keri nodded, her hair rubbing up and down against his shirt-clad chest. Suddenly, she started to laugh.

"What is it?"

"I think this is the longest I've been with you fully clothed."

After a moment, he joined in, his laughter rich and fluid. Then his laughter faded, his arms tightening around her again. "We can fix that."

The soft promise in his words sparked a firestorm in her blood, and suddenly she wanted to be completely naked, feeling her body writhing against his. "Yes," she whispered.

"You'll need to be blindfolded again."

Suddenly, she hated her promise. It was one thing not to see his face when he was her mysterious Master, giving her the best sex of her life. But she wanted to gaze into the eyes of the man she loved. Maybe not during the sex—she liked being tied up, tied down, and pushed around too much to forego the pleasure just for the benefit of seeing her lover's face while she came—but before, seeing his expression of anticipation mirroring her own, and after, seeing how satisfied she'd made him. That's what she wanted.

But if it was a choice between seeing his expression as he said good-bye, and not seeing his expression as he taught her body new meanings of the word "ecstasy," the choice was simple.

She closed her eyes and released him. "Whenever you're ready, Master."

Soon, the blindfold was blocking out all light, and his hands were moving over her body, undressing and caressing her. But in the back of her mind, she wondered why he insisted that his face remain hidden. What was he afraid she'd see?

She kept recalling a scene from the *Charmed* episode when Paige first learns that Cole is half demon. Paige had asked her sister, "How's Cole? Morphed into any demons lately?"

The words repeated in Keri's brain, endlessly looping. Morphed into any demons lately? Morphed into any demons lately? She loved Alex. But that hadn't been enough to save Phoebe and Cole from the disastrous effects of their doomed love. Would her love be enough to overcome Alex's secrets? Or would those secrets eventually drive them apart?

* * * * *

Keri woke to darkness. The rubber sheet beneath her stuck to her sweating skin, so she knew she was still in the dungeon. But where was Alex?

She swept her arm across the bed, searching for him. Nothing.

"Alex? Master? Are you here?"

Her voice was swallowed by the cavernous room, the special paint and ceiling tiles absorbing the sound.

She closed her eyes and rolled over, wincing as she pressed against one of the bruises on her ass. Alex had tied her to the massage table and shown her the wonders of whipping, which had made her forget all her doubts and fears as the sensations flooding her body consumed her. By the time he finished, her back and ass were on fire with desire, although he'd been careful not to break the skin or cause any serious damage. He assured her that the few small bruises would fade by morning.

But that didn't stop them from hurting now. And not in a good way. In a way that kept her from getting back to sleep.

And now that she was awake, she realized she needed to go to the bathroom. The more she tried to ignore it, the more urgent the need became.

"Fine. Not like I was sleeping, anyhow."

Careful to avoid any additional pressure on her bruised ass, she put her legs over the side of the bed and stood up. Extending one hand like a player in Blind Man's Bluff, she stumbled toward the bathroom. The door was already ajar, and she reached out, fumbling for the light switch.

The overhead bulbs flared to brilliance, just as Alex was coming through the connecting door to his bedroom.

"Oh my God! It was an accident! I didn't mean..." Keri's apology stuttered to a halt as her sleepy brain recognized the man in front of her. Andy Thibodeau. "You!"

Keri sagged against the doorframe, landed on one of her bruises, then winced and pulled away. She turned back to the dungeon, light from bathroom seeping past her to pool on the floor allowing her to see the bed, although the rest of the room was still in shadow.

The bed where she'd gone down on Thibodeau earlier, thanking him for her successful day at work. She groaned, burying her face in her hands.

"Keri, please, it's not what you think."

"What, that it wasn't all just some sick joke? God, you knew exactly who I was, you knew what happened today, and yet you let me..."

He came up behind her, placing his hand on her shoulder, but she shrugged him off.

"Don't touch me."

"Keri, please—"

"How long have you known? Since the beginning? Is that why you approached me at the party?"

Sickness churned in her stomach. She'd felt so sexy and desirable in her costume. Had it all been a lie? Had he approached her only because he knew he'd be competing against her for a client, and wanted any advantage he could get? It was a low, dirty trick, but something she wouldn't put past The Shark.

"No. I had no idea who you were until you took off your mask. I approached you because you were beautiful, confident, and sexy as hell. Just looking at you from across the room was enough to make me hard."

She'd had proof enough of his desire while dancing with him. And their bodies had never lied to each other. He had desired her. But she remembered his strange hesitancy when she'd removed her mask, and her fear that she'd done something wrong.

"Why didn't you tell me when you found out who I was?"

"Because I wanted you. I wanted you so badly I could hardly think, and I didn't want a simple vanilla affair. I wanted to be your Master, to rock you to your core with the feelings I inspired in you."

He turned her to face him, tipping her chin up so that she had to look him in the eyes. Well, she'd gotten her wish, to look into her lover's eyes, and it made her as miserable as every magically granted wish ever did.

"Answer honestly, Keri. If you'd known who I was, would you have trusted me enough to allow me to do what I did?"

She bit her lip, then shook her head. No. She'd never have trusted The Shark with her body, let alone her heart.

"But then why did you leave the next morning? Why didn't you explain who you were?"

"I admit to being conceited when it comes to my work. I'm damn good, and I know it. You're good, too. That's why, when Steve said he was in trouble on the Uninational account, I jumped at the chance to face off against you. I wanted to see what you were made of."

She nodded, encouraging him. It's what she'd wanted, too. He sighed, and ran his fingers through his hair.

"Saturday morning, I had every intention of telling you who I was, figuring now that you'd had a chance to get to know me better, you'd know I could be trusted to care for you as my slave. But then I started worrying about how it might affect your work. When I defeated you, I wanted it to be because I was the better consultant, not out of any misguided feelings of servitude on your part."

Keri smiled grimly. "Instead, I kicked your ass."

"You did not kick my ass." His eyes glittered for a moment with anger, before he Mastered his emotions. "You had the better product. And you did a hell of a job preparing for the pitch. You deserved to win the bid, although if you'd been a lesser consultant, you might not have. You beat me, but just barely."

She considered his rationale. Would she have fought as hard as she had if she'd known she was facing Master

Alex across the table, and not Andy Thibodeau, The Shark? She'd had enough trouble keeping her thoughts away from Alex during the meeting, although now she realized her subconscious must have made the connection between the two men, even if her conscious mind hadn't.

She frowned, disturbed again by what looked like his obvious pattern of deception.

"But at the meeting, I didn't recognize your voice. You sounded nothing like you do now."

He shrugged. "Professional radio voice. I took training in how to sound sincere, convincing, and corn-fed American back when I started in sales. For some reason, many people were disinclined to trust a salesman with an accent, unless it was British."

"I think it's sexy."

His smile lit up his entire face, and she realized she'd spoken in the present tense, giving him hope that his lie had not destroyed her feelings for him.

"Ah, but sexy is not the same as sincere. And sincere is what sells."

"What kind of accent is it, anyway? I've never been able to place it."

"My father was in the amusement park business. I was born in Florida, then moved to Paris and Australia while I was growing up. So my accent's a sort of Outback French Floridian."

She glanced over her shoulder at his dungeon. "Amusement parks, huh?"

"Let's just say that a passion for satisfying fantasies runs in my blood."

Her blood hummed at the thought of the fantasies he'd already satisfied, and the promise of all the ones he would satisfy in the future. If she let him.

"But there's still tonight. We'd already had the client meeting. You'd already lost. Why insist on the blindfold tonight?"

"I almost told you after the meeting, but you ran away before I got a chance. So I planned to tell you, preferably after you were tied up so you couldn't run away before I explained. But you looked so distressed by the whips that I couldn't add to your pain by revealing the secret then. And once you told me how you wanted to thank me, well, I couldn't resist the opportunity to have one of my own fantasies fulfilled."

"It wasn't what you expected, though, was it? I—what was your phrase?—rocked you to your core."

"You did. And I panicked."

Keri blinked. That wasn't the admission she expected to hear. "You panicked?"

"I'd known we were good in bed together, and made an awesome Master/slave team. But those sorts of relationships come and go all the time. People grow, they move on, their needs no longer mesh the way they did. If you'd changed your mind about being my slave after finding out who I really was, I'd have been saddened, but would have shrugged it off and looked for my next slave."

"But...?" she prompted.

"Something changed tonight. We connected, in a way that took me completely by surprise. I couldn't lose you. I wouldn't lose you. And if the price of that was continuing to hide my face from you, it was a price I was willing to pay."

"I fell in love tonight," she said softly.

His eyes widened, brightening with hope, then his gaze fell and his head drooped. "And I destroyed that by lying to you, didn't I?"

Keri took a deep breath, knowing any possibility for a future in their relationship hinged on her answer. Slowly, she walked forward, until she could feel the heat radiating from his body, then reached out and clasped his hands. Startled, he looked up.

"You didn't lie to me. You gave me a choice, to be with you, allowing you to keep the secret you wanted to conceal, or to insist on knowing all your secrets and having nothing more to do with you. I chose to be with you." She smiled at him, putting all the love she was capable of in her expression. "And if the price of that was you continuing to hide your face from me, it was a price I was willing to pay."

His hands tightened on hers. "Then, we're good? We can still keep seeing each other?"

"I'd like that." She gazed at his body, then stared into his eyes, drinking her fill of the sight of him now that she could. "But one last thing. What am I supposed to call you? Andy? Alex?"

"My real name's Alexander. I hated it as a kid." He drew the name out in an over-the-top French accent. "*Ah-Leek-Sahn-Dre*. So I insisted everyone call me Andy. The name stuck. But I like the way you say Alex. Or Master."

"Master," she whispered.

He closed his eyes, breathing deeply. "I was afraid I'd never hear you say that again."

"Surely someone who enjoys fairy tales as much as you do believed in the happy ending," she teased. "What would this one be, Sleeping Beauty?"

He flipped on the overhead light for the dungeon, then turned her to face the painting on the wall. Walking behind her, he urged her closer until she could see that it was not just a painting of a rose under glass. There were reflections in the glass.

She bent closer, trying to see them better, then gasped as they finally came in to focus. A masked man, dressed entirely in black leather, even his jutting cock, with a wild mane of hair and two lethal-looking horns, held a long black whip in his hand.

Across from him, a beautiful woman was tied naked to some sort of rack, her body crisscrossed with red welts. Her head was thrown back as she uttered a cry of intense passion, her ecstasy visible in every quivering line.

Alex's hands wrapped around Keri's waist, fitting her naked body close against his. "I've always been partial to Beauty and the Beast, myself."

THE END

About the author:

A pinch of this, a smidgen of that... and lots and lots of anything sparkly! Whether it's cooking, decorating, or writing books, Jennifer Dunne is never one to do anything the same way twice, allowing her wide-ranging interests to lead her where they will and trusting that sooner or later, it all comes out in the writing. Her strategy has paid off, earning her three EPPIE awards as well as a host of lesser awards, and devoted fans who eagerly wonder where her next story will take them. Her fiction spans the fantasy, romance, and science fiction genres, but wherever one of her stories goes, it can always be counted on for an exciting ride.

Jennifer Dunne welcomes mail from readers. You can write to her c/o Ellora's Cave Publishing at P.O. Box 787, Hudson, Ohio 44236-0787.

Also by JENNIFER DUNNE:

- Sex Magic
- Luck of the Irish – with Kate Douglas & Chris Tanglen
- Tied With a Bow – with Dominique Adair & Madeline Oh

TRICK OR TREAT

Madeleine Oh

Chapter One

"But I told Andrew you would, darling. He's counting on you."

Katie Fairfax took a deep breath. "Mother, did it ever occur to you to ask? What if I happened to be going away that weekend?"

She pictured her mother's raised eyebrows. "You're not, are you, dear?"

Katie sighed. 'Yes, I am,' entailed lying to her mother, 'No, of course not, ' meant she got stuck cat sitting. What a choice! Pity she couldn't plead allergies. "Tell Andrew, I'll keep his cat."

"I think it will have to be in his house, dear. Moving Elise will upset her, she's expecting"

Sheesh, her sister, her cousin, and now the cat. At least Mother hadn't started on, 'Isn't it time you found a nice young man, Katie'.

"Okay, Mom. Tell Andrew I'm game. But he darn well owes me!"

"I knew you would dear, now don't forget Sally and Tim's shower. You do have a gift don't you?"

Yet another cousin getting hitched-not that she'd have Sally's Tim if he came gift-wrapped, "Not yet, Mom, but I will. See you there then. Bye, I love you."

Katie hung up the phone with a sigh. One of these days she'd toughen up and learn how to tell her mother 'no'. Meanwhile, she was committed to spend a weekend in her favorite cousin, Andrew's, almost obscenely luxurious house, and possibly midwifing a cat. That was in two weeks. More pressing was getting a shower gift for Sally and her intended. A quick trip to the mall one afternoon after work would take care of that. As for the cat, she'd manage. If Andrew had asked, she'd have agreed like a shot, but when her mother asked, she felt honor-bound to push a bit. Mind you, Andrew never nagged her about still being single, and didn't ask prying questions about her social life.

He did however, call her the next day. "So your mom and mine put the screws on you. I didn't mean them to shanghai you."

"What did you intend?" Just curious of course...

"I asked my mother if she knew anyone who'd house and cat sit while I was away. I'm driving down to Atlanta to pick up Sophie." Sophie was Andrew's sophisticated, but quite agreeable, intended.

"No prob, Andrew, but you owe me!"

"Forever!" he agreed. "What can I get you?"

"A gorgeous, exciting, bedworthy man to make all my wildest dreams come true." Good luck Andrew! She'd not managed it herself in twenty-seven years.

"That's a tall order!"

She chuckled. If her mother knew what she'd asked, she'd pitch a hissy fit. "Too hard?"

"No way! Give me time!"

"Never mind, Andrew, if you can't, I'll settle for pizza."

"I think I can find the man for you." He gave a teasing laugh. "Tell you what, you come help me shop for a gift for Sally and Tim, and I'll take you to the new brick oven pizza place at Five Points."

"Sounds great. Shall we stop by the mall?"

"How about the Rose and Leather Boutique?"

The new, kinky sex shop out in Rosewood that certain city counselors had been trying to close. "I thought I'd get them scented candles or perfumed massage oil."

"They have oil, and scented candles, and other stuff. It'll help broaden your horizons. Pick you up at seven, tomorrow."

Mom and Andrew seemed to be taking over her life. She'd suspect them of being in cahoots-but the kinky boutique was not, she was certain, her mother's idea. Still it might be fun. She had been curious about it, with Andrew she'd not get hit on by perverts looking for entertainment, and it would up her street cred with the twenty-year-olds at work.

Andrew was there on the dot, complete with his sporty Mercedes and a smile. Pity he was her cousin, and taken already. On the other hand, did she really want to hook up with someone she'd played kidnap and 'tie up the princess' to his dragon, when they were kids?

"I might have another client for you," he said as his car purred away from the curb. "I gave your name to a man at work for his sister."

"Great! What does she want?"

"Not too sure. She's a writer. Just sold a book, and decided she needs a web site. I've got her card in the glove box."

Not a name that rang any bells, but if she'd just sold a first book, it wouldn't. "Thanks,"

"Have to help keep my little coz solvent."

"I'm two days older than you!" They'd had this argument a dozen times. It was about the only edge she'd ever had.

He glanced away from the road and grinned. "Maybe, but I've got a bigger one than yours!"

She spluttered. What next? "I've managed very nicely without one for twenty-seven years."

"That's not what you told me on the phone last night."

She'd live to regret that little confidence. "Maybe, but can you provide one?" She was sorely tempted to slug him one and wipe the smirk off his face. But he was driving, and a major collision would delay getting pizza.

Marvelous pizza it was too: pesto and assagio with shrimp, piping hot from the brick oven. The tiny restaurant was cozy from the warmth of cooking. The air redolent of garlic, and cheese.

"Thanks for the referral about the website," Katie said as she chewed on a particularly toothsome mouthful of shrimp. "Every one helps."

"How are things going?

"Not bad really. I may even end up making a profit this year."

"Wonderful!"

"Not a massive profit you understand-about a hundred, if I'm lucky, but it's way better than a loss, and I can tell my mother that Fairfax Web Design has had a profitable year."

"She's still giving you a hard time over it?"

"Pretty much. I think I'm a major disappointment to her. Susie is a tax accountant, properly married, and producing grandchildren, while I'm single, eking out an existence with a retail job, and playing with computers in spare time that would be better spent finding a husband."

"Quit acting like a sad sack! You'll be the successful one. Your web sites are marvelous. Each one is different, not cookie cutter sites from templates."

"Thanks for the vote of confidence, but I can't convince Mother."

"My mother adds her fuel to the fire. I'd better warn you, they have both decided you need a 'nice young man'. They've seconded me to find one."

She'd been joking, sort of. Her mother and Aunt Mary weren't. "Darn them!" She reached for a second slice. Pizza momentarily satisfied a lot of needs.

"How's your love life?"

From him it didn't sound like a cliche. "According to my mother, unsatisfactory. I'm too particular. I need a man made to measure. After all Sally is getting married and she's two years younger than me! I should be getting worried." It was enough to make a saint cuss.

"Are you too particular?" He grinned. "Don't throw that slice at me! The cheese will fall off. Just wondered. After all you've had plenty of dates over the years."

Katie shrugged. She'd never admit this to Mom, but after all, Andrew was the closest thing to a brother. They'd shared confidences and secrets since they were kids. "I've met some nice ones, yes. A couple Mom thought perfect."

"But you didn't?"

She shook her head. "No one who lit my fire."

He looked at her a long minute. "What was wrong with them?"

"Nothing really! They were nice men, but..."

"The sex just wasn't right?"

"Yeah." She chuckled. "You can just hear me telling Mom that, can't you?"

"I'll find you someone. I think I know the perfect man for you."

"I'm pretty picky, you know."

"But I know you, Katie. Remember when we were kids and I'd kidnap you and carry you off to the dungeon?"

"Yeah! And remember when you tried to kidnap Sally and she ran screaming to Aunt Jenna?"

"God, yes! I had to apologize for scaring her. She was a whiny brat." And hadn't changed much, only now it was her fiancé she griped about. "You never complained."

"Just planned on punching you when I'd had enough!"

"I don't remember you ever punching me."

"Neither do I."

He went very thoughtful, looking at her in a way that sent an odd shiver down her back. It wasn't sexual. Couldn't be. Heck, she and Andrew had had diapers changed together. Attraction wasn't anywhere in the deal.

They finished the pizza in companionable silence, sharing the last slice. Andrew eyed the empty platter. "That was worth the trip down here, now shopping, right? It's why we came, wasn't it?"

"I've got my Visa card ready."

He hadn't been joking about the Rose and Leather Boutique. The black leather bikini and fishnet stockings on the model in the window, set the mood. The whip in her plastic hand left little doubt that this was not your everyday gift shop.

But despite her misgivings, Katie was fascinated, and couldn't help noticing Andrew seemed right at home as he went over to the cash register and bought a gift certificate. That would be an easy way out, but she caught sight of a row of costumes. All grown-up sizes, for Halloween, she supposed. She was looking at a pirate outfit complete with black breeches, spotted kerchief and a white shirt with flowing sleeves, when a young woman clerk came over.

"Looking for a costume?"

"Just looking, thanks."

Andrew came up behind her. "Found something you like?"

"I don't dress up for Halloween." She spent her energies and money handing out candy to the children in the neighborhood.

"They're not for Halloween."

Katie looked from Andrew to the young woman. "Fancy dress?"

She shook her head. "Acting out fantasies." She pulled out a couple of hangers. "The French maid and the nurse are popular."

The idea was preposterous, and utterly fascinating. The nurse and maid did nothing for Katie, but the empire line Jane Austen style dress the clerk now held was lovely. Apart from the slits up to the high waist.

"Like it?" Andrew asked, as the clerk wandered off to talk to another customer.

"I do rather, but it's revealing."

"That's the whole point."

"You could get arrested walking down the street in that."

"Sweet coz, it's not meant to be worn walking down the street. It's for acting out your fantasies in the privacy of your boudoir."

For when the pirate came and carried you off... It took her back to their old games of make believe as kids. "You've got a pirate one?"

"Not the pirate." He chuckled. "I go for the black leather look myself." He looked up at a model suspended against the wall. "Like that."

'That', was skin-tight, black leather pants with a vest that showed pretty much all of the model's wide chest. "I can't see you wearing that for Sunday lunch with your parents."

That sent him off in a great peal of laughter. "I'll let you into a secret, only Sophie has seen me in it."

Perfectly understandable. Or was it? What was she doing here? Fascinated to tell the truth. The price tag on the Jane Austen dress was reasonable enough, but when would she every wear it?

"You like it don't you?" Andrew asked.

"Yes, but I came to get a shower gift, not fancy dress." But she spared a final glance for the Pirate. It even had a leather eye patch dangling from the hanger. Enough! She turned and all but knocked over a table of whips and riding crops. She stepped back, but not before noticing one made of royal blue suede. Fascinated, she reached for the smooth handle, and ran her fingers through the soft tresses, until she noticed the price tag, and put it down very carefully. Way above her price level.

"Like it?" Andrew asked. "It's a nice piece of workmanship: French. They make very nice quality things over there."

"They make the best crystallized fruit too."

He raised an eyebrow at that. "Marrons Glacés to you too, Katie me girl. Never thought I'd find you with a flogger in your hands."

This was getting too much. "Let up, Andrew. I need to find a gift for Sally."

"I've paid for mine. You're the one playing with the merchandise."

Undeniable, but... "You brought me here.

"Yes, I did!"

"Why?"

"Just curious, Katie, and I do so love yanking your chain." He rattled a set of manacles and chains hanging from a display case.

There was no point denying her fascination. Andrew read her too well, but the shop was more crowded than a few minutes earlier. What if one of her clients walked in, or someone she knew? Time to beat a fast retreat. She grabbed the nearest article that wasn't leather or metal: a pair of red velvet, fur-lined handcuffs, and made for the check out.

If the pimply youth at the cash register dared any smart ass comments... He barely glanced at them, just scanned the tag and took her plastic. Why not? If customers regularly bought chains, whips, and the odd-looking leather swing hanging in the window, a pair of handcuffs were pretty banal.

"Do you gift wrap?" She wasn't sure what made her ask that, but...

"Sure," he indicated a roll of paper behind him. It was shiny black with tiny gold and silver handcuffs.

"Never mind." She'd drop by the card shop later and pick up something with flowers or wedding bells. Much safer.

She was ready to beat a fast exit. Where was Andrew? Over by the books and videos, talking to a tall, dark-haired man. A sumptuous-looking dark-haired man. Okay, a kinky dark haired man, given he spent his evenings here, but on the other hand, maybe his cousin had dragged him here too.

At that moment, Andrew looked her way. "Ready?"

"Yes!"

He-and the scrumptious other-walked over.

"Katie, this is Jud Carlton. Jud, Katie Fairfax."

"Hi, Jud" He had a lovely firm handshake, and his eyes crinkled at the corners when he smiled.

"My pleasure." His voice was warm and confident. Yikes! What a sexy smile, did the man have any idea what he did to any woman over puberty? "You're with Andrew?"

"He's my cousin. We're shopping." Sheesh! That sounded twerpy and now Jud was eyeing the black shopping bag in her hand.

"I dropped in to look around, too. You never know what you'll find here. Or," he paused, "who you'll meet."

"We're done, Jud," Andrew said. "On our way for coffee. Want to join us?"

It was the first she'd heard about coffee, but caffeine wouldn't go amiss. She had a web site to work on when she got home.

She ended up in a booth next to Jud, while Andrew went off to pick up three lattes, and to make sure hers was hi-test.

"Planning on staying up all night?" Jud asked.

"With a bit of luck." He nodded expectantly and she went on. "I have a web design business on the side."

"So you stay up all night working?"

"Not every night. Just when I have someone paying extra for a rush job. I wasn't about to say 'no'."

"Do you ever say 'no'?"

How was she supposed to take that? His dark eyes didn't look as if he were hitting on her, but hell if she knew. "When it's in my self-interest, yes. What about you?"

"Me? I believe in self-indulgence and discipline."

"Aren't they contradictory?"

Jud shook his head, and a lock of dark hair fell over his high forehead. "Not in the least. Doesn't one need both in any venture? How would your business on the side be without discipline on your part?"

"It wouldn't be, and yes, my mother considers it self-indulgent."

"Proves my point!" She wasn't sure it did, but... "So, Katie, what do you do when you're not building web sites, or shopping for kinky toys?"

"I wasn't shopping for..." Hell, she had been. "For a 'day job' I work retail. It pays the rent, and gives me health insurance."

"Retail? Hmmm... Not at the Rose and Leather?"

"No way! I'd never even been there before."

"Big bad, cousin leading you astray?" His eyes twinkled. "Tell me what did you buy?"

"Handcuffs."

"Ever had them used on yourself?"

"Good grief, no!" That sounded ridiculously prim. "They're for my cousin, as a gag gift for her shower."

"If it's a 'gag' gift why not get her a gag?"

"They sell gags? What for?" Dumb question.

"Same reason as handcuffs, chains or ropes: to restrain a lover." Had to be something about his voice, but her throat went tight and she felt the bag beside her crackle as her fingers gripped the top. "You think your cousin would like that?"

Highly unlikely! "It's just for fun. She'll never really use them." It was actually hard to even imagine prim Sally making out, but...

"Why not? People do, you know. It adds to the excitement and pleasure."

"Being made helpless?" This was approaching incredible, and fascinating.

Jud nodded. Three seconds later, Andrew arrived with a tray and three mugs. She almost hugged him. Jud was making her nervous, but on the other hand if they now started talking basketball, or football...

They talked about cats, or specifically, Andrew's pregnant one.

"Katie's holding the fort for me while I'm away. She can be godmother to the kittens if she likes."

She didn't really like. "I'm going to will that cat to wait until you get back."

"Don't sweat it," Jud said. "If you need help delivering, just give me a call. My mother bred dogs, cats can't be that different."

"I might just call you to come over so you can worry for me."

He'd obviously been waiting for that. He produced a printed business card, and wrote a number on the back. "Here's my cell phone."

"You make house calls?"

"Any time."

This was getting out of hand! Trouble was, she wanted this Jud she barely knew to make a house call... and stay the night. She was nuts! She knew nothing about him, other than he was one of Andrew's friends-or maybe just an acquaintance. "I'll remember that, Jud." She slipped the card in her jacket pocket, finished her latte, and reminded Andrew she had to get home.

They didn't talk much on the way back. She sensed he was waiting for her to say something-about Jud perhaps. She didn't. Not having any idea what to say, and wasn't sure she wanted to talk about him. He rather unnerved her.

"See you at the shower," Andrew said as he dropped her at her front door and drove away.

Chapter Two

Aunt Sarah's house was packed when Katie arrived.

"Katie! I'm so happy you're here. Come in and get some wine." Sally was glowing with joy, as she hustled Katie into the kitchen where, Tim, her intended, was dispensing jug wine, and talking to Mary, her cousin Jason's very-pregnant wife. Yes, the family was increasing.

Katie took the offered wine, and Mary grabbed a can of pop before they both elbowed their way towards the living room. As Katie noticed and waved at her also pregnant sister, Susie across the room, Uncle Jimmy, Sally's father, called from the doorway. "Okay! Everyone in the living room and get a seat. Time to open the goodies! Part the crowd please and let Sally and Tim through!"

Balancing her wine, Katie moved sideways. Mary followed turning her belly as best she could.

"Excuse, me," a voice said behind them. Katie turned and stared. Jud smiled. "I thought it was you, Katie." He smiled at Mary. "I think in your condition, you deserve a chair. With a courtly bow, he stood and offered her his.

Mary was no fool, eight months gone and swollen ankles. She sank into the wing chair with a grateful smile. "Thanks."

"My pleasure," Jud said, and closed his hand over Katie's and eased them both away.

Smooth mover was an understatement. They were squashed in a corner, and as more people moved into the room, she found herself penned in behind the sofa.

"Didn't expect to see you here. You know Sally and Tim?"

"No. Sophie's out of town, so Andrew brought me instead."

She couldn't help laughing. "Think anyone noticed the difference?"

He nodded with mock seriousness. "I suspect so, but three bottles of good Merlot helped ease the way."

"Is this sort of affair your idea of an evening out?" She was here half on sufferance. She'd have heard about it from her mother until Christmas if she hadn't put in an appearance.

"I understood you'd be here."

He was direct. "I might not be staying."

"You see a way out?"

Short of climbing over the back of the sofa and stepping on the four people occupying it-no. "This wasn't accidental, was it?"

"Not much that I do is accidental."

Sheesh, what had she ended up with? Besides a voice like warm Kahlua, and looks to stop traffic or change the weather. "Planned it all out did you?"

"Yes." She was tempted to shove him for his arrogance, but elbow space was at a premium right now. "After I got home Thursday, I called Andrew right away, and he said you'd be here. I came. Waiting for you to call was too iffy. I was afraid you'd chicken out."

She almost spluttered red wine all over Aunt Mildred's new hairdo. Jud offered her a handkerchief. It was perfectly ironed, hemstitched linen, darn good thing she didn't really need it.

"Thanks." As she handed it back, their fingers brushed, his dark eyes watching her intently. His gaze bothered her, or more precisely, excited her. She turned away, making a point of looking intently at the stack of wrapped and ribboned gifts. "They should start opening them soon."

"Can't wait to see them open your present," Jud said, "and to watch your reaction."

"My reaction?" It was what the entire family would say when Susie opened it that was bothering Katie. And heaven help her! Her mother was now standing by Susan, and at a nudge from Susan, Mother looked across the room. She waved, her eyes all but popping out on stalks when she noticed Jud. Katie groaned inwardly, she was headed for the maternal inquisition now. "Hi, Mom, Susie!"

They both waved back, eyeing Jud as if he were the first man they'd seen in twenty years. And he, drat the man, nodded politely and smiled! Susie simpered in reply. Darn it, her sister was married with two and seven-ninths children, she had no right ogling her man. Hey, wait! Jud wasn't hers. He was just the man imprisoning her in the corner behind a rather nice, chintz-covered sofa.

"Your mother?" Jud whispered, his breath warm in her ear.

She nodded. "And my sister."

"Am I the only person present who isn't a blood relative or in-law?"

"Yes."

"That gives me an edge, I hope."

"I don't think it gives you anything!"

Since Robbie, Sally's brother called for quiet just then, Jud was saved the trouble of replying. Everyone settled expectantly to watch Sally open her gifts.

But first they had to divide into three teams and blow up condoms until they burst. Since everyone else was suitably impressed at Jud's condom bursting ability, she pretty much had to be. Fair enough, he did burst their team to victory.

"That was interesting," Jud whispered "Do that often at family gatherings do you? Some sort of fertility rite?"

She not only stopped herself from laughing, she even managed to look him in the eye and reply, "Yes. It's a family custom."

"Hmmm." He raised his dark eyebrows and the corner of his mouth twitched. "I can think of much better uses for them."

"If they pop that readily I'm not sure I'd ever trust one around you!"

"I'll get super strength ones."

And Mom was smiling benignly in their direction. If she had half a notion what he'd just said, she'd have a conniption. "Think you'll need them?"

"Of course. I wouldn't want to get you pregnant, until you're certain you want to have my baby."

She asked for that one! But, she had to admit, she'd never had so much entertainment at a family gathering in her life. And she'd be up there with the angels, if she didn't get a charge out of all the admiring and curious glances cast their way. She was spared from answering by the start of the grand gift opening.

"I like the black lace one," Jud whispered as Sally opened yet another tap pants and camisole set.

Keeping her eyes fixed on Sally and Tim surrounded by wrapping paper and gifts, Katie shook her head. "I prefer the red satin one." "It'll look good on you, but even more, I'll enjoy taking it off."

Sheesh, try to be ornery and the man took it as come on. "Dream on!"

"Oh, I do, Katie. Don't you? Imagining you has kept me awake the past couple of nights."

"That explains it, you're sleep-deprived."

"It's not sleeping I plan."

Across the room, she caught her mother's encouraging smile. Mom wouldn't be quite so complacent if she knew what Jud was saying-or would she? After their last, 'Katie, do you think your attitude might be putting men off? You should try harder!' She wondered, Right now, it was Jud who was trying-in every sense of the word!

"After this, I'm going home to sleep-alone!"

"Good. That means I don't have competition!"

He got a punch in the ribs for that.

His hand caught hers. Very gently, he opened her hand, and stroked one finger across her palm. Quite against her will, her body broke out in goose bumps. He dropped her hand before she had a chance to pull it away.

"You're pushing your luck, Charlie!"

"It's Jud, and I'm looking forward to pushing more than that."

"You flatter yourself that you even have a chance."

"I know I do, Katie, and so do you. If you were really annoyed you'd have moved away. You're enjoying wondering what outrageous thing I'll say next."

She was sorely tempted to deny that soundly. But lying was a sin, so she settled for a glare, suspecting it wouldn't have the slightest effect, and darn it, he was right! She was enjoying his company. This was one family get together she'd remember for the rest of her natural born days.

"Alright, Katie?" Jud asked after they watched in silence while Sally opened a gift basket of massage cream and scented candles, and Tim opened an electric can opener. Obviously Aunt Anita and Uncle Joe hadn't approved of the idea of a 'honeymoon' shower.

Katie looked at Jud. His dark eyes were serious, not a glint of amusement or tease. He looked worried, unless he was very good at acting. "Why wouldn't it be alright?"

He smiled. "Shh, they're opening your present now."

Damn it! They were. What had seemed fun in the shop wasn't quite the same with her mother and aunts and uncles looking on. But Sally seemed happy enough. "Just what I need when Tim gets out of line!" she announced to a chorus of ribald laughter. "Thanks, Katie," Tim added. "Let me know if you need to borrow them!"

More laughter all around, then thankfully they moved on to Helen and Jimmy's gift of *The Joy of Sex*.

"You know," Jud whispered, as everyone gave their attention to a long package wrapped in silver paper, "when you look at those cuffs, your breath catches, and your heart beats faster."

A denial rose to her lips, but the words never came out. "You imagine it!"

He shook his head. "I noticed that evening in the coffee bar, and in the Rose and Leather. The thought of handcuffs and manacles excites you."

Talking about it was a bad idea. "Jud..." she began

"I do understand, you know. They excite me too. Kidnap, hostage, princess in the tower, fair maiden in the dungeon are fun games to play."

"Children play games! You grow out of it."

"Some of us never do."

Jud took her hand again. Lightly. It would take no effort to pull her fingers from his. She didn't.

"I won't disappoint you," he promised. For some inexplicable reason, she was wet between her legs.

Katie expected her mother to be hovering by the door. She was dead right. "Katie, dear," Mom enthused. "You will introduce me, won't you?"

Since saying "Hell, no!" to your mother was not an option, Katie smiled. "Mom, this is Jud Carlton, a friend of Andrew's. Jud this is my Mom, Angie Fairfax."

"Pleased to meet you, Mrs Fairfax."

Mom beamed at Jud. "Lovely to meet you! I hope we'll see you at some other family gatherings." Not quite an invitation to dinner, but why did Mom have to act so eager?

A couple of gracious comments from Jud (she had to grant it to him, the man was slick) and they did the last round of good-byes and left.

Together.

She might as well have put an announcement in the morning paper.

He walked her to her car.

"Can I convince you to come and have a drink? Coffee?"

She shook her head. "I'm not making it up, but I have to get home and work. I've..."

"A client waiting for a rush job?"

"Modifications to the rush job."

"I'll accept it's not an excuse if you meet me for lunch tomorrow."

Tomorrow was her day for visiting Gran, as much as the old ladies would love the novelty, Katie was not taking Jud. But she didn't want to brush him off. Ridiculously she was drawn to him, outrageous comments and all. "Tomorrow lunch is out, a family commitment, but if you're serious about wanting to see me, give me a break from playing kitty doula the weekend after next."

"You feel Andrew pulled a fast one on you?"

"To be fair, no, it was my mother."

Jud had a wonderful laugh, and out of the confines of the house, he let it roar in a wonderful rich peal that echoed in the frosty night. Heck, a couple of cousins turned from unlocking cars to listen. "I doubt many people refuse her. She gave me a good once over. I half expected to be asked my career prospects, and whether there was insanity or feeble-mindedness in my bloodlines."

It was her turn to laugh. "That will come when you get invited to Sunday lunch."

"What are my chances of getting an invitation?"

One hundred percent, if she left it up to her mother. "Aren't you going a bit too fast?"

"Far too fast, but what have I got to lose? I made up my mind that night in the coffee shop. I want to see you again. No, what I really want to do is take you home and make love all night... but you have modifications for your clients rush job."

"Jud..." She made the mistake of hesitating.

His knees brushed her thigh as he placed his hands on the car roof, either side of her shoulders. "Katie," he whispered, his voice husky, while she stared up at him like a damn rabbit caught in the headlights. His lips came down, warm and moist in the October night. His mouth closed on hers with a gentle pressure that sent wild desire spiraling through her. Ridiculous! It was only a damn kiss, but his lips caressed, like a warm tide along a smooth beach. Each pressure on her mouth sent another rush of sensation flooding her mind and body. Wetness gathered between her legs, as he pressed his body against hers.

Katie vaguely wondered about people passing by or traffic or Aunt Mary seeing, until his lips opened hers and her mind shut off. She couldn't think, didn't have a need to. She opened her mouth and welcomed his tongue as it gently caressed hers. Blood pounded in her ears. Her heartbeat echoed inside her skull, as she wrapped her arms around Jud Carlton and pulled him close. Her legs parted at a tipping of his knee. She pressed into him, and he pinned her to the car with his body. He was hard. She was hot. And he deepened the kiss. She wanted this kiss to last forever, to spend the rest of her life locked in his embrace, but in a far corner of her reason, she knew there was more, much more. This man would take her to undreamed of places, give her unimagined pleasure, and with that hope, she kissed on.

She was wobbly by the time he broke off.

He too was breathing fast and looking down at her with glazed eyes. "We must stop."

"Why?"

"Because I say so." Her heart skittered at his hoarse voice.

"Jud."

"Not here, Katie. What I want to do to you would get us both arrested, and utterly destroy the wonderful impression I made on your mother. I could take you home with me but..." The damn web site! She was two hairs from consigning her client to the devil but... "Business is business, Katie. You can't let a customer down. We can wait. I'll see you this weekend"

"When?"

"I'll call you." He took the keys from her sweaty hand, and unlocked the door. He even buckled her seat belt for her, and dropped a soft kiss on her cheek. "This weekend, be ready."

He shut the door and walked away while her confused brain processed what he'd said. She was half-tempted to call after him, but they'd put on enough of a display for one evening.

Chapter Three

"What have you done to Jud, Katie?"

Andrew was darn lucky he was across town. As it was, she could only snarl down the phone. "What have *I* done?" her voice rose quite satisfactorily. "I went to Sally's shower, and got opportuned!" Good word that.

"Ah!" The way he laughed, he was lucky he wasn't within kicking distance. "Like Jud do you?"

"I really don't know." Might as well tell the truth. "He comes on a bit too fast."

"Is this the same woman who complained about wishy-washy men?"

"There's a wide range between wimpy and indecisive and Jud Carlton!"

"So, he turns you on just a tad?"

Little did Andrew know! She'd been so fired-up after that kiss, she'd pulled out her trusty vibrator even before stopping to make coffee. "I'm not sure what to make of him." Safe and non-committal seemed best.

"He's smitten, Katie. He just burned my ear off for over an hour. I don't think it's so much lighting his fire as the setting of a conflagration."

"Yeah, right!" Jud had been in control every inch of the way.

"I'm not kidding, Katie-coz. I've know Jud three years, and never seen him like this. I thought you'd hit it off, but never imagined he'd get ensnared so fast."

Flattering but... "Hey, wait a minute! You thought we'd hit it off? You set us up?"

"Guilty as charged." He ignored her angry splutter. "Hold on, Katie. I thought you might suit. He's a good guy, and I thought you needed a good man."

"You're sounding like Mom!"

"Heaven forbid! But who asked me to find them a nice, bedworthy man?" Okay, but she hadn't expected him to take her seriously. "Give him, and yourself, a chance. I think Jud's just what you need." The man certainly knew how to kiss, maybe... "He'll call you, okay?"

"Can't he call and ask himself? Why this John Alden act?" Jud hadn't exactly been hesitant so far!

"You want him to call?"

"I'd like to run my own life without you or my mother orchestrating everything." Arranging a meeting in the kinky shop!" True, Mom wouldn't have set that up but...

"He suggested it!"

Sheesh! "So, he's into that sort of thing?"

"Yes, so am I."

"Andrew!" That sort of squeaked out. It fascinated her, yes. But looking and doing were too very different things. And much as she dearly loved Andrew, she did not want to think about what he and Sophie did in bed. "I'll call him!" she said and hung up.

And didn't call. Heck! What was she going to say? 'You fascinate and scare me all at the same time, and now Andrew's told me you're into kinky sex. I don't know which direction to run.'

Jud was going to have to wait. Web site clients paid good money. Jud looked likely to cost her at least some peace of mind.

Client satisfied, Katie stripped off her clothes and fell into bed, remnants of make-up still on and teeth uncleaned. She'd treat them to double brushing in the morning-and just about passed out. Until she woke climaxing in the middle of the night, still high from a wild dream that featured Jud, red velvet handcuffs and enough wild sex to fill a couple of X-rated videos with original storylines. She lay panting, sweating, and gasping, and convinced she'd better never get that far with Jud, as the reality could never match up. It never had.

After a restless half-hour, she got up, finally cleaned her teeth and showered. She was wide-awake, and this was as good a time as any to start the next job. By five am, she had created a series of sexy graphics that she could never, ever use on a web site for a Methodist church preschool.

What now? She knew damn well she couldn't sleep. She couldn't work, it seemed. And while it was hardly fair to blame Jud, there was no one else available.

She found his card still in her jacket pocket, and punched his number on her cell phone.

It wasn't until she heard his "Hello?" after the fifth or sixth ring she realized it wasn't yet seven, heck, it was barely six-thirty.

"Jud?"

Silence for several seconds. "Katie?"

"Did I wake you?"

"As it happens, no."

He'd been awake, too. Given the feel of his hard body, he probably worked out for two hours before breakfast. "You said to give you a call sometime." Dumb line but...

The phone amplified the richness of his deep laugh. "I did, didn't I?"

"Sorry if I'm disturbing you." Eeek, that sounded wimpy.

"Not in the least, Katie, but tell me, for future reference, are you in the habit of calling men before breakfast?"

She wasn't much in the habit of *ever* calling men, but now was not the time to go into that. "Only good kissers with sexy, dark eyes!" What made that come out?

"I knew you were a woman of sense and good judgment the minute I saw you caressing that suede flogger."

He would have to bring that up! "I was just looking. Anyway, it was too expensive."

"Nothing's too expensive for you, Katie. It fascinated you, didn't it? I was watching you."

"Jud..."

"I watched your lips part and your eyes get bigger." Sheesh! "Were you imagining how it would feel? How those soft tresses would caress your back? How they'd stroke your skin as they trailed over your ass, and down the back of your legs. How they'd feel brushing behind your knees? You're very sensitive there, aren't you?"

Her throat all but seized up. Her heart raced and the hand on the phone was damp with sweat. As were other parts of her body, she didn't want to think about. Why was he talking like this? Even more to the point, why was it turning her on?

"Jud, please..."

"I will, Katie, I promise."

"Listen!" She had to say something, but her mind was awash with sensual images and her cunt was throbbing faster than her magic wand at high speed. This was nonsense, ridiculous, and... "Look here, Jud, I..."

"We need to talk. Lunch is out. Can you meet me this evening, just for an hour?"

After the past five minutes she should run the other way. "There's a deli, at Five Points, Knish and Tell."

"I know it. What time?"

She was working late tonight. "How about nine-thirty?"

"I'll be waiting."

"Okay." Was it really?

"And Katie..."

"Yes?"

"Don't be scared. I understand." Damn good thing he did, because she was completely confused. "I'll be waiting for you."

He was. Sitting in a table by the bay window, watching. For her. Waiting like a lion for his prey, or a lord for his lady. He was turned away, watching up the street, so she paused, half-tempted to run, knowing there was no way she could. No two ways about it, Jud Carlton fascinated her. It wasn't just the sexy voice or the way his eyes sparkled, and wrinkled at the corners when he smiled. There was something about him that drew her, despite his outrageous conversation. But if he really thought she was going to let him whip her, he had another think coming! He turned as she pushed the door open, and stood up, his face breaking out in a broad smile. Had he been worried she'd stand him up? It might have been the smart thing to do, but smart held little appeal.

"Katie!" He stepped towards her, taking both hands in his. A gentle grasp, but very confident, as he pulled her close and kissed her on the cheek.

"You found it okay?" Duh! Of course he had! He was here, wasn't he?"

"Yes, now let me take your coat." He had it off before she had time to suggest she was quite capable of taking off her own coat. As he draped it over a spare chair, on top of his jacket, he asked. "Coffee? Soda? What can I get you? A sandwich?"

Food! She needed to think about food, not the way his hair curled behind his ears. Or did she? The ache in her gut was something far more basic than hunger. "I don't know." What was wrong with her?

"Have a seat." She sat down in the chair he held. "I'll get you something. Are you vegetarian, or anything like that?"

"No!"

He dropped a kiss on her forehead. "Don't get so wound up. I'm not bringing out whips or chains in here."

That was supposed to calm her!

Her deep, relaxing breath came out like a sigh from her gut. She leaned back and stretched out her legs, and doing so, nudged a black plastic shopping bag that looked suspiciously like one from the Rose and Leather. She was tempted to look, but it really was none of her business. Did she really want to know? Yes!

Another deep breath. Why was she here? Because Jud asked her. No, because she'd called him before dawn and had the most outrageous conversation. She needed a couple of weeks to sort this out. He fascinated, and scared the willies out of her. He was into whips and chains, and heaven knew what else, and she wasn't interested. Intrigued, maybe.

Particularly by what was in the bag, less than an inch from her left foot. She could peek, but that would be on a par to his looking in her purse, and she drew the line there.

Better not to know. But she'd have to be made of stone not to wonder. The suede whip? She didn't think so. Handcuffs? Chains? Most likely a couple of the kinky magazines she'd not had the guts to look at with Andrew there.

"Here you are." He was back fast. Just as well she didn't have her nose deep into his shopping. "The soup looked good, and on a damp night like this, I thought it might appeal more than a sandwich."

"Thanks."

Appetizing aromas of garlic, herbs and onions rose up from the bowl of vegetable soup. He set his own bowl on his side of the table, and sat down opposite. "Bon appetite!"

It was delicious, and after the second spoonful, her appetite came back with a rush. "It's great, thanks."

"You're more than welcome, Katie. I enjoy erotic torture, but I've never starved a woman yet."

It was only luck that she happened to be between spoonfuls. "Can we talk about books, or movies, or the weather, while we eat?"

"By all means. May I take that to indicate you're willing to talk about sex after we both finish eating?"

"That was not what I said."

"No, but if you really were offended, you'd be halfway down the street by now. You're not. You're just uneasy."

"I'm not sure it's 'just' anything."

"I'm not either." He paused to take another taste of soup, his lips puckering against the side of the spoon. His eyes met hers, as he slowly sipped without a sound. He rested his spoon on the side of the plate. "Tell me, Katie, Have you read the latest John Grisham?"

She had, and he'd read the latest P.D James. A good start. But after she discovered he'd read all Laurel K Hamiliton's Anita books, and was in the process of collecting Chelsea Quin Yarbro's backlist, Katie felt she'd met a soulmate. "I'm so thrilled you like reading the 'weird' stuff," she said. "Most people I know think I'm odd."

"Maybe we both are. We're not alone, are we?"

It felt as if they were, tucked in a warm corner, with the night outside. It was as if the other customers and the shop around them receded. Jud had her complete focus. She made herself look away and taste her soup. It seemed to have lost most of its flavor. "What else do you read?"

"Erotica."

She should have expected that! But to be truthful. "So do I."

"I thought so. Katie, I'd love to have a look at your collection."

"Sure you don't want to see my etchings?"

"Katie, it's not a pick up line. Looking at your books would tell me a lot about you."

Too much. She wasn't ready to have him see her collection of Laura Antoniou, or her limited edition, leather-bound, Story of O. Not yet. If ever. "If you did, then I'd be entitled to look over your shelves."

"Be my guest, any time. We could trade favorite reads. Have you discovered Ellora's Cave?" Had she just! He'd never get a peek at her hard drive. "They have some quite impressive BDSM works."

"I know."

That smile put a dimple in his right cheek. "I'm damn glad, Katie." He reached across the table, and rested his hand on her forearm. If his touch was meant to be reassuring, it wasn't working. Just feeling the warmth of his fingertips through her sweater sent her body temp up several degrees. "Have you ever told anyone about your interest in kink?"

"I'm not sure I am interested."

He smiled, and lifted an eyebrow. His attitude tweaked her already heightened nerves. "I am, aren't you?"

She wasn't sure about anything any more! The man had her so twirled up inside, she was lucky she knew which end of the spoon to put in her mouth. Just to make sure, she scooped up a spoonful of soup. Definitely lukewarm. About the only thing for a yardstick that was. She was hot under her skin, and the look in Jud's eyes suggested minestrone was the last thing on his mind. "Fifteen minutes of conversation with you, and I'm not sure of anything any more!"

"That was what I was hoping for."

"You get your thrills confusing people?"

"I don't want to confuse. My aim is to help you sort things out."

"How?" Come to that, what did she need to sort out? Whether to walk out now, or in three minutes?

He hesitated, just a tad. "I think, you want things I can offer."

"You sound pretty certain!"

"I am." Was he some sort of weirdo or lunatic? He was Andrew's friend! "I could be mistaken," Jud went on, "but I don't think so."

"Mistaken about what?"

"That you're intrigued by kink, but your only experience is vicarious."

"Aren't you making a wild assumption?" And wasn't she crazy to sit here and discuss it?

"Yes," he agreed amicably, "but I'm not often wrong about these things."

"This could be the time."

"Is it?" In the silence that followed he asked, "Want a fresh coffee? Yours has gone cold."

"I need to go home." But she didn't want to. As much as Jud disturbed her, he was also offering something she wasn't sure she had the nerve to accept.

"Do you? Right now?"

No, but it might well be judicious. "Jud, how about come out and say it? Seems you're beating around the bush, making oblique suggestions. What are you trying to say?"

"I want you to let me take you to bed, and show you the reality is far, far, better than the best kinky fiction."

She'd asked for direct. She got it. What now? Run a mile? Better catch her breath first. He was waiting for a reply and her tongue had fused to her teeth.

Chapter Four

Jud wanted to swear, or at least bite off his tongue. She'd asked for it point blank, but hadn't been ready. Heavy duty damage control needed. She was so wonderful, and so eager, but didn't understand what she wanted. He was dead certain he hadn't been wrong. He'd watched her face as she looked at the toys in the shop. Her reaction to the handcuffs she bought was clear as daylight. It turned her on, but wasn't ready to acknowledge her needs. She would. "You've gone very quiet."

"Are you surprised?" She had her voice back, good.

"No. I imagine it's the first time a potential lover suggested that."

"You're right the first time! And I'm assuming that this isn't your standard courtship conversation."

"Not in the least. There are very few women I'd have this conversation with. Most women would run a mile, the magnificent ones, like you, don't."

"You mean the crazy ones."

"Not in the least. You are wonderfully sane, just a bit reluctant."

"Hardly surprising."

"Yes and no. Kink fascinates you, Katie, but you've never had a lover tie you to the bed. Never known what it is to let go completely. Never felt the sweet kiss of a flogger."

"Hell, no! I'm not into pain!"

"I'm not talking pain. I'm talking about massaging you with scented oil, before stroking your smooth flesh with the tresses. I'd open your legs, and caress the insides of your thighs with the flogger before kissing you where you want it the most. You'd have the best climax of your life and want more."

"Jud!" It came out like a shocked gasp. Her face was flushed, and it wasn't all embarrassment. "I just met you five days ago. We've had three casual meetings --as if they really were casual -- and you're talking about getting me naked, and doing things to me!"

"Is the prospect so abhorrent?"

"It scares me witless, to be honest!"

They were getting somewhere. "A little bit of fear ups the arousal, and you are turned on, Katie. I can smell you even over all this garlic." She blushed beautifully. Would her cunt be that same luscious shade? Her nipples as sweetly blushed? He longed to find out. "I'll make no secret of it, Katie, I want you in bed. Naked. I want you to submit and give your body over to me. I want to give you incredible pleasure. And I suspect you want that too, don't you?"

"Yes!" She gasped, her eyes wide with shock. "I don't know why I said that!"

"Because it's true, and against all the odds, you trust me."

"Beats me why!"

"Instinct, Katie. You know in your heart, I'm what you need, and I won't let you down."

Instinct might not let her down but common sense had. Jud walked her home after she'd said she lived round the corner, but hadn't even asked to come in. He kissed her sedately on the cheek and walked away, once he was sure she'd gone inside. From talking dirty, they wound up like a date out of Happy Days. She wasn't sure she needed to get involved with him. But she was desperate to see him again.

Two days later, she ran into him-or rather he spotted her. He pulled his car up to the bus stop where she was waiting, rolled down the window, and asked, "Need a ride?"

"My mother told me never to accept rides from strange men!"

"Hop in!" He leaned over and opened the door. "I just heard all the buses are on strike."

"Idiot!" she said, as she sat down, hauling her tote bag after her. "They're not on strike, one just pulled up right behind us." The driver was glaring for all he was worth. "There are laws about stopping in bus lanes."

"Buckle up and we can go." As he spoke, he reached across, pulled the webbing across her chest.

"Bondage, I see!"

"Rot!" he said, as he clicked the buckle into place. "It's called observing the law. Trust me, you won't click out of any bondage I put you in."

"Dream on, Sonny!"

He laughed so hard, he had to steer sharply to avoid a cyclist. "I can see I took the wrong tack with you the other night. You like a direct approach."

"I like getting home in one piece. So far you've violated a bus lane and almost shaved the hairs off a cyclist's legs."

151

"It's worth it to run into you like this."

"You'll run into the pedestrians if you aren't careful!" That was unfair. He'd stopped at the crossing but... "Who told you I'd be waiting there?"

"No one. It was fortunate happenstance." He ignored her grunt and went on. "I planned to call you tonight, but when I saw you standing in front of the bank building, I took it as a sign from Providence."

"More a sign I was late. I missed my usual bus."

"You don't drive to work?"

"This is a better deal. If I drive, I have to pay for parking. By taking the bus, my employer pays for the bus pass."

"Ah! An ecologically aware employer."

"Not particularly, just short of parking places in the mall garage."

He did have a nice laugh. But... "Why did you want to call me tonight?"

"To ask you for a date."

Reasonable enough, or was it? "Where?"

"You'll come? I thought you might run a mile."

"If it's a night out at some kinky club, it'll be two miles."

"How about a night in."

"When?" And come to that..."Where?"

"Halloween. I thought I'd invite myself to your house for trick or treating."

"Along with the goblins and the ghosts? You want candy?"

"Just what you keep between your legs."

Sheesh! But she'd be lying through her teeth to say she didn't want him. "Thanks for the compliment. What sort of tricks and treats?"

"You're smart enough to figure that out, I think. We both dress up, we act out parts, and I give you the best sex you've ever had."

"What do we dress up as?"

"You pick mine, and I choose yours. Once we're suited up. I lead and you follow."

"What if I don't fancy following?"

"You say 'no'."

Couldn't be that straightforward, not with Jud Carlton! She needed think time. "Not to change the subject or anything, but would you make a detour at the next corner for the cleaners? It'll save me going out later?"

"By all means." He slowed and turned left. "But only on the condition that you have dinner with me."

"When?"

"Tonight. I'll bring it. Do you want Chinese, Indian, or Turkish?" The car pulling up at the curb saved her from replying. She unsnapped the seat belt and opened the door.

"I'll be back in a minute."

It was nearer ten. Half the city seemed to be waiting for cleaning or shirts, but the delay gave Katie time to think and get even more confused. No doubt about it, Jud was sexy and attractive, fascinated her with his promises, but he also scared her witless. Could she trust him? Andrew said Jud was a good guy, and she trusted Andrew as much as she did anyone-or had until he admitted to tying Sophie up regularly. The thought of poised and sophisticated Sophie tied up and getting spanked was getting Katie's panties damp. She hoped to the heavens the chemical smell from the machines in the back hid it from everyone else.

It was her turn, Katie handed over her claim check and her plastic money, signed the slip, and grabbed her cleaning and walked out into the October afternoon.

Jud was standing by the car, in a no parking area of course, and opened the door for her. As he got into the driver's seat and put the key in the ignition, Katie turned to him. "I prefer Indian, medium hot, and please don't come before eight. I've something I have to get done."

"I'll be there, Katie."

Neither spoke a word for the next couple of blocks. Jud turned left and took a short cut to her apartment, as if he'd studied the route. She suspected he had. He'd studied her, hadn't he? He pulled up right in front of her apartment. She did manage to get out of the car before he got around to open the door, but Jud got her cleaning before she reached in. Unnecessary for a liberated woman, but she wasn't in the mood to argue. But she was not about to relinquish her key to him, which he clearly expected. Heck, it was her front door. Jud stepped in behind her, giving old Mrs. Brown next door, plenty to think about.

Once inside, he just stood and smiled, looking around in a not too pointed way-he got a few brownie points for that. Katie was half-tempted to tell him to just stay and she'd fix omelettes.

He reached out for her hand, and stepped closer, her heart took on a pulse of its own, and what her blood pressure was doing was anyone's business. The sight of

Jud, watching her with his beautiful dark eyes, and the twitch of a smile in the corner of his wide mouth, had her biting her own lips. A nice, hot kiss would be very welcome. She looked up at him and smiled.

"I'll be back at eight, on the dot." Katie's breath caught as he brushed her cheek with his finger, trailing slowly to caress the point of her chin. Her lips parted in anticipation, her heart did a little flip, and her chest heaved as their eyes met. "Medium hot, right?" he asked brushing the hair off her forehead before dropping a quick kiss.

Sheesh! Her first kiss in High School had been more passionate than that! But it hadn't left her quivering and wet. This was nuts!

"I'll be back!" With that, he opened the door and walked out while she gaped like a dimwit. He paused to wave and blow a kiss before getting into his car and driving off.

Katie slammed the door.

He said he was into games, and brother had he told the truth! She was panting for it, aching between her legs, and her bra felt two cup sizes too small. Damn him! She was half-tempted to grab the phone and call every friend or acquaintance until she found someone to go to the movies and be gone when eight rolled around, but she wasn't that stupid.

If Jud could do this to her with a brush of his lips, or a caress down her chin, he had to be worth the trouble.

And it was time for her to take some trouble.

She hadn't shaved her legs since the pool closed on Labor Day. Time to defuzz. She also had time for a face pack, a leisurely soak before shaving her legs, and a shower to wash her hair. She indulged herself thoroughly by digging out the basket of bath goodies she'd received on her last birthday, and now her tiny bathroom smelled like a summer garden. She finished off by slathering her body with a good third of the bottle of lavender lotion, and wrapped herself in a clean bath towel to dry her hair.

She was clean enough to stand up to scrutiny, or better still lie down for it.

Teeth brushed, mouth washed, hair next to perfect and a bod smelling like the perfume counter at Marshall Fields. Time to get dressed, and what the hell was she going to wear? Her seldom-worn black lace gown was way too obvious. Sweats, what she usually wore around the house, a bit too casual for seduction. After prolonged indecision, and a lengthy contemplation of her wardrobe, that left her convinced she had nothing wear suitable for a seduction. She settled for a very skimpy, white lace bra and panties she seldom wore, blue jeans and a silk shirt.

She set the table in the kitchen, before realizing she didn't have a bottle of wine in the house. Too bad! It was too late to run out and buy a bottle. She lit the gas logs in the fireplace, gathered up the stray papers and old magazines and shoved them under the sofa, and plumped up the pillows. Back in the kitchen, she found a half carton of ice cream in the freezer that looked reasonably edible, topped with chocolate topping it would make a sort of sundae.

Perhaps for afterwards...in bed.

Chapter Five

The doorbell ringing had her rooted to the floor for several seconds. He was right on time. She opened the door. Yup, it had been a while since she'd had a man like this on her doorstep. And yes, she'd done right to stick with jeans. He'd changed into black jeans, a black sweater that looked like cashmere, and a black leather jacket. He also had his arms full, with a sack that emanated wafts of spice and garlic.

Jud kissed her on the check, and strode into the kitchen as if he owned it. Setting the bag on the table, he reached out for her hand, drawing her close. "Katie," he murmured and lowered his mouth to hers.

How could lips be cool, hot, wild, and gentle all at once? Jud's were soft and insistent as he pressed his mouth against hers. Wild excitement flooded her mind and body. Her skin tingled where his fingers touched. Her heart sped. And when his lips opened hers, her brain all but zapped out. She gave a little moan, pressed herself into him, until she flattened her breasts against his hard chest, and wrapped her arms around him. His hand was in her hair, another caressed her between her shoulder blades, but they were mere background sensations to the kiss she felt down to her knees. She was aware of his body hard against hers, her racing pulse resounding in her ears, and the wonderful joy of a kiss that took her flying-literally. Her feet were off the ground, as Jud's hands on her waist lifted her so they were level. Katie gasped as she caught her breath, and angled her mouth for more.

And got it.

She was shaking. Whimpering under her breath. Her hips pressed into his, as arousal burned deep in her belly. Her nipples were hard, her pussy wet and throbbing. As far as she cared, curry could wait. She was so hot, she'd never notice if it got stone cold.

"Enough," Jud whispered, and set her back on her feet.

"I don't think so..." She grinned up at him, anticipating so much more.

"Yes," he insisted. "I came to bring you dinner, not fuck you."

Nothing like being pulled up short! "Say it like it is, eh? What happened to making love, or old-fashioned, good sex?" Sheesh had she really said that? She was too darn hot to think straight, and, hell, she'd forgotten to change the sheets. Seemed it wouldn't matter. She'd just made a fool of herself again.

The way Jud was looking at her, who knew? He didn't appear shocked. Why should he be? He'd used a four letter word, but... "What is it?" she asked, irritated at his scrutiny.

"I want to make love, have great sex, and fuck you, but not tonight."

"Why not? Got your period?"

He shook his head. "I want to be certain you really want it."

And that little interlude hadn't convinced him? "Did you detect reluctance back then?"

"Not in the least. I detected passion, desire, and a woman worth having, but I'm not sure you really understand what I need from you."

And some women claimed all men were after was sex. "You've utterly confused me. You kiss me so I almost climax, and then decide you don't want sex!"

He grinned. "Did you really almost come?"

The blood rushed to her face. Great! Now he thought her fast and easy! She turned to the table and lifted off one of the cardboard lids. "Aloo Ghobi, one of my favorites..." She looked up at Jud. "Did Andrew tell you that too?"

"No, it was a lucky guess. It's one of my favorites."

"So, we have that much in common."

"I think, Katie, we have a lot in common. I just need you to be sure."

She was rapidly getting more unsure, but she was hungry. "Look, Jud, you have me so confused, I'm ready to give up. Can't we eat? I don't have any wine I'm afraid," She'd half-hoped he'd bring a bottle, but...

"Just as well, I think we both need clear heads."

It couldn't hurt. She was out of her depth with Jud, knew it, and decided drowning might be fun. If she ever got her nerve up to take the plunge. Meanwhile... "Hadn't we better eat before it goes cold?" Of course, he could always warm it up the way he did her - with a look and a smile.

"Good idea? Want some Rogan Josh?"

They piled their plates with the lamb curry, eggplant, cauliflower, and lentils, and sat down opposite of each other. Katie making a concerted effort not to brush knees under the too small table.

"You forgot to light the candles," he said. Light them? She'd forgotten they were even there! "Never mind." He produced a cigarette lighter and lit them. No, he seduced the darn things. Holding the flame just over each wick and watching until the flame leapt up and burned steadily before moving to the next one. "I love candles," he said as the second caught alight and he snapped the lighter closed. "They add to the atmosphere, and these..." He sniffed the air. "Vanilla?" She nodded, locking eyes with his. Heck, they could be old gym-sock scented for all she knew. "Romantic and sexy," he went on. "Like you."

Her throat went tight, and she had to swallow hard on her mouthful of Aloo Ghobi, and clear it down with a long drink of water.

As she set her glass back on the table, he asked, "Katie, how would you like a love affair?"

"Who with?"

He scowled. "Don't be obtuse! Who do you think I mean?"

"You, presumably?"

'Well, would you?'

Nothing like coming to the point. "Perhaps." Why play hard to get? "No! I'd say, yes, definitely, I would." She tore off a corner of the Nan, scooped up a morsel of eggplant, and looked him in the eyes.

She almost choked on her Bhahn Bharta.

Jud's eyes had gone dark as the night outside. His lips parted just enough to show the tip of his tongue, and his chest rose and fell as his breath caught. He'd been telling her to wait, and right in front of her eyes was one aroused male. There was nothing but sheer male desire in every fiber of his body.

"I'm delighted, Katie," he said at last, "but I need to be totally sure."

"Hell! How much surer can you get than, 'Yes, I would!'"

"I'm not sure you know what you're agreeing to."

"What am I agreeing to then?"

"Whatever you want."

"This sounds like a riddle."

"It is, in a way. I want to give you the best sex of your life. You agree to obey me, and do whatever I ask, and in return, I agree never to do anything you don't want."

She was right about the riddle bit. It was a ruddy brain teaser. "Look Jud, you're into kinky sex, right? Handcuffs, etc." She'd forget about the whip. He said only what she wanted. Andrew insisted he was a good guy...so... "I'm curious." Or stupid.

He set his fork down, and reached over to curl his fingers over hers. She felt his touch up her arm, down to her knees, and several places in between. "I won't disappoint you, Katie, I promise, now eat up."

Suddenly, she was ravenous. Probably her mind's way of blocking out what she'd just agreed to. But the candlelight, the aroma of spices in her small kitchen, and the brush of his knees against hers, all combined to hoist her senses to hyper-alert.

It was nuts, but she might just skip the questionable ice cream in favor of hot sex.

But Jud seemed in no hurry.

And reached over to tear off a portion of Nan. He dipped it into his portion of Dahl, and popped it in his mouth-all while looking at her.

"This is great." She scooped up rice and cauliflower on her fork. "Did you get it at the Bombay Palace?"

"The Taj Mahal on Western Boulevard." He took anther taste of curry. "I'm looking forward to getting you naked, Katie."

At least she wasn't chewing this time! "Maybe, I'll get myself naked."

"Good idea! I'd enjoy watching you undress. I'd sit on the end of the bed while you stand in the middle of the floor, and one-by-one strip for me. Everything: your shoes, jeans, panty hose, tee shirt, underwear, until you stand there, naked."

"And what about you being naked?"

"I will be, but I want you naked first. Perhaps I'll have you kneel by my side so I can stroke your head. I find the prospect of you naked and me fully clothed rather exciting." He paused to take another mouthful of food. "I'm imagining candlelight flickering over your skin, watching the lights and shadows across your breasts, and the curve of your belly, and the softness between your legs." He paused. "Are your nipples large?"

As if she'd ever thought about it! "I don't rightly know!"

"Something for me to find out."

"Seen a lot of nipples have you?" A bit tart, but heck was he measuring them up?

"A beautiful sufficiency. I'm not a virgin, Katie, any more than you are."

Fair enough, but she suspected he was way ahead in experience. "That's good news!" Sheesh, she sounded snippy.

"Am I arousing you?"

"Yes!"

"Underwear damp yet?"

This was getting out of hand. "Yes!"

"I thought so. Take them off!"

She almost choked on her Basmati rice. "Take them off?" She managed after a long drink of water.

His smile could only be described as disarming. "You want to sit there in damp panties? Besides, you might as well get used to doing what I tell you."

He had to be able to hear her heart thumping across the table. This was ridiculous! Or was it? Wasn't this what she'd half-agreed to? The thought of following his lead excited her. "Okay." Throat tight, palms as wet as her pussy, she stood up and took two steps across the room.

He grabbed her wrist. Not tightly, not to hurt. But he held her securely. To move away she'd have to yank her arm free. "Where are you going?"

"To the bathroom!" He looked up at her, a little quirk in the left corner of his mouth, and shook his head. "You asked me to take off my panties!"

The quirk became a lop-sided smile. "Yes, I did. Go ahead."

"Not here!" Sheesh! In the middle of the kitchen!

"Why not? The blinds are drawn. No one can see you but me."

"I'd rather take them off in the bathroom."

His thumb, gently stroked the inside of her wrist. He had to feel her racing pulse. "I know you would, my dear, but this is where you start obeying, but since this is new for you, I will give you a choice. If you prefer, you may take them off in the bathroom." The sigh she let out was sheer relief. "But if you take that option, be prepared, when you come out, to lay yourself across my lap and accept a spanking for failing to meet my request."

Chapter Six

Heaven help her! The blood in her ears roared so loudly, she could barely think. Her chest tightened and her throat all but seized up. What would it feel like to have his hand hard on her soft bottom? For a split second she was tempted to walk into the bathroom just to find out, but she wasn't that stupid. Judging by the grip on her wrist, his hand would pack a punch.

Nodding, because she wasn't sure her mouth could form words any longer. She eased her hand from his grasp, and unsnapped her jeans. She fought the urge to turn her back, instinctively knowing that was not what he wanted. She unzipped, eased her sneakers off, and stepped out of her jeans. She hung them over the back of her chair before pulling down her panties, which were so wet the cotton gusset gleamed. This was bizarre, but to say she wasn't turned on would be a bold-faced lie.

"Give them to me."

He was holding out his hand.

Without a word, Katie handed them over.

He shoved the scrap of cotton and lace into his pocket while she stepped back into her jeans and zipped them up. The denim rubbed rough on her aroused flesh, catching to her clit as she sat down. She squirmed a little to shift the seam off her tenderest spots.

As she reached for her fork, hoping she could still swallow solid food without choking, Jud caught her hand, and raising it to his mouth, kissed it. "Perfect! Katie, I think you will be a dream come true."

Every bit of tension in her body eased at his touch, discounting the throb in her groin that itched to the point of ache, and it sure wasn't all denim abrasion. Taking advantage, of the calm she suspected was merely temporary, she asked. "Do you collect panties?"

"Only from women I intend to tie up."

"You're not tying me up!"

"That's something we need to negotiate."

"You have to be kidding!"

"Not in the least. If the idea didn't intrigue you, you'd never have bought those handcuffs."

"That was a joke. A gag gift!" He raised an eyebrow. That just about finished her. "I'm not letting you make me helpless!"

"The thought of being helpless is arousing, isn't it?" Reluctantly, she nodded. "I won't do anything you don't want. Trust me Katie, you'll enjoy being helpless."

For some insane reason, she believed him. "Okay. But..."

"But what, dear?"

"You're not spanking me!"

He thought about that a minute. "I might. Don't scowl so, dear. I won't do anything you don't want, and nothing you won't enjoy."

"How on earth can you tell?"

"I'll know, Katie. I can read your face, catch the flush of excitement on your skin when you say 'no' but think 'maybe', feel your pulse race when you're aroused. Even now, I can smell your need and curiosity."

She'd been afraid of that. "Jud, I'm getting out of my depth here."

"I'll be your safety raft and life belt."

There was something oddly appealing about the prospect but... "I've never needed a life raft before."

"No one's ever offered what I'm offering."

"What exactly are you offering?"

"More pleasure than you can imagine. Complete and utter satiation." He grinned. "I guarantee satisfaction."

"You offer a written warranty?"

"I offer my word and my body, and my utter, undivided attention, is that not enough?"

"That's more than anyone else offered, or gave."

"You need me, Katie. You want what I'll do to you. You crave the excitement I offer. You even long for the fear."

"I'm not too certain about the fear!"

"I am. I watched your eyes when I threatened to spank you. The prospect horrified you, but intrigued and aroused you at the same time. You dreaded it, but wondered how it would feel, and if it would be as exciting as you imagined." He kissed the tips of his fingers, and reaching across the table rested them against her lips. "Am I right?"

She nodded, her throat too dry and tight to speak. "Why?" she croaked with effort.

"Because you're submissive, and need a strong man to dominate you."

That got her voice back in a hurry! "Jud, I have news for you. I am *not* the sweet, obedient, submissive sort." His quirked eyebrows were maddening, and somehow appealing. "Look here, buster..."

He grabbed the hand that pointed right at his chest. "Katie, I never said you were the 'sweet, submissive sort'. In fact, according to Andrew, you 'have balls and attitude'. I agree, it makes you attractive and sexy. You're sexually submissive, a very different thing entirely."

"What makes you so damn certain?"

"I'm a dominant male, I know these things." Oh, please! "You question that?"

"Yes, I do." She leaned her elbows on the table and looked him in the eye. Let him explain that away.

"Alright, dear, answer me one thing. If another man had told you to stand up and take off your underwear, would you have?"

"Hell, no!"

"But you did for me." And had been wondering about that ever since. "You responded to me as a dominant. Your sexual intelligence recognizing what your rational mind balks at."

"Maybe..."

He shook his head. "There's no 'maybe' about it. I'm going to prove it so thoroughly, you'll never question again."

"You talk a good spiel about all the wonderful things you'll do to me. How about putting a little substance behind your words?" Sheesh! What had she done? Agreed to? Asked for?

"By all means, Katie. Next time."

"What do you mean 'next time'?"

"I mean not tonight. You have to be certain you want this, and right now you are too horny to think straight."

"And who got me that way?"

"I did!" He was so darn smug-and so right. "Don't worry, dear, I won't make you wait long. Watch for me on Halloween, I'll come with your very own tricks and treats."

Two whole days. Damn good thing she had her magic wand upstairs beside her bed. "If I agree, right?"

"I'll call you tomorrow. Think about it. Very carefully. I won't harm you. I'll give you a safeword to use anytime you want me to stop. I will tie you up, and I may spank you if necessary. You promise to submit, and in return I'll give you the best sex of your life."

"What about you? I imagine you'll have a bit of fun too."

"Of course! You don't think I'm getting a charge out of the prospect of you lying helpless and a little bit anxious, and the thought of you sucking my cock has me hard already."

In his dreams! And in hers! "This is getting out of hand."

"You're overloaded." He stood up. "I'm going home. Call me with any questions? I won't force you to do anything you don't want to. Pleasure, yours and mine, is what this is about."

She got his coat out of her small closet, which now smelled of expensive leather. He shrugged it on and gave her a quick kiss on the cheek. "Think about it, okay?" The man was a comedian. She doubted, she'd think of anything else for quite some time!

As she went to open the door, he stopped her. Pulling her into his arms, he pressed himself against her. He hadn't been kidding about being aroused. It felt like he had an oak branch in his jeans. Why would he walk out if he was this hard? "See?" he said. "I want you, but not until you're certain."

His mouth came down, hot and sweet, and tasting of curry spices and garlic. Her lips opened by instinct. Before she drew breath to sigh at the sensation of his mouth imposing on hers, his tongue took over, caressing, stroking as his hand found her breast. She responded with wild need, and urgent passion. Grinding her hips so his erection pressed hard into the softness of her belly. His arms held her tight, smoothing between her shoulder blades. One hand went up to cup her head, his other hand eased down, to stroke her ass. She sighed and whimpered in her building need. Her hips rocked. Her desire surged into a wild need, as he slowed the kiss and pulled away.

"You want me, Katie, and in two days, I'll give you what you've needed all your life."

"Jud..." It came out like a mewl, as she grasped his lapels, not wanting him to go.

"I know, dear, but it'll be more than worth the wait. You have my word."

"I'd much rather have a damn, good fuck!"

"You will. Now, two things before I go." What now? The catch? "I want you to pick my costume."

"For Halloween?"

He nodded. "Which costume from the Rose and Leather do you want me to wear? Your choice."

Hell, what did she remember? Not the spacesuit. Too odd. She tried to visualize the row on the rack... "The pirate!" Knee breeches and eye patch seemed to suit him.

He bowed. "As you demand, lady so shall it be. You'll be the pirate's captive, subservient to my every demand.

I'll pick your costume. You wear what's in the box, I send, and nothing else."

She hoped it wasn't the Princess Leia at Jabba the Hut's den outfit. "I'll have a zillion grade school kids knocking on my door that evening."

"You're not wearing it for them! Trick or Treating stops at nine, right? I'll knock on your door at ten. Plenty of time for you to get ready." Seemed fair enough. "One last thing, Katie. And this I absolutely insist on. You're forbidden to masturbate between now and then. No nice session with your electric friend. No touching that lovely clit to ease the tension. I'm taking charge of your body. That includes your climaxes. I give them. You are forbidden to pleasure yourself."

She'd never heard such nonsense in her life! If she wanted a climax, she'd damn well have one. Her Magic Wand waited upstairs. She was hot, horny, and ready for it. She needed a nice mind-numbing climax. She looked up into his face. "I promise."

His dark eyes glowed, as his mouth curled into a sexy smile. "That was a hard promise, wasn't it?"

"It was hell!" It took all she had not to sock him one for leaving her like this.

"You'll go to sexual heaven for your reward." He stroked the side of her cheek, Just that simple touch upped her need another notch. "You'll learn the ecstasy of obedience."

He brushed his lips on her cheek, and was gone.

Katie stood by the open door watching as he strode down her short front path, and turned left towards his car. He paused, waved, and called, "Shut the door, it's cold out!"

She hadn't even noticed.

Chapter Seven

She felt bereft without Jud's presence, his overbearing presence, she amended to herself. His fascinating presence, her emotions insisted. All that remained of the strange evening was her still high-pitched arousal, the aromas of curry spices in the air, and a heap of almost-empty aluminum containers. Trying to ignore the first one, Katie scraped the remains onto a plastic container and cleared the mess away. Now the place seemed even emptier. She snuffed out the candles, remembering how Jud had liked them. Most men never noticed these things. Most men would have had her upstairs long before now. They'd be naked between her sheets, and sometime towards dawn he'd go off home, leaving her vaguely satisfied and wondering if that was all there was to it.

Jud, she suspected, wouldn't leave her wanting. In that hope, she'd keep her promise about do-it-yourself sex. A cold shower would no doubt help. An early night in bed, reading the convoluted prose of her employers' new health care benefits would dampen her ardor.

Jud called, next morning, while she was swigging down her second mug of caffeine between bites of toast. "Did you sleep well?"

She swallowed a seemingly enormous mouthful of crust. "Yes."

"Are you telling me the truth?"

She eased the last of the chunk down with a mouthful of coffee. "Yes, I am. I admit I was a trifle hot and bothered after you left, but I put myself to sleep reading about my new health insurance plan."

He had a particularly sexy chuckle for this early in the morning. "Katie, I admire a woman of resource. I'll have to put it to good use."

"Maybe."

"There is no 'maybe' about it, dear. I'm looking forward to discovering you. Tell me dear, have you ever had anal sex?" Damn good thing she'd set her mug down. Coffee all down the front of an ivory silk blouse was no way to start the morning. "Have you?" he persisted, while Katie contemplated hanging up on him. She couldn't. The soft, insistence of his voice held her. "Once," she replied. It was a memory she tried hard to forget.

"Did you enjoy it?"

"Let's put it this way, if I had the choice of a root canal or anal sex again, I'd jump at the chance of a root canal."

"Was it that terrible?"

"Yes!"

"It won't be with me."

In his dreams. "Jud, if we're going to get into bed together, let's get this straight, you're not coming anywhere near my back door. Understand?"

"Completely. I'll respect that limit. There's plenty more I will enjoy with your lovely body. I'll call you tonight, and we'll talk about what you like best about sex. I do hope you'll like sucking my cock." On that parting shot, he hung up.

What now? Jud was outrageous, demanding, so damn full of himself he deserved a good kick where it would hurt most. Drat him! He excited her, and to be honest, not that she'd admit it to him, the thought of sucking his cock was anything but unwelcome. If she'd had her way, she'd have had that pleasure last night.

As it was, if she didn't get a move on, she'd be late for her appointment with a prospective client.

Jud was not one of the men who promised to call and then fell mute. By the time she got home from work, he'd left three messages on her voice mail. The first sounded like his usual cocky self, the second had a tinge of annoyance, but the third sounded downright concerned. "Katie, please give me a call. If you've got cold feet or worries, tell me. Okay?" A pause... "I was beginning to think you were a dream come true. Just let me know one way or another, my number..." and he repeated it for the third time.

A dream come true! Either Jud was a slick talker, or...or what? She wasn't sure, but she punched in his number.

"Katie!" He half-sounded as if he'd been waiting by the phone. "Is everything alright?"

"Fine!" Okay that was a lie, but... "It's fine between us, I mean. I just got in. Had to work extra hours."

"Does this happen often?"

"Only when another clerk has to take a sick kid to the Emergency Room. I offered to stay and cover for her,"

"I see." A pause. "So you're still prepared to celebrate Halloween my way?"

"I think so."

"You've doubts?"

"Yes, but isn't that the whole point?"

"Not doubts, no. I want you secure with me, certain I'll never do anything without your consent."

So he kept saying. "Just how does that fit with 'trust and obey me'?"

"Perfectly! After tomorrow night, you'll begin to understand." She wished she felt half as confident as he sounded. "I bought the pirate costume this evening, and yours too. They're delivering it tomorrow. Get ready to obey. Good night, dear."

"Good night."

"Tomorrow," he promised, his voice soft and suggestive, "will be the best Halloween of your life."

Time would tell. If it was half as good as he promised she'd not complain, but right now, she was dead on her feet. If she didn't get any sleep tonight she'd end up snoring through her night of passion.

Katie overslept, luckily she was working short hours, and not due at the shop until one. She took a leisurely shower, eyeing her legs for overnight appearance of fuzz, and gave them a quick shave, figuring this time it would be worth the effort, and deciding to treat herself to a real breakfast. She was in the middle of scrambling eggs when the front door bell rang. As she signed the receipt, her hand shook. The name 'Jud Carlton' as sender, told her what was inside.

She left the eggs to overcook, while she grabbed a kitchen knife and slit open the tape. Inside the carton, was a shiny, black box. She lifted off the top, black tissue rustled as she pulled out the costume. Not the Princess Leia in captivity, or the harem outfit she'd half dreaded. This was the Jane Austen one from the Rose and Leather:

all pastel pink and white muslin, with little pink rosebuds, a low-cut neck and high waist. Demure and sweet looking, until she shook it out and remembered the slits all the way to the high waist. And if that wasn't revealing enough, the back was wide open. She'd had more butt coverage in the open-back hospital gown she'd worn when she had her tonsils out.

Not a trace of underwear. Hardly surprising! He'd shown he preferred her bare under her clothes. This was going to be some trick or treat. In her heart, she didn't doubt Jud would deliver on his promise.

When the last bunch of little goblins scampered down the path, Katie gratefully turned off the porch light. It was five past nine. It's time the juveniles were back home eating candy until they bounced. She had an hour to get ready, and given the quantities of Milk Duds and Tootsie Rolls she'd munched between doorbells, she was fired up with energy. Heck she was more than ready! When it actually got to showering and changing, curiosity and courage did bit of a flip. Was she sure what she was doing? No! Was she willing? Sort of... How could she tell Jud 'no', when her heart raced with anticipation?

If she backed out of this, she'd spend the rest of her life wondering 'what if'.

That decision made, she toweled off briskly, slathered her body with scented lotion, and gave herself a generous spritz of perfume for luck. She dried her hair and fluffed it up. Gave her eyebrows a last inspection for stray hairs, and slipped on THE DRESS. This beat any costume she'd seen tonight. The elastic waist fit snugly, showing off her breasts, heck, showing off her nipples! The fabric was soft against her skin, and the skirt hung gracefully from the high waist, the hem brushing her ankles. The skirt didn't reveal as much as she'd feared. Until she moved. Sheesh! It left *nothing* to the imagination, and the back let in chilly night breezes. She felt so exposed behind. He'd promised no anal sex, and she trusted that, but what about a strong, male hand, stroking and squeezing her very available flesh?

She was getting hot just thinking about it.

Downstairs, she skipped her leather sofa, in preference for a velvet-covered armchair as much cozier to the rear, only the nap brushed her exposed ass and thighs every time she moved.

Nine fifty! Ten minutes. She could last. A nice stiff drink might help, but she remembered Jud's dictum about not letting alcohol dull her wits, and passed. The house was silent, as was the street outside. She listened to the chiming clock on the mantle, and the hum and drip of the refrigerator as it started the defrost cycle. She flicked open a magazine, but gave up trying to concentrate on environmental protection laws, when she saw the print came off on her sweaty hands.

The last thing she needed was smudges on the rosebuds. Come to think of it, the last time she'd worn rosebuds, she'd been five and flower girl at an aunt's wedding. But she was wearing flowered muslin because Jud had ordered it. That realization, sent a weird thrill down her spine, but it didn't solve her dirty hands. She ran into the kitchen and washed them in the sink. Now, they smelled of lemon fresh dish detergent, but what the...

Her mind and body went into shock at the sound of the front door bell. What if it was a last contingent of trick or treaters? She couldn't open the door to local juveniles dressed like this. It couldn't be kids. The porch light was out. It was Jud.

She peered through the spy hole, at a tall figure in the dark. She flicked on the porch light, a pirate, complete with red spotted kerchief and eye patch, looked right at her.

"Open this door," he said. "Or feel my rope end where you don't want it!"

Chapter Eight

Her body tensed. Her throat jammed shut. She could barely hear for the blood rushing in her ears, but she opened the door.

And stood there, staring.

He was incredible. Dark knee breeches and over-the-knee boots accentuated the strength and muscles in his legs. He wore a purple silk sash round his waist, and the full sleeves of his shirt billowed in the night as he stood, feet apart, and hands on his waist. The knotted kerchief over his dark hair, and his eye-patch completed the picture. With hair a little longer, and shirt hanging open, he'd fit right on the cover of a romance novel. And come to that, bent backwards over his arm, she'd show a prodigious amount of bosom and leg. Maybe there was something about those paperbacks she covered before reading on the bus.

"I didn't come to stand on the front step all evening," he said. "Although the sight of you in the light was worth the trip."

She stood aside and let him in. In the bright light of her sitting room, he stood even more magnificent. He smiled and she smiled back, until she noticed the whip tucked in his sash.

She gulped, staring like a mouse caught in a snake's eyes. "Why?" she asked.

He rested his hand over the top of the handle, his long fingers rippling the tresses. "I brought it for you."

She shook her head. "You're not whipping me!"

"It's purely for pleasure, not chastisement," he said, as he pulled it out of his belt.

The sight of the long, blue tresses dangling from his hand both horrified and fascinated her. "If that's your idea, you'd better go right now!" And if he did, she'd be desolated.

"Bear with me long enough to prove what I say."

"How can being hurt be pleasurable?"

"It's very pleasurable in fact, but that's not where we'll start. Trust me in this, Katie," He took hold of her hand. "Let me show you." He looked up at her, his lips parted in the beginning of a smile. "It won't hurt."

"Okay." What the hell had she said that for? Because she was as fascinated as she was scared. She gasped as he lifted the whip and tickled her wrist and the back of her hand.

She stared. The tresses were bright blue and green to match the braided handle. Some looked like fine leather, others were ribbons. As Jud gently flicked his wrist, the tresses caressed her skin. A little sigh came unbidden, as he brushed back and forth on her arm. "You like that?" It was more statement than question.

Katie nodded, unwilling to commit herself by agreeing but wanting him to continue. He didn't disappoint. He trailed the soft thongs, up her arm to her shoulder. He merely brushed a few inches of leather and satin over her skin, and she felt it deep in her pussy. "Why?" she whispered.

"Why not?" he replied. "You like it don't you?"

She nodded.

As if waiting for that agreement, he brought the whip up to her shoulder again, but this time, he trailed the tresses across her breasts, until her nipples hardened to little points of sensation. Her head dropped back against the wall, and she let out a low moan. She wanted this to go on forever. Every touch, every little brush of ribbon and leather, sent wild thrills of pleasure across her skin, until all sensations seemed to be pooled between her legs.

"Jud...," she whispered.

He squeezed her hand and kissed her wrist. "Turn around."

She obeyed without hesitation, wanting more, needing the caress of the whip on her shoulders and back.

It wasn't until the tresses trailed down her back and over her ass, she remembered just how much naked flesh this costume revealed, and by then she didn't much care. When he whispered, "Part your legs," she spread them wide. Moaning with sheer bliss as leather and satin kissed the inside of her thighs.

She was leaning into the wall, breathing fast and losing herself in the wild sensations, when she realized with disappointment, he'd stopped. "No! I want more!" she cried as she turned to look at him. It took a few seconds to realize she'd been shouting.

"Katie, my love, there is so much more," he replied. "Much, much, more, and we have all night." He dropped the whip and reached out to pull her into his arms. "You looked so terrified of my flogger, and I wanted to reassure you."

"You succeeded in making me horny!"

"I'm so thrilled." He kissed her forehead, her cheek, and the swell at the top of her left breast. "Before we start playing in earnest, we need to talk."

The man was always talking! Right now what she wanted was a good fuck, not chatter. "You get me hot and horny and then want conversation?"

"Trust me love, after this conversation you'll be even hornier." An arm round her shoulders, he started towards the kitchen. "A nice cup of coffee will perk us both up. Seems to me you're feeling a bit wobbly."

"You did that!"

"I know." Damn him, he was smirking. But if the past few minutes were any indication of what she had to look forward to, he was entitled to be pleased with himself. "Where do you keep your coffee?"

"In the cabinet."

She reached to open the door, but his hand on her arm stopped her. "I'll make it. You'd better sit down. Give those shaky knees a break. Save your energy. I'm going to ask a lot of you once we get upstairs."

"I can manage to make coffee."

"I never doubted, but I'm doing it. Now if you want to help, bring in the bag I left on the front porch."

She bit back the comment that if she was too weak-kneed to make coffee, where did he think she'd get the strength to go to the front door and back? Perhaps this was all part of obeying. She wasn't too sure she'd be that good at it, but she might as well try. It had been part of the deal after all, and if the rest of the night was anything like the little interlude with the whip, she'd go along--all the way.

With great care she peered out the front door. If fetching his bag involved stepping out onto the porch, he could do it himself. She wasn't freezing her butt off-literally-for anything. Not even the promise of kinky sex.

The brown paper grocery sack stood just inches from the threshold. She reached out for the bag, grabbed it, and made sure the door was locked behind her and the porch light off. Late night trick or treaters could go elsewhere.

"Thanks, dear." Jud looked up from pouring boiling water into the press pot. "Please put it on the table, we can go through it while we have our coffee."

She set it down, just inches from the blue flogger that he'd arranged on the table, like a peacock's tail. Gingerly, she ran her fingers through the spread tresses. She'd been right, some were soft leather, some ribbons. They slipped through her fingers as gently as they'd stroked her arms and shoulders earlier. Was he going to use it again? Her crotch came alive at the thought. Oh, Please!

"You like it after all, don't you?" She turned to find him watching her. "Don't you?" he repeated. She nodded. "Katie, speak to me. It's important. Part of any dominant/submissive relationship is communication."

Mentioning 'submissive' just about dried up her tongue along with her throat. "Is that what we have?" she croaked.

"Not yet, but I hope we will one day. I believe you will make a perfect submissive--with a little direction. You like the touch of the flogger on your skin, don't you?"

"Yes." It was more of a long sigh that a word.

Jud grinned as he pressed down the plunger in the pot. "I'm so glad, Katie." He reached for two mugs off the hooks, and poured the coffee before carrying the mugs over to the table, and reaching in the fridge for milk. "Sit down. I want you to feel that polished seat against your bare ass." It touched off nerve endings she didn't know she had. Against her soft flesh, the wood felt hard and smooth. "Open your legs. Wide." She stared, but obeyed.

She wrapped her hands round the mug and looked up at Jud. "What's in the bag?"

"Toys. Have a look."

Did she really want to? Yes. Time to stop hesitating. The whip she dreaded, had turned out to be a sensual delight, so would everything else in the bag.

Like the scarves. Three of them, in shades of blue and green. They were silk, light in her hands, and warm to her skin.

"Why do you think I brought them?"

"To tie me up." Her cunt tingled with anticipation. Was he right then? This would be pleasure, not discomfort.

"I might blindfold you with them." He tilted his head on one side and watched her. "Would you like that?"

"I'm not sure."

"Tell the truth."

Deep breath first. "The thought scares me, but it also excites me."

He grinned with sheer delight. "Oh, Katie, I think I've found my dream woman."

"You dream of scaring me?"

"No, I dream of having wonderful, thrilling sex with you. I dream of you whimpering in my arms, begging for more of what only I can give you. I dream of you naked and bound, legs spread open. I dream of trailing my flogger over your naked back. I dream of the sighs and grunts you'll make when I bring you to climax, and I dream of holding you, limp, and sweaty and soft in my arms as we both fall asleep."

"Want to go upstairs right now?"

"Take out the rest of the stuff in the bag."

A bottle of massage oil. Nice. Her shoulders tightened at the prospect of Jud's long fingers rubbing jasmine-scented oil into her skin. Or was she the one intended to massage him? No hardship there, she couldn't wait to see him naked. At the bottom of the bag, a smaller white one, containing a tube of lubricant, and a small rubber article. She looked at the bullet-shaped object, with its flared-out base and frowned at Jud. "Look here, Buster! I clearly said, no back door. What's this for?"

"Apologies. I thought you meant no anal sex. Didn't realize you meant no sex toys either." He stood up, picked the tube and plug up and walked over to the trash and dropped them in. "If you don't agree, we don't do it."

The sight of the full dress pirate pumping the lid of the pedal bin made her smile. "Are we going upstairs now?"

"Soon." He walked over and stood beside her. She made to get up but his hand, strong on her shoulder stopped her. "Just two more things. I want to explain our roles, and give you your safeword."

"What's a safeword?" She could guess. The thought of needing one had her fists clenched. Was this really a good idea?

How could she doubt it when he smiled down at her, his dark eyes twinkling. Sex with Jud would be fun. If they ever got that far! 'Make her wait' seemed to be his modus operandi.

"A safeword, my dear, is the most important communication between us. If I do anything you want me to stop, use it."

"What happened to 'just say no'?"

"In the fantasy we'll be playing out, 'no' will be part of the fun. I'm the big, bad pirate, abducting and ravishing my virgin captive. I expect you to say 'no' a good few times, and I will totally ignore your pleas for mercy, and have my wicked way with you."

Her chest went so tight she gasped. "Why?"

His hand eased up her shoulder to the base of her neck. She couldn't hold back the shiver. "Because my beautiful, the prospect excites me and judging by the flush on your face, and the sparkle in your eyes, it arouses you too. No matter how much your reason says 'no'."

It's not so much reason saying 'no'. Force and rape are horrific."

"I agree, dear. So does any decent, right-thinking human, but this is play. I could no more rape you than cut off my own head. I want to play subduing you. I want to pretend to overpower you. To make believe you're helpless, but you'll be in control of the action. At the word from you, we stop."

"If that's the case, how come you call me submissive? Seems I'm the one controlling the action."

His cool lips on her forehead underscored just how flushed and hot she'd become. "Right first time, Katie. You do. It's all a big game, for our mutual pleasure. I act the big baddie. You pretend to be the frail, little captive, and together we have a marvelous time."

If they didn't she'd need a conversation with her vibrator! She was so hot for it that his fingertips stroking the neckline of her dress had her itching inside. She was so wet between her legs. She could smell herself over the coffee in their mugs, and his musky aftershave. "Let's get started then, Long John Silver."

"I'm Black Jack Tar, and you'd better remember that, my pretty! But first, the safe word. What's your full name?"

"Katherine Marjorie Fairfax."

"Use that. Say your full name, and I'll stop whatever I'm doing."

"Okay." Maybe that rotten middle name would have its use. "I say it. We stop. What happens next? You go home?"

"Hell, no! I ask what's the matter, and do something else." He put both hands on her shoulders and looked down at her with need-dark eyes. "I'm not walking out on you, until you are so sated, you don't know what day it is. Heck, I'm not leaving then. I plan on taking you out for breakfast."

"I'm going to live that long then? You don't make your captives walk the plank?"

"Nah! I'd much rather strip you naked and ravish you, Lady Katherine, my virgin prisoner."

"I've news for you, Black Jack Tar. I'm not a virgin!"

"Thank God for that!"

He pulled her close, angling his hips into hers. Yes, he didn't need a shy virgin! He had a raging hard-on, and if the pressure on her belly was anything to go by, he was enormous. His hands heated through the thin fabric. His fingers splayed on her bottom, pulling her even closer as he worked his hips, grinding his hard cock against her.

"Get ready, little prisoner. I have no mercy on my captives."

She tilted her chin up. It wasn't quite what she hoped as it gave her an eye lock with him, but... "Indeed!" She tossed her head and put on what she hoped was a haughty air. "Unhand me! How dare you so threaten me! My Father, the Royal Governor, will have you hung from the yard-arm!" What ever a yard-arm was.

Black Jack's hand eased up to cup her breast. The pressure made her gasp. "He and his ships have been after me for ten years, Missy. My ship is faster than the fastest frigate, and sweeting, do you think he will fire on me while I have you aboard? There's nothing he or you can do!"

"No!" She tried to pull away, but only succeeded in getting herself pressed against the counter top. She leaned back, but he grabbed her shoulders and yanked her close. His face was so near to hers she felt his breath, just for a second until his mouth closed down.

It was a hard kiss, his lips forcing hers apart as she fought his grasp. Her attempts only served to press herself closer to him. A knee came between hers, his breeches rubbing against her skin as her skirt fell open. His tongue forced between her lips, and met hers, gently, caressing, teasing with a promise of more, until she whimpered, and he broke the kiss. He was gloating as he looked down at her, "Like it don't you, little prisoner? Open those legs wider, get ready for Black Jack's cock in yer lovely cunny!"

"Indeed, Sir, you presume too much!"

His wild laugh made her toes curl. Thank heaven it was only a game. "I have not presumed enough, little one. Seems you need to learn who is master on this ship."

"A saucy pirate. An impudent rogue. A brigand who presumes too much."

His eyebrows almost met as he scowled. "And the captain who has you in his power! Never forget that." His roar sent a cold thrill down her back. In real life it would be terrifying, but now..."

"Why should I remember?" She was pissing him off royally, but why not? It was play, wasn't it?

"This is why!" He grabbed her by the wrist, dragged her over to the table, and spun her around, flattening her face down on the table top. Her nose was just inches from her coffee mug, and the pile of silk scarves. "This will help you remember!" Before he stopped speaking his hand came down on her ass. She yelped, more from shock than hurt. Her ass throbbed a little, that was all. Immediately he spanked the other side, then back and forth, just hard enough to send offended thrills coursing through her body. This was terrible, wonderful and exciting, but why was she letting him do this to her? She tried to wriggle out of his hold but a hissed, "Be still or I'll use my belt!" had her lying still while he landed anther couple of hard swats to her sore rump.

She was panting as he pulled her upright and turned her to face him. "Are you in my power?"

"Yes!" The tremor in her voice wasn't put on.

"Yes what?"

"Yes, Captain, sir!" What was the right answer?

"Captain, will suffice."

"Yes, Captain."

"Are you my prisoner?"

"Yes, Captain!"

"Will you obey me or risk punishment?"

"Yes, I'll obey you Captain!" In real life this would be hell, but his hands grasping her upper arms, and the little shakes as he fired his questions, stirred unexpected emotions. She was scared, but thrilled deep inside. She wanted to obey him. Wanted to be ordered. Wanted to be coerced. As he released his grip, without pausing to think she fell to her knees at his feet. As she bowed her head, a feeling of utter peace, and wild excitement flooded her mind. All she could see were the polished toes of his black boots, but she felt his personality and presence, like an enveloping joy.

Her breath quickened and her chest heaved as she waited, with no idea why she was on her knees, but knowing it felt right. She sighed with pleasure and submission, as he stroked her head.

"Nice," he said, in an almost-Jud voice. "I think you've learned your place!" That was back to Captain Jack. "Captives belong on their knees. You just stay there while I finish my grog." His boots moved out of her line of vision but he was still close. If he'd left the room she'd have known. His presence filled the room and her mind.

A strange peace filled her as she waited. She bent lower, until her forehead touched the cool tile of the floor. What was he doing? Finishing his coffee? She rather regretted her half-finished mug, but captives didn't get coffee or grog, they... A gentle tap on her ass caught her attention. "Get up, prisoner!"

She did, and turned to face him. "Who told you to look at me?"

"No one, Captain."

"Then turn back!"

She did but not before she noticed him reach for the pile of scarves. "Seems I need to chastise you a little more. Lay you across the table and let you taste the end of a rope's end."

Her throat went dry. One spanking was enough. Time for Lady Katherine to kick in the traces. "No!" she yelled, and spun to face him. "I'm not afraid of you! You're nothing but a common criminal!" He'd wanted a reaction. He had one. Black Jack scowled.

"Just wait til you feel..." She didn't wait to hear what he intended her to feel. Her heart racing, blood pounding in her ears. Cunt throbbing with fear and excitement, she ran as he reached out to grab her and raced up the stairs.

Chapter Nine

He was so close behind she could feel his boots on the stairs. As she dashed into her bedroom, he grabbed her by the waist and threw her face-down on the mattress, and landed on top of her. His weight pressed her into the mattress. His cock felt harder than before, and he made a point of grinding his erection into the crease of her ass. "Seems I may have to subdue you completely," he growled in her ear. "A cock up your insolent ass would keep you in your place."

"No!" It came out as a panicked wail. He was playing, right? He'd promised. "Please, Captain please, no. I beg you!"

He didn't move except to stroke her head and ease it down into the pillow. "Since you begged. I won't bugger you, Lady Katherine, but I will chastise you. You need a lesson in obedience."

Before she could even think what 'chastisement' involved, he pulled her hands over her head, and tied them to the bed. He never said a word as he twisted the silk scarves though the ornate headboard she'd thought so stylish and interesting. He tested the knots, easing his finger under the scarves to gauge how tight her bonds. She wasn't uncomfortable, just incredibly undignified...and excited.

His hand cupped her ass and kneaded her flesh. "Didn't learn the first time I spanked you, did you?"

"No, Sir, I need another one!" What the hell had made her say that? Stupidity? Or the wonderful sensation between her legs at the thought of his hand smacking down and warming her butt.

She got what she asked for, hard on one side. "That's for not remembering to call me 'Captain'!" Before she could correct herself, or apologize, another landed, hard enough to make her gasp. "I'm sorry, Captain," she cried, the warmth spreading across her cheeks, until cool air brushed her heated ass as he parted her skirt.

"So!" he roared. "You purported to be a decent woman. Only whores from the dockside walk around without pantaloons. His hand stroked her ass. "I can see you need severe attention." She sensed his eyes gloating over her lower back, and legs. "Open your legs!"

She debated disobeying, for a second, but thought better of it. Legs spread wide, she lay there waiting, and hoping, for whatever came next.

"Seems you can learn. Good! I left my flogger downstairs. Don't go anywhere until I get back!"

It wasn't just the sound of his boots on the stairs that told her he'd gone. She felt his absence. She missed his all-enveloping presence. She wanted him back. She didn't even care if he used the whip on her-hell, yes she did! A few spanks, okay... After the last episode she'd expected that, but no way was he laying that flogger thing on her. If he tried, it was safeword time!

If he ever came back.

How long had she been lying here? It seemed ages, but by her alarm clock, when she turned her head, it was only a couple of minutes. No, three as she heard his measured tread slowly up the stars. Silence. She sensed him watching. Waiting. She exhaled and let her shoulders sag into the mattress. He was her captor. She was his prisoner. Whatever he wanted, he could do. He had her helpless, and it thrilled her.

The bed sagged to one side. His knee nudged her thigh. "Did you disobey? Did you move while I was gone?"

Her throat went tight with fear. "I looked at the alarm clock!" An anachronism, but what could she say? It wasn't an hourglass, and that was...

A single finger traced a slow line up her spine, leaving a trail of goosebumps in its wake. "And why, little prisoner, did you do that?"

"I wondered how long you'd be gone."

"You wanted me to come back?" The finger came back down, and rested just above the top of her crack.

"Yes, I did." She burrowed her head in the pillow at the admission.

"And now I'm back and look what I brought." She didn't dare move, didn't need to. He set the flogger on the pillow by her face, a stray tress, brushed her cheek, sending warm shivers across her skin. "Cold?" he asked.

"No, Captain."

His hand went between her legs to cup her mound. One, long finger intruded deep into her cunt. What would Lady Katherine do? Katie bucked, trying to dislodge him, but his free hand came down in the small of her back, pinning her down. The finger in her cunt withdrew, and came back, deeper and harder. She suspected there were two this time. He moved, pressed and poked until she squirmed from excitement, arousal, and a half-imagined fear. "You will learn to submit, Lady Katherine. By the time I've finished with you, you won't dream of resisting!"

She hoped he never finished with her, but for good measure she bucked her hips. And felt teeth nip her ass.

The squeal was entirely involuntary. "You hurt me!"

"Good! Lie still while I play with your pussy."

As if she'd resist that! Once she relaxed his touch gentled. His long fingers, pulsing deep inside, until she sighed, "Like that do you, little captive?"

"Yes, Captain." He could go on all night if he wanted.

"Good!"

She let out a moan as he pulled out. "I want more!"

His shirt brushed her bare butt as he leaned close. "Prisoners don't ask. They take what comes."

"Yes, Captain."

"Want to use your safe word?"

Did she? No way! "No, Captain."

"Good!"

The bed shifted back as he stood up. His hands grasped the back neckline of the dress, and the sound of tearing muslin shocked her into a shriek. "No!"

"Oh, yes! I paid for this dress. I'll rip it off your body if I choose." Strong hands pushed the fabric off her shoulders. Before she'd felt exposed. Now she was completely vulnerable. "Nice little body you have, prisoner. I'll enjoy having my wicked way with you, as soon as I get you ready."

She was tempted to tell him she'd been 'ready' for twenty minutes or more, but Captain Jack made the rules.

She waited.

Something cool landed on her back and dribbled down her spine. The aroma of jasmine filled the room.

Strong hands spread the scented oil across her shoulders and down her back. The sigh of pleasure was utterly involuntary.

"Like that do you, wench?"

"Yes," she sighed.

His hand came down on her ass. "Yes, what? Have you forgotten where you are?"

"Apologies, Captain!" Sheesh, her left butt smarted even as his hands resumed their wonderful caress. How could his hands give such pleasure and hurt her at the same time? Did she care? She'd take a whole lot more on her exposed rear, if he'd keep up the massage. She let out a whimper as his fingertips brushed her ass, almost touching the fading ache from his slap.

"I want you like this often," he said. "Naked, helpless. Bound and exposed for my delectation." There was a little chuckle as his hands cupped her ass. "I can see, reach, and touch everything I want." As if to prove his point, his oil-slick fingers eased up the sensitive flesh inside her thigh, and darted in and out of her cunt before coming back to massage her ass. "Available. Just as you should be." Fingertips trailed up her spine, his touch was gentle, or at least it was this minute. Who knew what would come next? "Nice body, little captive. Relax. Submit completely, and accept my flogger."

She'd almost forgotten that damn thing! The tresses disappeared from her line of vision. "What are you going to do with it?"

"Enjoy watching your responses. Your pale skin marks up beautifully. My hand left a lovely red mark on your butt. It's faded now but I could soon renew it." His lips were so close to her ass, she could feel his breath.

Unable to resist the temptation, she bumped her hips upward to his face. His hands grabbed her hips. His oiled fingers didn't grasp that tightly, but it was enough. "Shouldn't have done that," he said, and bit her.

As she yowled with shock and real pain, his fingertips eased away the hurt. Just as before, the sweet caress after the hurt sent her mind whirling. She was enjoying this, the good, the hurt, and the unexpected.

Once she relaxed again, he let her back down on the bed. "You're turning into a troublesome captive. Time to subdue you with a good whipping."

"No!" A protest about the promised whipping? Or the loss she felt as he moved off the bed? She had no idea.

"Do you want to use your safe word?"

Did she?" No, Captain."

"Remember what it is? Tell me?"

"Katherine Marjorie Fairfax."

"Good." In the silence, she heard something scrape on the floor, and a clink like glass. The bottle of oil? Something else? She resisted the urge to look. No point in earning another spanking. The whip would be bad enough-or good enough if he used it as he had downstairs. She longed to feel its caress. Would he start on her back or her legs?

"Get on your knees! Keep your head down!"

Easier said than done on a soft mattress. She managed in the end by putting her weight on her forearms and scooting her knees up. Lord alone knew what she looked like from the rear. The ultimate in ungracefulness, but in a few minutes she was in position: knees bent, ass up in the air, and her shoulders still on the bed. If she'd been 'available' before, she was exposed to the world now.

It felt wonderful.

"Good girl! Just what I ordered."

She sensed movement. He pulled off the spare pillows and shams, and pushed them under her belly. "I don't want you uncomfortable. Except when I intend you to be."

Thrills of expectation radiated out from her clit. She was so aroused it hurt, but felt wonderful. "Please, Captain..." she whimpered, and had no idea what she was asking for. But she wanted it, and soon. Heaven help any real captive in this position, but as a fantasy... She shut her eyes and sighed with anticipation.

Her legs had come together in her efforts to get into position. Gently Jud stroked the back of her thighs, priming nerve endings as pleasure skittered up her spine and her cunt went humming. "Open your legs, dear." The bad Captain's voice took on the tone of a caress.

The pillows helped, as she hastened to obey. She wanted to please him, to keep this kind captor, to take what he offered and promised.

She felt the air between her legs a second before the flogger struck. Again and again it landed and she yelped each time. Three cries of shock and outrage that echoed in the quiet room.

There were no more, but she lay gasping, and blinking tears away. "That hurt!"

His hand tickled up her inner thigh. "It was meant to. But doesn't it feel better now?"

Maybe it was his hand cupping her crotch, but everything felt wonderful. The hurt of a few seconds back turned into wild desire. Talk about needy! She was close to begging for it. If only he'd put his fingers in...deep...as he had earlier. She rocked her hips in an attempt to bring his fingers closer. A fingertip on her clit was all she needed.

"Naughty girl!" he said and moved his hand away. "Not how a submissive captive behaves. I've a good idea to leave you here. Alone, to calm down and learn better manners."

She couldn't bear it. "No, please! Don't leave me!"

"You're not quite ready yet. I want you begging for my cock!"

"Isn't 'please' begging?"

He laughed. "You're getting there, little prisoner. You're wet between your lovely legs, and you smell of horny woman, but I want your luscious cunt running when I fuck you. I need to work you over more."

Could he really make her wait? Hell, yes! And he was no doubt enjoying every minute. If he hit her between the legs again she'd probably come and she didn't want to, not without his cock inside her. She let out a long sigh as he ran his hands over her back. If only he'd massage her again. The scent still lingered in the air, and just catching a faint whiff, she imagined his hands on her back, easing down her spine, and gently stroking the curve of her hip. Hell, she could almost feel his hands on her flesh.

"I'd like to use the flogger on you again, Lady Katherine. Do I have your permission?"

Chapter Ten

He was asking? She lifted her head off as far as she could with arms bound. "Yes!" Why the hell had she said that? She didn't want that again, or did she? Her cunt throbbed in anticipation. The hurt would be worth it to feel the pleasure that followed. The hurt was the pleasure.

She relaxed into the pillows as best she could, and waited. Willing herself to relax as she waited for the thrill that came on the heels of pain.

The tresses of the flogger, slapped her shoulders gently before trailing down her back, over her rump, and down her left thigh, eliciting a sigh of total pleasure and submission. This was what she wanted, what she loved, and what only Jud, and his alter-ego Black Jack Tar, could give her. The soft leather and ribbon now kissed her other thigh. Tickling the tender spot behind her knee before sweeping up and back to her shoulders. She almost cried out with delight, but bit her lips together. If she said she liked it, he'd do something else.

He continued. She lost count of how many times the flogger swept up and down her willing body. She tried to stay still, but gave up the effort, her body rocking with the movement of the tresses, her back arching as the trails of sweet leather wrought their magic on her body. This she could take all night. This was pleasure she'd never imagined. She'd be his prisoner any time he asked. She'd walk naked in the snow to have him do this again. As the flogger brushed across the back of her thighs, wrapping softly around the sensitive skin, she realized it was possible to faint from pleasure. She was giddy with desire. Her entire world became a whirlpool of sensation.

Until she realized he'd stopped.

"Why?" she cried out in disappointment.

"I can't wield the whip, and unbutton these damn, authentic pants!"

A gasp of anticipation came out louder than intended. If he was undoing his pants, he had to be getting ready to...

His hands grabbed her hips, stopping any movement. The warm head of his cock brushed the crack of her ass. For one horrid moment, she feared he would bugger her after all his promises, but no...with a hard thrust he was in her. Deep and hard and hot.

Nothing she'd imagined had ever been this incredible! Not even her wildest dreams compared to this. He pistoned in and out. Slowly, each motion adding to the sensations flooding her mind. Either he was larger than any man she'd had, or he was discovering nerve endings she never knew she possessed. Little involuntary whimpers accompanied his rhythm. Her hips rocked of their own volition. She was climbing, as she reached each level of sensation, he pulled her higher. Never before, ever, it was incredible, fantastic! She'd surely come soon...

She cried out with frustration when he withdrew, slamming her head into the mattress, and tugging her hands in an effort to release herself but his knots held. "Why? How could you?" She was screaming, but didn't care. This was sheer torture. The man was a sadist. She hated him. Once she got free she'd clout him, right where he'd never forget.

His lips on the base of her spine and the gentle hand on her hip set her whimpering. "Why?" She sagged into the mattress, almost beyond caring.

"I intend to look you in the eyes as I fuck you, Lady Katherine. You need to know who's mastered you. Acknowledge who rules you. I want to break down your last resistance.

"You're about to break down my sanity!"

He kissed the back of her knee.

She was so far gone, only the pillows kept her upright. She could barely think any more. She cried out as his finger brushed her clit. It was sheer torture. It was heaven as his lips brushed behind her other knee.

He pulled away the pillows, so she collapsed on her belly. Her legs were pretty much good for nothing. What did he expect? What did she expect? His fingers closed over her ankle as he lifted it crossing one leg over her other, and rolling her limp body over. She was on her back, arms still pinned over her head, but now she looked up at him as he stood beside the bed. At some point he'd lost the eye patch and kerchief. His eyes were almost hazy with need. She wasn't the only one near the edge.

He didn't say a word, just pulled his full shirt over his head. Giving her the sight of a magnificent broad chest, with just enough dark hair to set her wondering how it would feel pressed against her naked body.

Except she wasn't quite naked yet. As he'd rolled her, the tattered remnants of her costume fell in a twisted heap around her. One breast hung out of the torn bodice, her legs were twisted in yards of printed muslin.

She gave up worrying about her clothes, when he sat on the bed and rested one foot on his knee.

Restrained as she was, her vision was limited, but not so restricted she couldn't see quite clearly that he wore nothing under his breeches. He'd left them undone, and she got a glimpse of his magnificent cock. The sight was enough to send her cunt churning.

Her mind wasn't in a much better state. He was taking forever-purposely she was certain. But why complain? Just watching the muscles in his arms as he yanked down his boot and tossed it on the floor, and then proceeded of peel off the other one, was enough to make her heart race. And when he stood up, and loomed over her, every nerve ending in her body sang.

Magnificent wasn't the word. No wonder she'd almost climaxed earlier. He was enormous. Relief flickered through her mind, that she'd refused to let him bugger her. He was too damn big to enter her that way. If he hadn't already been there, she'd be worried about him filling her cunt, but it had been marvelous. She needed him right back there. Moisture flowed down her inner thighs at the sight and promise of his erection.

"Please," she began. "Oh, please, Captain! Please!" She was begging, and didn't care. Her entire body tingled at the thought of that beautiful cock ramming deep inside.

"Don't worry, little captive, I'll please you and myself. I might just keep you tied to that bed forever."

Her mind sang at the thought! What wouldn't she give to stay in his power like this. "Oh, Captain!" she whispered, as he pulled down his breeches and stepped out of them.

Now she saw him in full glory. She stared at his naked beauty. His beautiful, broad chest, with a fine down of dark hair, narrowing over his flat belly, and rising from the dark tuft at his groin, a cock of wondrous size. Katie licked her lips in anticipation and sighed. It was arrogant perfection, rigid, wide and long. Her hands fought the bonds in her need to circle the turgid flesh with her hands, and feel his male power under her fingers. "I want to feel you," she whispered. "I need to feel your cock."

"You will," he promised. The bed shifted under his weight. She needed him so much. She could smell her own arousal, mixed with the male scent of his naked body. She lay there, submissive, expectant and longing. She closed her eyes, readying for his thrust deep in her cunt.

His knees brushed the sides of her chest. Warm, smooth flesh brushed her chin. "Suck me, Lady Katherine!" His cock was centimeters from her lips. His thighs straddling her chest and his arms loomed overhead as he braced himself on her headboard. He leaned forward, brushing her lips with the warm head of his cock. "Obey!" One word sent wild sensations flooding her mind. "Obey! Or feel my whip harder than you can imagine."

Fright and excitement thrilled her. She let out a whimper of delight. "Oh, my captain," she whispered "I love to obey!"

Her lips enclosed the smooth pink head of his luscious cock. Her tongue lapped the warm skin, and the hard flesh beneath. Wild joy coursed in every pore and nerve. How right this felt! How marvelous her body's response! Never, in her wildest dreams, had she imagined anything could be this incredible.

She lifted her head off the pillow, and swallowed him down to the root.

His hands cupped the back of her head, easing the strain on her neck. She arched higher, taking even more of him in. She was beyond thought, no longer Lady Katherine, or even Katie. She was an inspired, aroused woman, servicing her captor, and the fantasy thrilled her, deep in her cunt. Her entire will, her total consciousness, and utter reason all focused on the sensation of her lips working his cock. Her tongue circling the rim, teasing the sweet ridge of muscle under the head, and caressing the sweet opening where his pre-come flowed.

Gently, he eased her head up and down so her lips caressed the length of his cock. He tasted of man, and power, and sex. To be thus used was all she'd ever wanted, what she'd been made for. She'd waited her entire life for this moment. Without ever realizing it, she'd longed to be thus bound. Helpless, as she serviced her captor, her lord, her captain, her lover.

She wanted to lie there forever, her lips around his hard flesh, his hands directing her and his cock possessing her mouth.

"Enough, little captive," he said. His voice almost gravelly. She'd have smiled at his obvious need, but her mouth was far to stretched. "Fucking your mouth is heaven, but the smell of your needy cunt is too much for me."

She cried out with disappointment as he pulled away. "Patience!" he ordered, his voice sterner now.

He moved down the bed, pausing to suck each nipple until she whispered with need, frustration, and sheer joy. The kisses between her breast and down to her navel were incredible and arousing, but she wanted more. She needed that cock of his thrust deep, but he was enjoying making her wait. Let him! She wasn't begging, or was she?

Her mind all but zapped out as his mouth moved between her legs. He grabbed her hips with both hands, to bring her closer as his tongue used her. Gentle laps from fore to aft and back, sweet flickers of the tip on her clit, and sharp thrusts into her cunt. He had her moaning, thrashing from side to side on the crumpled sheets, and finally, begging, "Please, please, I can't take any more, I need you inside."

"You'll take what I give you!" he growled, his voice muffled by her bush. "You'll lie there and accept it. It's what you're made for. It's why I have you at my mercy."

Her cunt flooded! Was it possible to be so wet, her clit so sensitized, or her mind so lost to anything but pleasure? She cared for nothing but the need to feel that massive cock stretching, pounding, and filling her with joy.

"I'll take anything you want. I'll obey any order, but please, please..." She was begging, and gloried in her capitulation. "Please, Captain!"

"What do you want your Captain to do to you, little captive?"

"Fuck me! Hard! Please, I beg you!"

He let out a great whoop of delight. "Since you begged so sweetly, my dear, you'll receive your reward." His hands shifted to her ankles, holding her firmly, he hoisted her legs so her ankles rested on his shoulders. She was open, exposed, utterly helpless, and panting with anticipation. He rocked, shifting the bed a little, as he rubbed his hot cock in the crease of her ass. For one, horrified moment, she feared he was about to bugger her, but just as the worry coiled in her gut, he said, "Not this time, love, Your moment will come before long, I can't let that tight little hole stay neglected."

She was about to tell him, 'Yes, he damn well could!' But just then, his fingers spread her cunt lips wide, and his thumb brushed her clit. He could do anything he wanted if he just brought her to climax. "I need you in me! Please, oh, please! I can't take much more!"

"You'll take whatever I tell you to!" Her whole body clenched with renewed awareness of her utter helplessness. Her shoulders and head sagged back on the bed as he rubbed his cock between her cunt lips, letting the head stimulate her clit as his hands stroked her ass and thighs,

She was lost in a fog of sensual delight. If he gave her this incredible pleasure, he could do anything he wanted. Forever. She tugged against her bonds. They held tight. She was utterly helpless, open and exposed. In a flash, her mind floated free, and he plunged in. Hard and fast. She cried out with sheer delight. He was even bigger than she remembered, or perhaps her stretched open position gave him deeper access. As he pumped her, she felt his cock rub every millimeter of her flesh. She was whimpering with pleasure. Wild cries echoed inside her head. Sweat, poured off her body as stimulation built to excess and beyond. She was keening, caught between the sweet force of his cock thrusting his power deep in her and the grip of his hands on her legs.

Her mind went hazy. All she knew was ever-increasing sensation, until she could stand no more, but needed him to never stop. Wild cries resounded off the ceiling overhead, as the mattress rocked beneath them. Higher he took her, and higher until with a chorus of joyful screams, she came. She was shaking, sweating, and gasping. His need intensified. Faster he pumped and harder until he lifted her from the rim of a fading climax to the crest of a second, as he came with loud grunts of satiation. Her mind and body flipped off the edge again, and again, in a crescendo of wild climaxes that left her limp and weak and utterly pleasure-racked.

She was close to fainting, only half-aware that he'd released her bonds, and was kissing and rubbing her wrists. His naked body was beside hers under the sheets, his arms around her as she passed out in a haze of sensual peace.

She woke to his lips on her eyelids as he brushed her sweat-dampened hair from her forehead. "Feel good?"

Good was totally inadequate! "Incredible! It was wonderful!"

"Yes." He was quite smug in his agreement, but in the circumstances, perfectly justified. "I haven't finished with you, Katie, my love. We have all weekend."

Oh, please. "You won't find me complaining."

"Didn't think so. I received the impression you couldn't get enough. You were begging me for more, several times."

"Yes." Why deny it?

"After we shower and have breakfast, I'm taking you to my house for the weekend. I've made plans for you."

Impossible as it seemed after the previous night, she was aroused again. Aroused and needy, "You can do whatever you want!"

"No!" His finger traced the line of her jaw. "Whatever *you* want. Will you let me tie you up again?"

"Yes, please!" She longed to feel again that delicious helplessness.

"I have a canopy bed with eye bolts so I can tie your legs high and spread you open." Her clit responded at the prospect. "I have a collection of floggers, there's a white and silver one I want to use particularly." She nestled against him and wrapped her arms around him.

"Want me to dress up again?" Wasteful as it was, having him rip the dress off her was something to be repeated.

"That can wait for next weekend."

"Next weekend?" He was planning in advance and she had a hard time thinking beyond right now, here in her bed, and..."Next weekend I've got to sit for Andrew's dratted cat!"

Jud stroked her face. "I'm coming with you. He has an impressive playroom, and he's invited us to make use of it."

Her mind went into a tailspin. "What playroom?"

"You'll find out. He has some specialized equipment I plan to strap you to." Was she up to this? She nodded. He kissed her. Hard. "Forget about next weekend," he said, his lips almost touching hers. "Think about what will happen to you after I get you in my house. I intend to keep you naked the whole weekend. Nudity will help focus your mind on what you are, my beautiful submissive. Want to come with me?"

"Please!" Her hips thrust and chest tightened with expectation. She wanted to please him so much.

"Better prepare yourself to kneel at my feet naked and suck my cock."

"Yes." If he went on much longer, she'd climax with his promises.

"Every time I command it?"

"Yes. You're my captor and my pirate." She leaned up on one elbow. "You're the answer to dreams I never knew I had."

He grinned. "Katie, my love. Dreams and fantasies are ours to explore. Now." he paused, his eyes twinkling. "Get the shower warmed up before I spank you!"

She was tempted to dally, but they had all weekend, and she did need a good shower. "Yes, Captain," she replied, and pushed back the bedclothes. "Whatever you say."

THE END

About the author:

Madeleine Oh is the pseudonym of a retired special-education teacher, who now lives in Ohio.

Madeleine Oh welcomes mail from readers. You can write to her c/o Ellora's Cave Publishing at P.O. Box 787, Hudson, Ohio 44236-0787.

Also by MADELEINE OH:

- Power Exchange
- Tied With a Bow – with Dominique Adair &
  Jennifer Dunne

LOUISIANA HEAT

Dominique Adair

Chapter 1

He had to have her.

David Hunter rubbed his thumb over the label on his beer bottle as he watched the slim blonde standing near the edge of the crowd. The condensation on the glass was cool against his palm, a sharp contrast to the sultry heat of the Louisiana evening. The sun had sunk over an hour ago but the drop in temperature was negligible, not that the crowd seemed to notice.

He propped his elbow on the edge of the makeshift bar, which was made of plywood sheets propped on sawhorses. The large crowd that had gathered to celebrate his cousin Remy's thirtieth birthday separated he and the beautiful blonde.

He smothered a grin as he raised the bottle to his mouth. Too bad his cousin wasn't here to celebrate with them this evening. Then again, eloping with a librarian from Fort Myers who knew how to wield a paddle with ease could do that to some men.

David set the bottle on the bar and nodded to the bartender, Etienne, to bring another. He definitely wasn't that kind of man. He'd never let a woman turn him into a submissive. No, not him. He was more inclined toward domination, not the other way around.

He picked up the fresh beer and turned to where he could see the blonde. His gaze zeroed in on her pale blonde hair, an anomaly in the crowd of peroxide-tortured hair, redheads and brunettes. Artfully streaked and straight as a waterfall, her icy locks reached the small of

Kay Glenn's slim back. She stood on the far side of the dance floor and, even from that distance, he imagined he could smell her subtle perfume. Dressed in a short, soft looking dress that hugged her womanly curves, the ripe apricot color made Kay look like a pale, aloof rose in the midst of a field of wildflowers.

The question of the hour was what was the manager of the elite Reicht Gallery in Atlanta doing here in Bayou Blue, Louisiana? This backwater town was hardly a tourist mecca, especially for a sophisticate like Kay.

His gaze moved over the crowd, lighting on a small group of women sitting at a corner table, huddled over their drinks. All of them were strangers to the tiny town and all of them had been invited by the absent birthday boy.

One woman, a redhead with enough freckles for three people, had told the bartender she'd met Remy online months ago and he'd asked her to join him for his birthday. One by one these women had arrived and, after being plied with drinks by the ever-thoughtful Etienne, had relayed similar stories. He'd directed each woman to the table until five of them were crowded together, probably comparing notes. With their heads close and their voices barely above a whisper, he had no doubt they were plotting the demise of one Remy DeLaughter.

His gaze returned to Kay. Was she another of Remy's online friends?

He pushed that thought away. Why would a beauty like Kay need to pick up men online? She was beautiful, accomplished and very well employed. Then again, the women Remy had invited to the party weren't completely regrettable. One, a blonde, could probably learn to use a little less hairspray and save the ozone layer some trauma, but other than that they weren't a bad looking lot.

But none of them came even close to Kay's icy good looks.

The object of his attention moved into the crowd toward the bar, a nervous smile on her pink lips. Her walk was graceful, elegant, and she grew more beautiful with each step. Her features were fine, bordering on delicate with soft pale brows, thickly lashed blue eyes and pale skin. She looked like an angel fallen to earth and his fingers itched to paint her. Her lips were full, perfect for kissing, and slick with pink gloss. She wasn't very tall, maybe seven or eight inches under his towering six foot three. Her figure was curvy like a woman's body should be. Her legs and arms were lightly tanned and her nails were polished in a color that matched her dress. Several silver rings and a slim watch were her only adornment.

Kay looked very different this evening than she had the last time he'd seen her.

It'd been almost six months ago when he'd paid a visit to the Gallery to approve the location for a showing of his work. He'd been sitting in the owner's office when Kay had arrived with a folder of documents. Dressed in black from head to toe with that beautiful hair pulled back into a militant twist, she'd looked cool and unapproachable. She'd done little more than nod and smile at him and produce the documents for him to sign when the owner had requested them, but she'd left quite an impression on him.

For weeks afterward, she'd haunted his dreams and he'd woken with a massive erection dedicated to her every morning. Though he'd been too busy to play while in Atlanta, he'd later kicked himself for not asking her out. In the gallery, she'd possessed a touch-me-not quality that had intrigued him, and turned him on more than he wanted to admit. But in Bayou Blue, that quality was stripped away and she looked very touchable now. Her skimpy summer dress left little to the imagination with its slim straps and above-the-knee hem. She looked like sin in sandals as she leaned on the bar just a few feet from him.

"Excuse me," she called to Etienne.

"*Bonjour, ma jolie fille*, what can I get for you?" Etienne's accent was as thick as David's forearm and his gaze was appreciative as they fastened on Kay's bountiful breasts. David noticed how her flesh strained the fragile chiffon bodice of her dress.

"I'm looking for Remy DeLaughter. Do you know him?" she asked.

David straightened in surprise. She was one of them. His gaze swung to the table of strangers, then back to Kay. How could this be?

Etienne chuckled. "*Oui* — "

David set his beer down hard on the bar and Etienne's surprised gaze swung toward him. David gave him a subtle shake of his head and nodded toward the gazebo situated near the river. Unlit and secluded, it was the perfect place for private…conversation.

Etienne gave him a wink and picked up a rag and began drying off some glasses. "*Oui*, I know dat Remy. I saw him headed 'ward the gazebo over dere a few minutes ago."

Kay glanced toward the secluded structure, then flashed Etienne a quick smile. "Thanks for your help." She turned away and walked into the dark, skirting the table of Remy's would-be dates.

David dodged the crowd and slipped into the shadows as the band broke into La Jolie Blonde. He smiled. How apropos. His pulse quickened as she mounted the steps of the structure.

"Remy?" she called. "Are you in here?" She vanished into the dim interior.

David waited a few seconds then stepped into the gazebo behind her. Kay stood in the center of the small building, indecision written in every line of her body. He moved behind her and placed his hands on her shoulders. She jumped beneath his touch and started to turn, but he tightened his grip.

"Don't turn around," he whispered. He dropped his head and inhaled the rich scent of her hair. He shifted silken strands away from her left shoulder and dropped his head to touch her with his mouth.

"Remy?" She shivered and leaned into him.

He pushed away annoyance at hearing his cousin's name on her lips. He wanted this woman and, if he had to use deception to get her, he'd do it. Her image had driven him crazy for the past six months and the need to possess her was too great to ignore.

"Kay?" he whispered.

He heard her sigh and felt her sag against him even as his conscience pricked him for deceiving her. The scent of her perfume curled around him, arousing him as never before. His cock throbbed and strained against the zipper of his jeans. It was all he could do prevent himself from pulling up her thin dress and taking her.

"I was starting to get worried." Her voice was smoky, her light northern accent filled with heat. "I didn't think

I'd ever find you. I'd ask people where you were and they'd just chuckle."

"Everyone has been looking for me," he lied.

She gave a throaty laugh. "Well, it is your party."

David made a non-committal sound, then slid his hands over her slim shoulders. Gathering the silk of her hair in both hands, he arranged it over her right shoulder, out of his way. A gentle breeze whispered through the trees, allowing quick snatches of lantern light to penetrate their sanctuary.

Reveling in her soft skin, he slid the thin strap of her dress from her shoulder. He heard her breath catch as the bodice slid down to bare the top of her breast.

"Remy—"

Irritated at the sound of his cousin's name, David whispered, "Call me Hunter." He didn't want to hear this woman crying out another man's name when he made her come.

"Hunter?"

"A childhood nickname." He ran his hand down her arm, nudging the material covering her breast to the side with his fingers. "Everyone here calls me that." Which was the truth for a change.

"Oh."

She shivered as the cloth slid over her erect nipple, baring the pale mound to his gaze. He cupped her breast, his tanned hand looking erotically dark against her pale skin. With his thumb, he caressed her hardened tip, watching as it tightened even more. Her breathing deepened. She was incredibly responsive to his touch.

"You're beautiful," he said.

They stood in the shadows, David pressed to her back, her bare breast in the palm of his hand. Behind them, the party continued. The band swept into an energetic version of The Bayou Stomp while the stillness in the gazebo was palatable.

"You've seen a photo of me—" She sounded breathless.

"Photos don't do you justice," he nipped at her shoulder, his teeth grazing her skin before he soothed her with his tongue.

She gave a soft laugh. "Flatterer. You have me at a disadvantage. You've seen my photo, but I haven't seen yours."

David stilled his thumb. Remy never sent her his photo? How could this be? "You haven't?" He kept his voice carefully neutral.

"You sent me the file, but I couldn't get it to open, remember? You laughed at me and said it was user error rather than a corrupted photo." He heard the amusement in her voice.

"*Mais oui*, I remember now." He chuckled and allowed his thumb to resume its lazy stroking of her nipple. "So you're saying you want to see my face?"

He felt her nod. He doubted she'd recognize him. The last time she'd seen him, he'd been groomed, his hair tied back, his face shaved and he'd been dressed in a black suit. Now, with his hair wild about his shoulders, two days of beard on his face and dressed in a white T-shirt and jeans so worn they appeared white, he hoped she wouldn't connect the two men. Who'd think that the world-renowned painter, David Hunter, would be residing in the back waters of Louisiana?

"You'll see me soon enough. Right now, I want to see you…naked." He whispered into her ear, his lips caressing her soft lobe, and she shuddered. "I want to feel my hands slide over your body like this." He removed the other strap of her dress and the bodice fell to her waist.

Kay made an instinctive movement to cover herself, but he prevented her by trapping her arm against her body with his. He had her at his mercy as he palmed one breast and covered the notch of her thighs with his other hand. Through the dress he could feel her heat. She was as aroused as he.

"Does this turn you on, *'tite bébé*?" he breathed, his erection hard against the small of her back. "The thought of having sex with me, right here, a few feet from a party where anyone can come in and see me fucking you?"

She moaned and tossed her head restlessly against his shoulder. Her palms were damp as she clutched his arm. Her left hand covered his and pressed it harder against her pussy in a rhythmic fashion as she bumped her lush buttocks against him. He ground his teeth. Much more of this and he'd throw her to the ground and fuck her then and there.

"Say it," he growled. "Tell me what you want."

"Please, please touch me." She shuddered.

David felt a surge of triumph rush through him. He released her and backed away. Almost immediately, he could feel her confusion and she started to turn.

"Don't turn around." Due to his heightened state of arousal and the fact his zipper was almost embedded in his cock, his voice came out harsher than he'd intended. Almost immediately she straightened and turned away from him. His eyes narrowed, fixing on the slim curve of her back. She liked being commanded, did she?

"Take off your dress." He moved away until she was little more than a slim, pale shadow in the dark. "Strip for me."

Her head dipped forward and he saw her shoulders quiver. She removed her tiny purse from over her head and laid it on the handrail. Slowly, she slid her arms from the spaghetti straps of the dress and slid it down over her hips. She wore flesh-colored thong panties and her buttocks were pale and lush, surprisingly so for someone of her size. They were just the right size to cushion a man's ride as he fucked her from behind.

She allowed the dress to drop to the floor before she slithered out of her panties. When she bent over to retrieve her clothing, he narrowly avoided biting his tongue as her thighs parted and offered him a glimpse of her sweet pussy. Impatient now, he tore off his shirt and tossed it over the rail before he approached her. On the tender curve of her hip he spied a dark spot about the size of a half dollar, but it was too dark to see very well. He dropped his hands to her waist and she jumped.

"Is this a tattoo I spy?" he whispered.

She gave a shaky nod, her breathing ragged as if she'd run a mile.

He squinted at the mark, trying to make out the shape. His eyes widened as he realized what it was.

Handcuffs.

Curiouser and curiouser.

He ran his hands over her silky skin to cup her breasts. Thumbing her nipples, she gave an excited hum and settled her plump backside against his crotch. He ground his teeth as she rotated her buttocks.

He grasped her shoulders and guided her to the far side of the gazebo, which faced away from the party. Earlier in the day, workers had been restoring the old building and had left some bricks behind, which David knew they could put to good use. Kay was too short for him to take comfortably from behind, so he urged her up onto a single row of brick, which raised her to the perfect height.

With thick fingers he tore open the front of his pants, groaning as his full cock sprang free from the opening. Thanking his lucky stars he'd kept the condom Old Man Pou had thrust at him when he'd arrived at the party, he tore through the wrap and slid the condom on in record time.

"Brace your hands here." He showed her where to place her hands on the white support pole to keep her balance.

Running his hands up her back, he positioned her hips just so before urging her to spread her legs, leaving her vulnerable to his touch. He dipped his finger into her wet pussy, relishing the moan and uninhibited thrust of her hips. He'd barely touched her and she was ready for him.

Removing his hand, he gripped her hips and thrust into her from behind. Her startled cry mingled with his earthy groan. She was tighter than a fist around his cock and he wasn't sure he'd be able to stand her snug heat for long. He grit his teeth and struggled to hold her still until he could catch his breath. But with her plump buttocks cushioning his pelvis, he was fired up and ready to go.

"Hunter..."

Her voice was heavy with desire and the sound of it inflamed his senses. Gripping her hips, he thrust into her, the sound of skin meeting skin and her moans mingled with the rousing piano of the Zydeco band.

As his cock hammered into her from behind, he reached around, parting her slick lips and his fingers zeroed in on her clitoris. With a few deft strokes, he had her bucking so hard beneath him, he had to grip her hips or she'd have pulled away from him completely. Her silky hair licked at his shoulders as she flung her head back and her body convulsed around him.

He gripped her hips, his fingers biting into her flesh as he struggled to maintain control. But the heat of the Louisiana night, the scent of sex mingled with honeysuckle and the damp heat of the woman surrounded him and drove him over the edge.

Her cries had barely faded before he was thrusting into her again. Lust rolled through his bloodstream as fire licked down his spine. Dimly he was aware of Kay's cries as the familiar sensation of orgasm trickled up the back of his calves.

His brain exploded into a red haze as his balls tightened and release tore through him. His breath raged in his lungs and his knees threatened to buckle as wave after wave rushed through him.

After the storm had passed, David laid his head on Kay's shoulder. Their bodies were as close as two humans could be with his cock still buried in her sweet pussy. Reality slowly reasserted itself and he became aware of the lack of noise from the party. Nearby he heard the distinctive twang of Old Collete, the town's retired librarian.

"Sounds to me like someone was having more fun than I."

David smothered a smile against Kay's shoulder. Fun did not even begin to describe what had just happened.

Chapter 2

How in the devil had she ended up here?

Kay propped her elbows on the picnic table, her overloaded paper plate untouched. The tables around her were crowded with people eating from a very generous buffet. As she watched, one of the older men standing over the grill brought a heaping platter of barbecue to the buffet table.

The people of Bayou Blue certainly knew how to celebrate a birthday.

Her gaze strayed to Remy — Hunter, she mentally corrected herself. He'd reached the bar and was now leaning against it after ordering their drinks. He talked with an elderly man on a tall stool. The older man smoked a hand-rolled cigarette and wore a grimy baseball cap, the company logo long since obliterated by the soaked-in grime that covered it.

Hunter said something to him and the man gave a harsh, braying laugh like that of a donkey before his amusement turned into a coughing fit. Hunter shook his head and thumped him on the back as the bartender set their drinks on the bar beside him.

Who'd have believed that twenty-four hours ago she'd been in Atlanta, processing paperwork for the gallery where she worked, and now she was sitting at a picnic table in the heat of a Louisiana night waiting for her lover to bring a cool drink.

Her lover.

She shivered despite the humid night. He wasn't quite what she'd expected. He was bigger, quieter maybe? Online, Remy—Hunter, she corrected again—was quite a talker, while in person, he'd barely said more than a handful of sentences to her.

What had taken her more by surprise was the sense of immediacy she'd felt with his first touch. They'd had a comfortable relationship online, sharing their lives in a way that only online friends could do, and she'd felt she knew him pretty well, or at least well enough to be comfortable coming here to meet him in person. While she expected some awkward moments, she'd been taken by surprise at the sense of familiarity, the sense of rightness. It was as if she'd known him before. They'd barely spoken, so far at least, but she didn't feel like the proverbial outsider here in his hometown. She smiled. This was a good thing as they'd had sex before they'd even been properly introduced.

Her cheeks warmed and she ducked her head when Hunter returned with their drinks. "One glass of tea, no sugar." He set it before her. The humidity had already created a thick layer of condensation on the glass.

"Thank you," she said.

"Drinking your tea like that is likely to get you kicked out of Louisiana," he teased.

Kay grinned and ran her finger down the side of the glass. "It's the Yankee in me, I guess. I just can't get used to drinking that syrupy stuff you Southerners pass off as tea."

"Iced tea is the house wine of the south." He raised his beer in a mock salute.

"I thought that was Dr. Pepper?" She lifted the glass to her mouth and took a deep drink of the icy beverage. She'd always drank her tea without sugar as her mother did.

Amusement shined in his dark bedroom eyes. "Dr. Pepper and RC Cola are akin to champagne down here."

She set down the glass and picked up her fork. "How continental..."

He tipped his head back and laughed. It was an unrestrained sound that sent a ripple of reaction down her spine. Her nipples hardened.

"You make us sound like a bunch of swamp dwellers who wrestle alligators for a living," he said. He picked up his fork and dug into a mountain of dirty rice.

"Not at all. Louisiana has some of the most beautiful scenery in the world and trust me, I've been all over. Your hometown is very beautiful and very rustic." She waved her fork in the direction of the band. "And you have to admit that seeing a violin player with two bloodhounds at his feet isn't exactly something you'd see in downtown Atlanta."

He glanced at the band, then shook his head. "True. Old Pete has had a hound at his feet for as long as I can remember. I can't imagine him without one."

"His idea of the perfect accessory?"

"Exactly." His teeth gleamed against the dark tan of his skin.

The silence was comfortable as they tucked into their meals. Around them, the party continued while they concentrated on the food and each other. Under the table, their knees brushed and their feet tangled. She shivered as he encircled her ankles with his calves. He'd trapped her to the point she couldn't move her legs.

"Comfortable?" His gaze was filled with meaning.

"Perfectly." She reached for her glass. "And you?"

"Very."

They finished their meal with little conversation though every gesture was loaded with sensual innuendo. They sampled food from each other's forks and he didn't laugh too hard when she almost choked on a rice dish that was so spicy her eyes watered. As she sniffed and dabbed her eyes, he asked, "Are you ready to leave?"

Kay looked at her unfinished plate, surprised she'd eaten as much as she had. Her body ached, her breasts felt heavy and the flesh between her thighs was wet and needy. It was all she could do to keep from squirming on the chair to relieve the ache. This man had given her a mind-blowing orgasm, fed her good Cajun food, and now it was time to indulge in appetites of another kind.

With slick palms, she pushed her plate away. His smile of satisfaction sent a rush of heat down her spine and she felt her face flush. Suddenly nervous, she looked away and fumbled with her string purse. Somehow it had gotten caught on the back of her chair and it was now hopelessly tangled. Mentally cursing, her hands turned to all thumbs as she wrestled with the strap.

"You'll break it if you keep yanking like that."

His sudden appearance beside her was startling. He dropped into a crouch and she was assailed with male heat as his hand covered hers and he gently untangled her purse from the chair. Their gazes met and he lowered their clasped hands to her knees.

"Why so nervous, *ma petite*?" He released her and placed his hand on the inside of her knee, his palm scorching her skin.

"I'm not nervous," she lied.

He leaned closer and whispered so only she could hear his words. "You've had me between your thighs. You've had me buried deep inside of you. We've felt each other reach release in the darkness." She shivered as his hand moved up her thigh and without thinking, she parted to allow him better access. "Soon, we'll be joined again." His lips brushed her ear and she gulped for air.

"I'll be buried deep inside you..." His tongue caressed her earlobe. "Fucking you..." He nipped at her jaw.

Of their own volition, her hands moved to his shoulders, her nails digging into the soft cotton of his T-shirt. She moaned as his fingers touched the needy flesh between her thighs.

"Hunt—"

Their lips met in a kiss of force, heat. It didn't start out gentle as most kisses do. This one was hot and dominating, almost overpowering in its intensity. She moaned again and her fingers tangled in his silky dark hair. She hauled him closer, relishing the heat of his body as his hips wedged themselves between her thighs. Their mouths ate at each other as his fingers parted her nether lips to give a bold stroke—

"*Mon Dieu*, get this woman a room," a voice cackled overhead.

Stunned, Kay froze and her eyes flew open as their lips broke apart. Over them stood the older man Hunter had been speaking to at the bar. His wrinkled face was stretched wide with a knowing smile.

"She too pretty to fuck at a picnic table, *mon ami*. What would your *maman* say?" He laughed. "You take her home, use a proper bed, boy. 'Dis one will keep you happy a long time." He turned away and shuffled toward the bar.

Cheeks burning, Kay looked around, relieved to see that most of the partygoers had paid no attention to their lewd behavior. The few glances she did catch were from women and they held more than just a tinge of envy.

Her gaze met Hunter's and she saw he wasn't in the least bit embarrassed. His gaze was dark as he removed his hand from between her thighs. She bit back a protest as his callused finger stroked her clitoris and sent a shudder of sensation through her abdomen.

Her eyes widened when he raised his hand to his mouth and licked her dampness from his fingers. His eyes darkened and his jaw clenched. She recognized the look of sexual need when she saw it and he definitely had that look.

"We go now." With an abrupt motion, he got to his feet and hauled her with him. He took her hand and led her through the crowd toward the bayou and away from the parking lot.

She wanted him more than she'd ever wanted another man in her life. He'd already taken her once and it wasn't enough. She wanted more, much more. As they wound their way through the dancers, she stumbled to keep up with his long-legged gait. It was obvious he wanted to make a fast exit and so did she.

She touched his arm and he stopped and looked down at her. "My rental car is in the lot. Is it safe here?" she asked.

"*Mais oui.*" He began pulling her through the crowd again. "It will be safe enough."

As they reached the edge of the crowd she heard someone call from behind them.

"Hey, HUNTER!"

Kay frowned and looked around, but no one seemed to be paying the caller any attention.

"Hunter...David—"

Hunter came to an abrupt halt and she ran into his back, hard. She would have fallen if he hadn't turned quickly and caught her by the arm.

"Are you okay?" he asked.

She nodded and he turned away, irritation evident on his face. He nudged her behind him and turned to deal with the fresh-faced kid that was running toward them.

"Make it quick, Gator," Hunter growled.

The boy launched into rapid Cajun, leaving Kay doubtful she'd be able to keep up even if she knew the language. She enjoyed listening, caught in the cadence and flow of the words, a blend of French and patois that was both elegant and guttural at the same time.

Her attention was diverted when someone tugged on her sleeve. She turned to see a short, round, black woman standing beside her. Dressed in a colorful muumuu that swept the ground and a matching turban, she gave Kay a wide smile. She removed the fragrant cigarette from her mouth and nodded toward Hunter.

"He no quite what you expected, is he?" Her eyes were sharp, knowing.

Kay cleared her throat, feeling a bit like Alice falling through the rabbit hole. "Well, no, not quite—"

"Pay no mind, he be genuine." She shrugged and took a deep draw on her hand-rolled cigarette. "We no know someone 'til we look into their soul and dat man, he hide his well." The woman patted her on the arm. "But you a smart woman, you'll see." She gave Kay a secretive smile, the kind women share only between themselves. "Besides, dat man, he know how to keep a woman happy for long time." She gave a deep, rumbling laugh. "Long, long time..." She turned away and swayed toward the buffet table, her cigarette still dangling from her mouth as she laughed at her own joke.

"Kay?"

Hunter's voice brought her back to reality and she looked up into his dark blue eyes. She frowned. Hadn't Remy said he had brown eyes?

He leaned down and gave her a quick, hard kiss. Her toes curled in her sandals at the instant rush of warmth she experienced.

"Let's go," he said.

Kay followed him toward the darkness of the bayou and the ultimate fulfillment of her darkest, deepest desires.

Chapter 3

"Why don't you have a real boat?"

David slammed the lantern door shut, the golden light strengthening as the kerosene burned. When he was alone in the bayou, he rarely ever used the light, preferring to find his way to the cabin by the light of the moon. As a newcomer to the mysteries of the bayou, he figured that using the lantern would make Kay more comfortable.

He dropped the lantern on the hook at the bow of the handmade pirogue, then looked up at her still standing on the dock. She stood so close he could smell her arousal. Just a few inches from his face, separated by the thin material of her dress was the heated flesh that wept for his touch. Flesh he wanted to feel against his mouth and taste with his tongue.

His cock throbbed, painfully constricted by his jeans. Now was not the time to take her, not if he didn't want to end up in the dark waters of the bayou. He cleared his throat.

"This is a real boat. It was handmade by my cousin R —" he stopped, irritated that he'd almost given himself away so quickly. To distract her, he caught her around the waist and pulled her down into the boat. She gasped as the narrow craft rocked beneath them and she flung her arms around his shoulders.

"You're safe, *ma petite*." He set her away from him, easing her onto the narrow seat in the bow.

"Are you sure?" She looked around nervously.

"*Oui*." He picked up the baire, a thin mosquito net that he carried in the bottom of the boat, and draped it over her. "Safe as a babe."

She ran her hand over the net. "What is this for?"

"Mosquitoes. Your perfume will bring them out in droves."

"Ah."

She sat huddled beneath the netting and her uneasy expression told him she wasn't reassured. David quashed his smile and moved to the other end of the boat. Picking up the pole, he stuck it into the water until he hit ground and shoved them off from the dock. The boat skimmed the water like a leaf on the breeze. There was nothing like traveling through the bayou in a handmade pirogue.

"Where are we going?" she asked.

"Home." For now, at least, it was home. He was using Remy's fishing cabin as his base here in Louisiana. "It's a mile or so down the bayou, as straight as the crow flies."

The physical exertion of poling was familiar and welcome as he moved out into the narrow waterway. While David didn't call Bayou Blue his home year round, he did come down as much as he could. This place occupied a part of his heart that his house in Boston could never touch.

The thick air of the bayou surrounded them as they moved through the darkness. On the banks of the river, life carried on as it had for thousands of years. He could feel the gaze of crocodiles as the boat slid past their resting places. The bayou was like no other place in the world.

It wasn't long before the soothing rock of the boat seemed to relax Kay and soon she was lying back against the prow, her eyes half closed and fixed on him.

She was beautiful in the flickering lantern light. Her lips were ripe and damp from his recent kisses. Her skin was pale and her legs were bare and, thanks to his quick hands, her panties now resided in his back pocket. Just knowing she was nude beneath that miniscule dress was enough to make him crazy.

She raised her hand to her mouth and allowed her index finger to follow the soft curve he longed to nibble. Her legs shifted in a restless manner, slight movements that spoke volumes and he wanted to know what she was thinking, though he suspected he already knew.

"Are you still wet for me?" His voice was low, heavy.

She gave a slow blink, then smiled a secretive smile that served only to warm his already heated blood.

"Show me."

She glanced around as if to find anyone who might be watching. He could have assured her that the only witnesses to her behavior would be a few crocs and some water snakes, but he didn't think that knowledge would keep her at ease. The thin netting did very little to shield her from his interested gaze. She dropped her hand and parted her thighs to reveal her sweet pussy. She looked beautiful, lying back and exposing herself to him, but it wasn't quite enough for him.

"Open yourself for me, Kay." His voice came out as a command and her eyes widened. He caught the flash of excitement before her gaze skated away.

She really enjoyed being commanded.

She spread her thighs further, her hand dipping to part her woman's mound. The dusky rose of her flesh glistened and her aroused clitoris peaked at him from its sheltering hood. He licked his lips when he saw her muscles clench under his interested gaze.

David's heart thudded in his chest and he shoved the pole into the water with more force than necessary, sending the boat to rocking. She gave a half-hearted squeal and released herself to clutch the sides. Mentally cursing himself, he steadied the craft and they continued their journey.

"Touch yourself, Kay," he commanded. "But don't come. It's up to me to provide your release. I decide when and where and for now, you must wait until we reach home."

Her dark eyes met his and she licked her lips. There was indecision written on her face and he held his breath. Would she refuse him? What would he do if she backed out now? Would he take her back to the bar? Could he release her after having had her only once?

Luckily, he didn't have to answer those difficult questions. He released the breath he'd been holding when she braced her knees on either side of the boat and exposed herself once more. With her pink polished nails, she began to stroke. Her movements were slow, sensual, as she dragged her fingertips over her clit, then down to tease the opening of her beautiful pussy. Her eyes narrowed and her hips rolled in accompaniment to her smooth strokes. Within moments, her breathing had deepened and her eyes slid closed. She drew up her knees to brace her feet on the edges of the boat.

The netting covered her only to her waist. It had rucked up around her hips as she'd moved. Soft cries sounded from her mouth as her back arched when she slid her fingers into her weeping cunt and began to finger-fuck herself. He could tell from her increasingly frenzied movements that she was close to the edge, much closer than he wanted her to be.

"Kay —" His voice held more than a hint of warning.

She didn't appear to have heard him and continued her sensual dance. Her back arched and a wild cry broke from her lips. Her hands covered her cunt, but he could tell from her slowing movements she'd already reached her release. He knew the sight of a woman's orgasm as well as he knew his own face.

Kay had disobeyed him. Had she done it deliberately? Did she expect him to punish her?

David tore his gaze away from her soft body, pushing his lust into a far corner of his mind and slamming the door on it. Fixing his gaze upon an unseen landmark in the darkness, he continued driving the boat forward, his pace urgent now.

The thought of giving this bewitching little minx a spanking was pleasurable, more so than he'd have thought an hour ago. Indeed, it was rapidly becoming incorporated in one of his favorite fantasies. With his mind filled with images of her butt pinkening beneath swats of his hand, he almost didn't hear her address him.

"Hunter?" Her voice was louder this time.

"Yes?" Sweat broke out on his forehead as Remy's private dock came into view.

"Are you mad?" Her tone was tentative.

Mad wasn't quite how he'd describe it…

"I told you to restrain yourself," he kept his voice cool, matter-of-fact. "And you chose to disobey me. How do you think I should feel?"

She was silent, her head bowed beneath the net. While he'd been imagining her stretched out across his lap as he swatted her, she'd sat up and composed herself with her hands neatly folded in her lap. Her knees were together and her heels were tucked under her seat. He could only hope she didn't find the box of paints and small canvases he'd stashed there earlier in the day.

"I suppose I should be punished," she said, her voice was low.

He caught the faint quiver that shook her shoulders. Was she afraid of him? She certainly gave every sign of being afraid with her head bowed and her shoulders hunched like that. Maybe he should—

Then she looked up and he caught the look of excitement in her eyes before she could mask it with remorse.

Well, that answered that question.

Hunter slowed the pirogue and met the dock with a gentle bump. Within seconds, he'd tied the boat off and helped her up onto the wooden planks of the dock. He started down the narrow gravel path toward the cabin and Kay hung back.

"What are you going to do?" Her voice was low.

"I haven't decided." He threw her what he hoped was a menacing look. "When I make that decision, you'll know shortly after I do. Right now, you need to get moving." He gestured to the path. "I think you're in deep enough as it is, don't you?"

She bit her lip and scurried past him, her excitement a palpable heat that clung to her body. David followed closely, his mind devising all sorts of delightful torment for his disobedient slave.

Chapter 4

Kay twined her purse strap around her fingers as she climbed the steps to Hunter's cabin. The narrow nylon braid had almost numbed them by the time she heard the creak of the front door.

Shrouded by thick shadows, he stood by the door, his arm outstretched, indicating his desire for her to precede him. All she could see was the gleam of his eyes.

It's now or never, girl...

Anticipation vied for a space among the nervous butterflies in her stomach as she stepped past him into the dark cavern of his home. She moved to the left until she was just inside the door leaving room for him to enter.

The darkness was thick, exacerbated by the heavy humidity. For a split second, she was frightened of the alien Louisiana night and the stranger beside her. It wasn't too late to turn back...

The click of a wall switch caused her to jump and she bumped into Hunter. His big hands caught her by the elbows and he hauled her against his chest.

"Looks like we're alone in the dark..." He nuzzled her neck.

Kay gave a nervous laugh. "You'd mentioned in your letters that this happens from time to time."

Hunter tensed and set her away from him with an abrupt move. She heard him flick the wall switch a few more times. He muttered a low curse then strode past her, vanishing into the dark. She heard rustling, the slam of a drawer, then the welcome screech of a match. Light flickered and Hunter held the bright tip to the wick of a glass kerosene lamp.

"Sorry about this, I'll have to restart the generator. It won't take but a minute." He put the lamp on a small kitchen table, then headed for what she assumed was the back door. After throwing a slide lock, he vanished into the night.

Curious and much calmer now that she could see her surroundings, she saw the cabin wasn't very large with everything contained in one room. To the left was a sitting area with a dark brown couch that had obviously seen better days. A laptop sat on the scarred coffee table and she smiled at the sight of it. That must be where he answered her emails.

A black and white TV, complete with wire hanger antenna, sat on a wooden Jax beer box near a large window. Next to that were some bookshelves where dozens of books, both paperbacks and hardcovers, vied for space. Scattered among them were framed photographs that she was itching to inspect.

Kay cast a nervous glance toward the door where Hunter had vanished. There was no telling when he could be back. Unwilling to be caught snooping, she moved away.

The kitchen and dining area was against the back wall. A sink, small stove and refrigerator were arranged on the right and a small table with two chairs was on the left. A glass Mason jar sat in the center, filled with an explosion of wildflowers.

Sections of the wood floor were covered with a variety of colorful handmade rag rugs. The wood between them gleamed and she was quick to notice there was not a dish or newspaper in sight. He was certainly tidy for a man.

In a corner of the cabin hung a sheer curtain. She moved to peek around it and there she found the door leading to the bathroom and the bed.

It was massive, made of some type of walnut. It stood tall, so tall there were several steps just to climb onto it. Thick pillows rested against the headboard and the clean white cases contrasted with the brightly colored quilt. She ran her hand over the covers. Soon they would be in this bed—

She jumped as the roar of a motor starting shattered her fantasy. Feeling guilty for some reason, she scrambled back toward the front door. Needing something to do, she shut and attempted to bolt it. She was bemused when she couldn't find a lock of any kind. Obviously Hunter didn't think his neighbors would break in his house.

"We're up and running." He came through the back door, his hands greasy from his work. He kicked the door shut, then walked to the sink and began washing. "The air conditioning should cool the place down shortly."

"Does that happen a lot?" She twined her fingers in her purse strap again.

He shrugged. "From time to time. We don't use it all that often—" An odd look crossed his face and he stopped speaking.

She frowned. "You don't live here all the time?"

"*Oui*, but I don't use the generator all the time." He picked up a hand towel that hung on the front of the oven and dried his hands. "Sometimes the old ways are best." He nodded toward the oil lamp.

She had to admit the golden glow from that one fragile flame was welcoming, more so than artificial light. Not to mention the fact that candlelight was flattering to female thighs—

"Come to me," Hunter commanded.

Her time had come.

Kay slid her purse off her shoulder and left it on the top of the television. He stood in front of the sink, his big arms folded over his chest and his expression remote. On wobbly legs, she forced herself to move to him. She stopped when she stood within arm's reach of him.

"On the way here, I gave you a direct order. I said you could play with yourself, but you weren't allowed to come." His dark gaze penetrated her soul. "I am the Master in this relationship and you've disobeyed me."

Kay bit her lip, her uneasiness forgotten as excitement raced to the fore. She could feel her pussy growing damp again.

"Yes, Master," she whispered.

"I think it's time to show you how a disobedient slave is treated, don't you?"

A whimper threatened to break free and she bit down hard to stop it. She gave a quick nod.

"Good, we're in agreement." He took her arm just above the elbow and led her to the table. Pulling out one of the wooden chairs, he sat down. "Now, you must take your punishment. We'll begin once you present yourself to me."

She tipped her head to the side, confused. "What do you mean?"

"Lay across my knees and pull up your skirt," he instructed. "I want to see your beautiful ass."

Her hands were damp as she moved to his side. Bracing herself on his thigh, she laid facedown across his lap. She gave a squeak when he shifted her body until her head was pointed down toward the floor and her buttocks were centered on his lap. She braced her arms on the floor.

"I don't relish punishing you, *ma petite*."

His impressive erection pressed into her left hip, belying his words. Either he had a potato in his pants or he was enjoying this just as much as she!

"But we must do this to show you who is the Master here." He laid his hands upon her upper thighs before flicking up her skirt and exposing her. "Now relax, Kay." He stroked her buttocks and upper thighs in long, soothing strokes. "I want you willing in this."

She forced herself to relax, but it wasn't easy. She wasn't uncomfortable, though the blood was rushing to her head a bit. Maybe this wouldn't take too long and she could—

Hunter nudged her thighs apart leaving her exposed to his touch, his gaze. She moaned as need streaked through her abdomen. She was so helpless, so wet…so needy…

He gave her a gentle spank on one buttock, then the other. She sighed. Well, that was easy enough—

His hand came down again, only this time it wasn't quite so gentle. She screamed, her back arching upward. He placed one hand between her shoulders, forcing her down again until she stopped struggling.

"Don't resist me, Kay. I will have my way with you." His tone was short and severe and, judging from the harsh jut of his cock against her hip, he was even more aroused than before.

Kay went limp, her lower lip caught between her teeth as he resumed her punishment, this time with lighter blows. The sound of his hand against her buttocks echoed through the room as heat spread through her tender flesh. He was careful to move his hand around with no two slaps in the same place as the one before. And with each stroke, her need increased until she was almost humping against his leg. She longed to grind her pussy against something hard, anything to relieve the unending arousal.

"Your ass is a beautiful shade of pink, Kay." His voice was strained, breathless.

The blows had slowed somewhat, but each one was more painful, thanks to the previous ones. She winced and spread her thighs in an effort to relieve some of the discomfort.

The slaps stopped and she felt his hands spreading her open.

"Are you wet for me, Kay?" he whispered.

She nodded, then jumped when he gave her another crack across the ass. Tears stung her eyes.

"Speak to me when I ask you a question, slave."

"Yes, I'm wet for you." The tears came faster now.

"Just one more—"

She screamed as his hand came down across her smarting buttocks. Before her scream died, Hunter flipped her upright in his lap and cuddled her as one would a child.

Confused and still aroused, she curled into him, burrowing her face in his neck. Was she hurt?

Embarrassed? Did she still want him to fuck her? Now she was too confused to tell for sure.

"Shh, *bébé*." He wrapped his big arms around her, his touch soothing, a sharp contrast to his spanking. "I hated that as much as you did, Kay, but it had to be done." He kissed her damp cheek. "Now I'll make us a drink and we'll continue with our plans."

He helped her up, not letting go of her until he was sure she was steady on her feet. Then he fixed tall glasses of lemonade with lots of ice. Kay remained standing near the table, ashamed that her buttocks were so sore she couldn't bear the thought of sitting on that hard wooden seat.

"It'll pass." He'd drained his glass before he pulled her into his arms. "In the morning, the burn will be but a faint memory."

She braced her forehead against his chest, drained. The pain might fade, but the confusion wouldn't. How could pain cause such arousal? Before she'd only had gentle spankings, maybe one or two swats. It had seemed like the more strident the spanking the more aroused she'd become.

His hands moved up and down her back in a slow, soothing motion. As they reached her hips, she gave an involuntary jerk and his hands stilled.

"I know what you need," he said.

He took her hand and walked her to the bed, then ushered her up the short steps at the side. Laying her down, he removed her sandals, his touch gentle, reassuring. She reclined at his urging and sighed when he spread her thighs.

As aroused as she was, it took only a few brief strokes to bring her to climax. Heat arced from his fingers to her spine as she screamed in satisfaction. Her fists knotted in the sheets as she felt the bed dip when he climbed in beside her. She kept her eyes closed as he slid his arm around her. Suddenly exhausted, she curled into his side.

"Rest, we'll talk in the morning." She felt him kiss her on the forehead and let herself slide into sleep, exhausted both physically and mentally.

Chapter 5

If it were possible, Kay was even more beautiful in the morning light.

With her face freshly scrubbed, she sat on the front steps of the cabin, drenched in sunlight. The golden rays of midmorning had turned her hair to silver and warmed her pale cheeks. Her eyes were closed and her chin was tilted up to receive the warm caress. On her lips was a dreamy smile.

David stood at the end of the porch holding two cups of coffee. He needed to capture this exquisite image in watercolors...no, they weren't strong enough for this image. Oils on an oversized canvas with thick, bold strokes might do her justice.

He shook his head. He worried about giving himself away by just talking to her. There was no way he could ask to paint her. As knowledgeable as she was about art, she'd recognize a Hunter original in four brushstrokes or less.

He cast a glance in the direction of the attic. There was no way he could let her wander into his temporary studio, either. The jig would be up in seconds if she entered the room. A jolt of panic struck his stomach. He wasn't ready to give her up, not yet.

"Is that for me?"

Her husky voice intruded upon his thoughts. Her beautiful gaze met his before it slid away. Something was wrong. Was she disturbed about last night?

He pasted a friendly smile on his face as he walked to her. "*Oui*, fresh chicory coffee. One cup will keep you up and going for the rest of the day." He dropped onto the top step beside her, then handed her one of the mugs.

She smiled her thanks and took a sip of the steaming black liquid. She gave an approving nod. "Just the right amount of sugar."

"So you don't like sweet tea, but you like your coffee sweet?" he teased.

She smiled and a soft blush colored her cheeks. "Yeah, well..." She shrugged. "How did you guess?"

"I didn't. This cup doesn't have any sugar." She laughed and he leaned closer. "I see you're wearing one of my T-shirts."

She nodded. "I hope you don't mind—"

"I don't. It looks better on you than it does on me." Her full breasts were neatly outlined under the thin, white cotton and he enjoyed the view.

"I didn't feel right putting my dress on again..."

There was definitely something wrong here. She was stiff and almost formal, not as relaxed as a woman should be after spending the night in the arms of her lover.

"What's on your mind, Kay?" He put his mug on the step beside him and propped his arms across his knees. "Talk to me."

She sighed. Her gaze was glued to the gravel path that led to the dock. Judging from the rising color in her cheeks, she was embarrassed to speak her mind.

"Is it about last night?" He leaned ever so slightly until his shoulder touched hers.

She ducked her head and nodded.

At last...

"It's alright, Kay. There's nothing to be embarrassed about."

"But..." Her flushed face came up. "I was so aroused when you spanked me."

"Some people are...the most responsive ones, at least." He draped an arm around her shoulder and urged her closer, pleased when she came without a murmur. "Do you know what the largest human organ is?"

Her gaze shot to his crotch and he laughed. "While I'm flattered, no, not quite. Skin is the largest human organ there is." He picked up her hand and opened it palm up. "It's also the most sensitive." He ran his finger over the thin lines that crisscrossed her palm. "It's possible to achieve orgasm without ever touching your sweet pussy. I've seen a woman come from just sucking her nipples. I've achieved orgasm from Tantric breathing alone, and you've seen that you can very easily achieve release from spanking." He kissed her palm and felt her accelerated heartbeat against his thumb. "All you have to do is let go."

"I just felt so out of control and ashamed to be so."

"In reality, the exact opposite is the truth." David smiled. "What most people don't realize is that, in a dominant-submissive relationship, the sub is the one who's really in complete control."

She tilted her head. "How so?"

"You call all the shots. If I go too far or you feel uncomfortable, you just have to say stop and it stops."

"You mean, if I'd said stop last night, you'd have stopped spanking me?" She bit her lip.

He nodded. "Do you wish you had?" He continued stroking her hand as she contemplated her answer. Her expression was distant, reliving the events of last night, no doubt.

"I wouldn't have told you to stop," she said. "I think I was just shocked to realize what my body was capable of. My rational mind was telling me this was wrong while my body was telling me it was right, completely right. I think I got scared and confused."

"We should've had this talk last night, but I was too carried away by you." He brushed her hair away from the side of her face and tucked it behind her ear. "You intoxicated me and I had to have you again."

"But you didn't." She gave him a shy smile. "Instead, you took care of me last night."

He shrugged. "True—"

"I think we should rectify this situation, don't you?"

David could scarcely breathe when she put her hand on his thigh, then pushed to her feet. Her shapely legs were bare as his T-shirt only came to mid-thigh. With the sun behind her, outlining her body beneath the shirt, she looked like a teenaged boy's favorite wet dream. His cock hardened in response.

"Come." She held out her hand.

He took it and rose, thinking she meant for him to follow her into the house. Instead, she guided him onto the porch until the handrail was at his back. She released his hand to unzip the fly of his jeans. He leaned against the rail just as she dropped to her knees before him. She pulled her T-shirt off and cast it aside before she pulled down his jeans. Unhampered by shorts, his cock sprang free. She made a sound of delight before she wrapped her fingers around his long, thick cock.

He groaned and his knees weakened at the first contact of her wet tongue across his head. He clutched the railing with both hands, then eased back enough to ensure he wouldn't fall off. His stomach muscles clenched when she cupped his balls. They tightened as she masturbated him with her hand while her hot tongue licked his balls.

"Damn," he muttered. Heat like none other moved through him. His breathing grew labored as he enjoyed the way she was sucking and licking his balls as her hand moved steadily over his cock.

She stopped and took his broad head into her mouth. Taking him deep, she sucked him into a pit of heated wet flesh and mind-blowing sensation. Again and again, she swallowed him, her pretty blonde head bobbing over his cock. Never had he seen anything as erotic as his cock sliding between her pink lips.

He wound his fingers though her fine hair, showing her the rhythm he enjoyed. "More," he hissed. "Faster."

She adjusted her pace without a break. She sucked on his cock like there was nothing beyond her world but this moment and him. Her fingers tightened around his base and he thrust his hips against her mouth, on the edge of losing complete control.

"Kay," he hissed. "*Mon ange —*"

She understood and increased her pace while she cupped his balls with her free hand. When she gave them a gentle jiggling squeeze, he knew he was lost. With an unrestrained roar, he came in her mouth. His hips jerked as his body released cum that had been building since last night. His knees folded and he'd have fallen if it weren't for the sturdy oak railing beneath his buttocks.

His chin fell forward and his breath raged in his lungs. His body felt numb, yet his mind was more alive and aware than ever. It felt like a cross between running a marathon and finishing a painting he'd slaved over for months.

He could feel her damp tongue as she licked him clean. She released him and he forced his eyes open. Kay stood before him. She slid her arms around his waist, her nude breasts warm against his chest and her nipples hard and pert.

Aroused, was she?

He folded his arms around her, tugging her closer, unwilling to move just yet. He braced his chin on her shoulder, allowing his gaze to travel over the curve of her back until her tattoo caught his eye.

The handcuffs were purple.

David smiled. It would seem his favorite fantasy would come true after all.

Chapter 6

For Kay, the rest of the day passed in a pleasant blur of sights and sensations. After the delicious blowjob on the porch, they'd showered and dressed. Piling into a battered pickup truck that was parked behind the cabin, they'd driven to New Orleans, a town she'd never visited before. They'd shared a massive luncheon at a popular restaurant in Jackson Square, then walked around to take in some of the touristy sights.

As night fell, Kay found herself in a bondage boutique on Bourbon Street. As Hunter had walked through the store, she'd clutched at his hand like a terrified child. Staring wide-eyed at the variety of clothing, toys and other apparatus that she couldn't imagine buying, let alone using, she'd followed, afraid to let him out of her sight.

In the end, he'd bought only one thing, a narrow band of black leather with a gold buckle like that of a dog collar. After they'd left the store, they'd stood on a narrow sidewalk on Bourbon Street and Hunter had put it on her. She'd seen the look of arousal in his eyes as he hooked the clasp. It excited him as much as it did her.

Kay rubbed her finger over the soft leather that encircled her throat. Beneath her cheek, Hunter's arm flexed as they turned the corner onto the rutted road that lead to Alligator Joe's. She'd learned that morning when they'd picked up her luggage that his cabin was just down the road from the bar, though the trip through the bayou had made it seem much farther.

She frowned. They'd had a good day together, though Hunter had remained stubbornly quiet about himself, the familiar chattiness from his emails completely absent. All day he'd stuck almost doggedly to questions about her life in Atlanta, reluctant to talk about himself at all.

To her surprise, she'd found he possessed a varied knowledge of art. Even though he'd known she worked for an art gallery, he'd never talked about his interest in art other than mentioning he had a cousin who was an artist. She thought that was rather odd.

While in New Orleans, they'd stopped at several small galleries in the center of the Quarter—at her urging, of course. It was a passion with her. When she traveled, she always made it a point to visit local galleries. The best way to keep her professional edge over the competition was to see what they were doing firsthand.

At one gallery, when she'd slipped off to the bathroom, he'd struck up a conversation about art with one of the local artists who was having a showing. They'd been deep in discussion about the merits of various types of paint—until she'd returned, that is. When she'd slid her arm around his waist, Hunter had clammed up and seemed almost embarrassed. Within moments, he'd hustled her out of the gallery.

Maybe her Cajun lover was shy about revealing his more cultured side?

She smiled. When she'd come to Bayou Blue, it was with the hopes of meeting Hunter and exploring the idea of a further relationship with him. She hadn't been prepared for this feeling of being swept away with the tide that was his personality. It was both frightening and exhilarating at the same time.

Right now, she was afraid she could be in way over her head. After this morning's talk, she'd felt comfortable again with him, like they'd reached a new level in their relationship. There was more depth, more feeling, a greater intimacy. Yes, they'd chatted online a great deal about their lives and their fantasies, both sexual and personal, but this was different. This was a feeling of familiarity that she hadn't expected.

While she was pretty sure he'd never come into her gallery, there was something about his face, his profile that was so familiar yet so out of reach...

The truck hit a bump as they turned into the dilapidated drive leading to the cabin.

"Almost there," he said.

She looked up and caught the quick flash of his smile. A rush of heat moved through her at the thought of the pleasures to come once they reached his home.

The headlights swept over the back of the cabin as he pulled to a stop near the rear steps. He turned off the ignition and set the parking break.

"Are you still full from dinner?" he asked.

Kay sat up and ran her hands over her rumpled hair. They'd dined at a seafood restaurant where they'd stuffed themselves silly on steak and seafood. Their dessert was in a carton sitting on the seat next to her.

She nodded.

"Good."

He threw open the door and climbed out. Before Kay could react, he hauled her out behind him. She was forced to make a wild grab for the container of cheesecake or it would have been abandoned.

She laughed as he tossed her over his shoulder and carried her caveman-style around the house to the front door. As he mounted the steps, his hand slid under her dress to give her buttocks a familiar caress.

Hunter opened the door and strode in. This time, when he touched the light switch, the lights came on. He strode to the bed and dumped her on top. She laughed until she caught the heated look in his eyes. Then her throat tightened as her abdomen grew liquid, warm.

"Do you want a few minutes to prepare yourself for me?" he asked.

Mute, she nodded, then scrambled off the bed. She shoved the box of desserts at him when she passed, then made her escape into the bathroom.

Her hands were trembling as she turned on the light. In the mirror, her face looked unnaturally flushed, her eyes large and luminous. Her gaze honed in on the black collar.

Tonight, Hunter wanted her at his command.

She wanted him any way she could get him.

Now.

Quickly, she stripped off her clothes and grabbed a washcloth to clean away the sweat from the day. Glad to have her makeup bag, she applied a tiny amount of fragrance to her wrists and the back of her knees. After a quick brush of her hair and a light application of lip-gloss, she inspected herself in the full-length mirror behind the door.

Dressed only in the black leather collar, she looked sexy, wanton. With her long, pale hair free, she resembled a submissive Lady Godiva. She grinned at the thought and turned the door handle.

Ready or not, here I come...

Hunter stood by the bed, his face impassive, though his eyes were hot and alive as they swept her nude form. He licked his lips and had to clear his throat before he could speak. "Come here."

Kay came forward, her shoulders back and her breasts jutting proudly, her nipples hard and begging for his touch. He slid his hand behind her neck and pulled her into a kiss so scorching her knees wobbled. She leaned into him, her palms against his chest as their mouths melded. It was the tiny snick of metal against metal that broke the spell he'd woven around her.

She moved back, her eyes searching when she realized she couldn't go very far. She reached up to her collar and her fingers encountered a metal chain. Her eyes widened when she saw he'd attached a chain to her collar. Her gaze followed the chain until she saw it was attached to one of the bedposts. He'd bound her to the bed.

"Your place is here," he said. He ran a possessive hand down her shoulder and arm. "This is your domain. You're mine to possess, to command. Do you accept your enslavement to me?"

Kay gulped as liquid heat rushed through her pussy. She could feel herself growing wet, swelling, preparing for this man's possession. Her breasts ached and she couldn't get enough air into her lungs. Her head felt light while her feet were firmly planted in the soft cotton rug.

She licked her lips. "Yes." Her voice was wobbly and she cleared her throat. "Yes, I accept my enslavement to you, Hunter."

A look of triumph flashed across his face and he quickly masked it. He gestured for her to climb onto the bed and, as she did so, she noticed the silk scarves he'd attached to the head and footboard.

She bit her lip against the rush of heat that assailed her. With shaky limbs, she stretched out, the sheets cool against her sensitive skin.

"With women, sensuality is all about seduction of the mind." He kissed the inside of her wrist before binding her with the scarf. "In order to seduce a woman, a man has to know how to seduce her mind first." He brushed his fingers over her temple. "Her body will follow." He tweaked her nipple, then bound her right ankle with another scarf.

"How about a man? How does a woman seduce a man?" She tried to press her thighs together as he took her other ankle.

"What's that old joke?" With a gentle tug, he spread her legs and secured her other ankle. "Show up naked with beer?"

Kay couldn't help but laugh. In her limited experience, most men she'd known were pretty easy to entice into bed.

"I see you've heard that one before." He kissed her wrist before securing the final tie. "We aren't exactly rocket scientists when it comes to sex. Almost anything will turn us on, even the day-to-day stuff that most women would never think about."

Kay tested the ties by tugging on them. She was securely bound, nude before this man and completely at his mercy. She closed her eyes and shivered as wave after wave of arousal washed through her. Had she ever been this turned on in her life? She opened her eyes in time to see him climb nude onto the bed.

"Do you know what turns me on more than any other sight in the world?" he asked.

Her tongue felt thick and disconnected from her body. She shook her head.

"You, like this." He touched her nipple, a faint caress that earned a sound of protest when he moved away. "You're the embodiment of every submissive fantasy I've ever had." He touched the thin collar and the chain that bound her to the bed. "You're so beautiful, I almost forget to breathe."

He lowered his face to her breast and suckled her nipples, first one, then the other. She moaned, her eyes drifting shut as she lost herself to his touch. Her pleasure leapt to the forefront as she pulled against the ties that bound her. Never before had it felt like this.

"Oh, Hunter," she breathed. She wanted him to touch her, harder. Everywhere. She arched her back, silently begging for more.

He moved between her thighs as he sucked harder on her nipple. She moved restlessly beneath him when he palmed her breasts, teasing her full globes until her nipples were stiff and wet from his mouth.

With his talented tongue, he traced a damp path of fire over her abdomen, pausing only to lap at her belly button. She moaned as he stroked his fingers over her pussy.

"I can't wait to get inside you," he hissed.

She cried out as his fingers penetrated. Thrashing against her silken bonds, she was both delighted and dismayed to find that they held her almost immobile. Her fists knotted as he began to finger fuck her.

"Your pussy is so tight." His voice was strained, guttural. "I want to sink my cock into you. I want to make you come until thoughts of any other man are obliterated from your memory."

At the first heated lap of his tongue, her hips arched off the bed. She moaned and tried to push against his mouth to increase the pressure, to no avail. Never had she been so aroused and so frustrated at the same time.

"God, you're perfect."

She forced her eyes open. The sight of his dark head moving between her thighs made her groan again.

"I have to have you," he muttered. He rose over her, his cock full, its tip damp with pre-cum. She sucked in a harsh breath as he sank the head of his cock into her aching pussy. "I won't last very long," he said. "You're too tight, too sweet." His eyes were closed, his expression strained as he sank into her, inch by inch.

She moaned when he buried himself to the hilt. She felt full, stretched in a way she'd never been before. He pulled out and entered her again with a slow thrust. Her head fell back and she groaned. As he moved forward, the wet sucking of her flesh around his cock aroused her more than ever.

"Hunter," she moaned. "This feels too good."

"How can it be too good?" He lowered his head and sucked on her nipples, first one then the other, as his hips continued their assault.

"I don't—" Unable to express herself in words, she gave a long, low moan as his cock hit her sweet spot. Dark spots danced before her eyes and she couldn't be sure she wouldn't pass out before she came.

He picked up the pace, thrusting in and out in deep, even strokes. His arms braced his upper body over hers. He slid his hands beneath her shoulders, taking a firmer grip on her body.

"You have a perfect pussy, Kay. So hot and we fit so well—" He gritted his teeth, and perspiration dotted his forehead as he increased the pace.

Kay was beyond words. She concentrated on the sensations of the man inside her as each stroke increased her desperate need for release. There was nothing more to say than, "Fuck me harder."

Her words broke his concentration. His dark eyes opened and speared her. Their lips met in a brief heated kiss.

"Is this what you want?" He sat up and released her ankles from their bonds. Guiding her legs around his waist, he adjusted his angle and plunged into her with a long, smooth thrust. She groaned as he hammered into her, back and forth in fast, deep movements, each one stroking her clit at just the right angle.

His expression was taut, his jaw hard as he fucked her pussy as if he meant to stay there forever. The erotic sound of flesh slapping flesh sounded throughout the cabin. Their moans mingled as she urged him on with her hips.

"What a beautiful sight," he panted.

Kay looked up to his gaze fastened on her pussy. She raised her head to see his thick cock fucking her. The differences in their skin color were erotic as his body continued its relentless assault upon her.

She groaned and closed her eyes, the tingling in her abdomen telling her that release was near. Every muscle in her body tensed, preparing to throw her over the edge.

"Come for me, baby. I want to watch you." He moved over her, grinding his pelvis against her clit as he fucked harder, faster. "You're mine, Kay. I'll never give you up."

She groaned and tossed her head back and forth, unable to do anything but feel him inside her, possessing her, giving her pleasure.

Her back arched hard, and she screamed his name as her orgasm broke. Her body had become a vessel for him to fill, to pleasure. Lightning streaks of release raced through her and she spasmed around him. His movements slowed and she sagged against the bed.

With his upper body propped on his arms, he cuddled her close as he plunged into her again and again, his pace never slowing. Within seconds, release burned bright and she came again. Over her, she could feel him tense as he sank into her, her orgasming pussy milking his cock for all she was worth. He came with a shout and his thrusts were no longer controlled, but jerky and out of control.

"*Mon Dieu*," he gasped, as his head fell to the pillow next to hers.

Neither moved. They simply lay together, their bodies in full contact and his cock still buried in her pussy. After a few moments, he reached up to release her arms from their bonds.

Free at last, they rolled to the side and Hunter massaged her arms until she was completely limp from head to toe.

"That was amazing." She settled her head against his shoulder.

"Mmm," he mumbled. His big hand settled on her hip and he guided her leg over his pelvis. "More than amazing..." His voice slurred then trailed off. A few seconds later, she heard him snore.

Kay smiled and snuggled against him, her body completely relaxed, sated for now. But in a few hours, who knew what they might get into?

Chapter 7

Early Sunday morning, Kay slipped from their bed. Hunter was facedown and still sound asleep. His arm was outstretched as if silently asking her not to leave. He was an amazing lover, everything a woman could ask for and more. She unhooked the slim chain from her collar and left it lying beside him.

After picking up his T-shirt from the floor, she held it up to her face, inhaling his familiar scent. Pulling it on over her head, she padded to the sink for a glass of water. She drained a large glass, then refilled it again and wandered to the bookshelves.

Packed with books, some of the titles surprised her. Many were on botany and environmental issues that were particular to the bayou, but it was the vast range of books about art that surprised her most. Expensive, oversized volumes that contained the work of the masters were piled on the bottom shelf.

She dropped into a crouch and selected the top one, a volume of works by Monet, and opened the cover. Female writing was scrawled across the inside flyleaf and she frowned as she read it.

To David, a man who is a work of art himself.

Love, Cherish

Who was David?

She skimmed through the pages, the glossy paintings shown in rich, full color and she smiled with pleasure. She'd always loved Monet —

The book flipped shut to the back flyleaf. A small white envelope fell onto the floor. She picked it up and tucked it back, but not before she saw the name typed on the front.

David Hunter

She glanced at the address and saw that it was in Massachusetts. How could a letter written to someone in Boston end up down here in Hunter's cabin in Louisiana?

Hunter? Were they somehow related?

Disturbed, she slid the book shut. Before she could think twice, she reached for the next, a thick volume on Rembrandt. She cast a hasty glance toward the man in bed, but he slept undisturbed behind the sheer curtain. Feeling oddly guilty, she opened the cover and saw it was blank.

Even as she chided herself for being suspicious, she pulled out the next title and opened it. David Hunter's name was printed on the bookplate.

It didn't make any sense. Why would Remy DeLaughter have books with the name David Hunter in them? Did he buy them at an auction? Maybe he got them at a used bookstore?

That had to be it. Shaking her head over being so silly, she tucked the volumes back onto the shelf and rose. The shelves above weren't quite as loaded because the books were interspersed with framed photos. She moved closer to check them out.

One photo contained two young boys, each with fishing poles, dirty feet and big smiles. She couldn't see anything of Hunter in that photo. Could they be nephews? The next one was of two laughing young men, one with thick black hair, the other with brown. Now this was more like how she'd expected Remy to look. The dark-haired man sat on the tail of a shiny pickup truck. Clad in a rumpled plaid shirt and worn jeans and boots, his grimy baseball cap covered most of his face but she could see it wasn't Hunter, the jaw line was all wrong.

But the man next to him was a distinct possibility. Dressed in cleaner jeans and a black T-shirt, this man's dark brown hair was windswept. While he strongly resembled Hunter, this man was thinner and there was something different about his eyes. Maybe it was an old photo? She stared hard at the picture. Something niggled at her, there was something oddly familiar about him...

The next one was definitely Hunter and the laughing black-haired man. Hunter sat on the steps of this cabin beside the other. Both were shirtless, wearing only jeans and wide grins.

She tilted her head to the side as she stared at Hunter's clean-shaven face. His hair was pulled back into a tidy ponytail and he looked vastly different from the man asleep in the bed. Handsome, yes, but there was something oddly familiar about the way he'd cocked his head. It reminded her of someone, but whom?

She stared at the photo a few more minutes, but no answers came. It was possible she'd seen him somewhere before, if he'd ever been to Atlanta, that was. But he'd told her in an email that he'd never been to Georgia, so it wasn't possible she'd ever seen him before.

She put the photograph down to look for her purse. Her lips felt chapped and she was in dire need of some moisturizer.

A quick search of the cabin didn't turn up her purse. She frowned, then remembered it was probably still in the truck. She smiled as she remembered their quick exit from the vehicle. Lust made Hunter move fast, that was for sure.

She crept to the back door and slipped on her sandals. Still sound asleep, Hunter lay in the same position she'd left him. After she retrieved her purse, she'd climb back into bed with him and wake him up with her mouth on his big, beautiful cock.

Holding her breath as she slid the bolt open, she stepped out into the early morning. The air was thick with recent rain, leaving the ground spongy. The truck wasn't parked by the back door so she headed for the barn. The door stood half open and she could see the bumper. She slipped into the gloomy building.

After allowing a few moments for her eyes to adjust, she approached the vehicle. Opening the door, she rooted around until she found her purse, which had slid under the seat. Retrieving it, she found the strap was caught on something.

Swearing under her breath, she reached in and pulled out a large, flat wooden box. It was obviously old and much used. The scarred wood attested to its use and near the clasp there were numerous paint smears. It wasn't very heavy and as she pulled her purse free, something inside rattled. She bit her lip, as she knew she shouldn't open it, but she badly wanted to. Opening this box would mean she'd officially crossed the line from hunting for her belongings into the realm of snooping.

Not cool.

Even as she had the thought, her fingers flipped the catch on the box and she opened it. Her eyes widened when she realized what she held in her hands.

It was an artist's box filled with battered tubes of watercolors, paintbrushes and rags. Was Hunter a painter? Was that what this was all about?

Tucked into the lid was a watercolor pad. She set the box on the seat and removed the notebook. She flicked it open and her breath caught as she saw what it contained.

Her breathing increased as she flipped through the pages. The colors and designs of the wildlife he'd captured in the bayou were exquisite. Each brush stroke was delicate, capturing the flora and fauna in rich color and texture. One was a landscape, the view from the front porch of the cabin as the sun awakened the bayou with its first rays of life.

This wasn't the work of a beginner; it was the work of a master. Only an accomplished painter could produce work of this magnitude.

A master such as David Hunter.

Her hands shook and she forced herself to flip back through the pages and scrutinize each piece. It certainly looked like it could be Hunter's work. The lines were clean and fresh, the touch of the watercolors light and delicate — the style characteristic of that which he was known for. She should know as she'd spent several months researching his work before the Reicht Gallery had sought to contract him for a show.

But where had this box come from?

She slammed the book shut and tucked it back into the box with great haste. If these were the works of David Hunter, that one little pad could be worth millions of dollars.

Millions.

Where would Hunter have come up with these? Were they related to the books inside?

With her heart thudding in her chest, she grabbed her purse and slammed the door of the truck. Her mind was whirling so fast that she almost failed to see the other car parked a few feet beyond the truck. Her steps slowed and she stared in horror at a forest green Jaguar.

She walked around the front of the gleaming car. There was no way Remy could afford this car and the Massachusetts license plate seemed to mock her with letters that spelled PAINTR.

A cry caught in her throat. Her Hunter could not be David Hunter, the painter, he just couldn't. The fates couldn't be that cruel to her.

Kay swung around and darted out the door. She had to see that photo again. It would prove once and for all that her Hunter wasn't *the* David Hunter. A man she'd met about six months ago at her gallery in Atlanta.

If it were true, her professional career would be over...

* * * * *

David woke slowly. He'd never been one to leap out of bed and greet the day with a smile. He was more likely to laze in bed a few minutes before opening his eyes. Of course, it was much more enjoyable when there was a warm, willing female in the bed with him...

Kay.

The thought of her beside him brought a smile to his mouth. With his eyes still closed, he reached for the other side of the bed.

It was empty.

Reluctantly, he forced his eyes open. The front door stood open and only the screen was closed. Already the relentless humidity was invading his sanctuary. Why would she have left the door open with the air conditioning on? Maybe she was outside on the porch? Remembering what pleasurable events had taken place on the porch just yesterday had him rolling out of bed.

He strolled into the bathroom and took care of his most urgent needs before he splashed cool water on his face. He grabbed a pair of old running shorts, then exited the bathroom. Maybe, after a bout of hot sex, he and Kay could drive along the coast for seafood and cold beer…

He came to a stop next to the kitchen table. His eyes widened when he saw the smears of red paint.

YOU LIED TO ME…

The art box that had been stashed in his truck sat on the table, the top open and the watercolor tablet open to the landscape he'd done of the view from the porch. A tube of red paint lay on the table near the words and he saw it had been squeezed dry. The brush she'd used lay nearby, its tip still damp with paint.

His heart aching, he picked up the brush and ran the tip over his palm leaving a trail of red, not unlike blood. She'd found him out.

David's eyes closed and he crushed the brush tip in his hand.

He'd brought Kay to his bed with a lie and had spent a few deliriously happy hours with her. Now he'd just lost her with the same lie.

Damn him for his deception.

Chapter 8

Six months later

Reicht Gallery

Atlanta, GA

"This is a disaster. These paintings are all wrong."

Kay paused, the phone halfway to her ear. What was Cissy going on about now? She set the phone down in the cradle. It was late Saturday morning and all her assistant had to do was inventory and sign for the delivery of David Hunter's art for his showing two weeks from today.

Her stomach quivered at the thought of Hunter. No, not Hunter, David. She'd shamelessly pawned any of the work for the Hunter showing to Cissy. Yes, it was completely unprofessional, but she couldn't bring herself to think of his name, let alone handle his work. It would be one of the most prestigious events of the year for the Reicht, but she didn't care. He'd lied to her, used her and she wanted nothing to do with him.

She rose from behind her desk and walked out into the receiving area off the main showroom. The crates had arrived early that morning and Cissy and the two men who assisted with setting up had already unpacked them.

Her assistant stood in the midst of the paintings, packing material and cases, her clipboard clutched to her skinny chest. Kay wondered if she realized she had an ink pen behind each ear.

"What's the matter?" she asked.

"These aren't the right paintings." The young woman spun around and shoved her clipboard at Kay. "Where's Dark Symphony? Where's Nightingale? Rapture? These aren't the ones we'd commissioned for the showing."

Kay frowned and took the board. On the left was the list of paintings they were expecting and on the right were the ones they'd received. A quick scan revealed none of the titles matched.

"I don't understand how this could've happened," Cissy wailed. "I just spoke to the shipping company. They said Mr. Hunter had everything packed before they'd arrived. It was most peculiar. I mean, they do the invoicing, packing and shipping. Why would he do this to us?"

"Well, let's take a look at these. Maybe we can do something—" Kay's words caught in her throat when she saw the first canvas.

He'd painted her.

Even though her face wasn't visible, it was definitely her body. He'd painted her lying on the bed, her body mostly covered by the white sheet, but her long blonde hair was evident. One breast was bared, the pert, pink nipple showing through the soft strands.

Behind her, she was aware of Cissy still screeching about programs and the costs of reprinting, but she didn't pay her any mind. Kay shoved the clipboard at her and told her to take a long break. As if in a daze, she moved to the next canvas.

This one was also of her, standing nude in the bathroom. She stood before the sink, her body leaning forward as she applied lip-gloss. The handcuff tattoo on her hip burned beneath her clothing when she saw that he'd left nothing out.

In the next, she was nude again, sitting in a demure fashion with her legs tucked underneath her body. Her long hair hid her face, but the black collar and gold chain were evident.

Her pussy warmed at the memory of his domination. She'd left the collar behind when she'd exited the cabin that morning. Many times afterward, she'd kicked herself for leaving it behind and wondering if another woman had worn it yet. Not that it should matter, but it did.

Next was a small watercolor. In this one, she was clothed in his T-shirt and sitting on the steps of the cabin. Her face was tilted to the rising sun and her eyes were closed, her features gently blurred.

Tears stung her eyes.

Damn him for making her remember again...

Frantically, she moved through the rest of the paintings. They were all of her and their few short days alone, and each one depicted her in various stages of undress. There was even one of them in the gazebo, their features hidden by tangled honeysuckle. It was painted from the front and over her shoulder; she could see David's shadowy form.

Warmth flooded her pussy at that particularly graphic painting. In it, her back was arched, her mouth open, her orgasm caught on the large canvas in vibrant oils. Just looking at it brought those times back with painful intimacy.

All of the paintings were her, every last one.

He must have spent every waking hour painting. Most artists couldn't produce this much work in a year, let alone six months. It was almost as if he'd been obsessed with capturing her image.

She turned and her foot hit one of the canvases. She caught it and prevented it from falling, only to reveal a smaller canvas behind it. With her heart in her throat, she stowed the larger canvas and picked up the smaller one. This painting wasn't of her; instead, it was David.

Nude, his big muscular body was painted in the submissive position with his face down and he wore her leather collar. The gold chain hung from the collar and the end sat on the floor near his feet, unattached to anything. In that moment, she knew he felt as adrift as she, that's what this painting signified to her. He wanted her to pick up the chain, to claim him as he had claimed her.

Her gaze blurred as the tears came. There was love in every stroke of each painting. Love and humility. Her knees wobbled and she collapsed to the floor hard, the evidence of his love for her surrounding her like a thick quilt. This was how he saw her. These images, all of them, were how he remembered her and their time together.

Yes, he'd lied and behaved as badly as a man could, but he was repentant. He'd probably half-killed himself over these paintings to prove his love for her.

Love that she returned.

She shook her head, calling herself every kind of fool in the book. She should've confronted him that morning but she'd been so angry and her only thought had been to escape him.

She'd hoped to have a wildly passionate affair with someone far removed from her world, someone with whom it was safe to explore the darker side of her sensuality. Instead she'd indulged in an intense affair with someone who moved in the art circles she could never aspire to reach.

After she'd returned to Atlanta, she'd lived in fear that he'd have told someone. She'd kept waiting for the knowing glances and leers, but none of that had happened. Life had carried on as before. With one slip of his tongue, he could've destroyed her career. Instead, he'd spent his time painting her over and over again.

Kay stumbled to her feet. She needed to see him, talk to him—

She came to a halt when a large, dark figure filled the doorway.

* * * * *

David stared at the woman he loved, his gaze drinking in her image as if to memorize a face he knew as well as his own. She stood a few feet away, her cheeks wet with tears and a shocked expression. Dressed completely in black, with her magnificent blonde hair locked into a militant twist, she looked more beautiful than he could have imagined.

"Hello." Her voice was soft, unsure.

"Hello, Kay. My name is David Hunter, and I'm the painter who's obsessed with you." He moved, desperate to touch her again. When she retreated, he stopped, not wanting her to move any further.

She looked confused. "What are you doing here?"

"I came for you, if you'll have me." He nodded at the paintings, the work he'd completed in a little less than six months. Never before had he churned out so much work in so little time. It was as if he'd been a man possessed with capturing her essence in oils, watercolors, whatever medium he'd found at hand. He'd barely eaten or slept and now, standing before her, he wasn't sure he'd done her justice in any of them. She was even more beautiful than he'd remembered.

"Why?" she asked.

"Because I love you."

Her expression turned wary. "Just because we're good in bed—"

He shook his head. "You make me laugh. You like beer as much as I do. You aren't afraid to give as good as you get. You're my perfect match and I can't imagine living the rest of my life without you."

As he spoke, he noticed that her eyes were welling up again. She gave a sniff and wrapped her arms around her waist. "You lied to me."

"I did. I panicked." He ran a hand through his unkempt hair. "When I met you last year, I'd wanted to ask you out then, but there wasn't time. I had to return to Boston and your life was here. But I never forgot you, not for a day. And when I saw you at Remy's party, I knew I had to do whatever I could to make love to you. I had to know if you were the woman I'd built you up to be in my mind."

"And was I?" Her voice was unsure.

"My fantasies didn't even come close to the reality," he replied. "You are perfection."

Her face crumpled and he stepped forward. The moment he pulled her into his arms and she leaned into him, he knew it was going to be all right.

"I was so mad at you." She cried into the front of his shirt.

"I know you were. If I could go back and change what I did—"

"Shh." She shook her head. "If I'd known who you were, you'd never have stood a chance. I didn't want to get involved with someone from my world here in Atlanta."

He laid his cheek on her head. "So you're saying I did the right thing—"

She gave an unladylike snort and slapped at his chest. "I wouldn't go that far."

He laughed and hugged her tightly, her fragrance surrounded him like a friendly handshake. "Marry me, Kay."

She slid her arms around his waist. "We still have a lot to talk about—"

"Marry me and we can talk for the rest of our lives." He nuzzled her ear.

"Mmm..." She sighed as he nipped her throat. "Don't think you're getting off that easily, buster."

"Just tell me you love me and I'll spend the rest of my life making it up to you."

"I love you." She sighed as he sucked her earlobe.

David felt a surge of triumph at her words. With a growl, he scooped her into his arms and carried her to the door.

"Where are we going?" She wrapped her arms around his neck, her expression bemused.

"To take care of something I should have done a long time ago."

She tangled her fingers in his hair. "And what is that?"

"Seems to me that you removed your collar without my permission." He nuzzled her neck as he carried her into her office. He'd put her collar and chain in his pocket before leaving the hotel, and he meant to see it on her in the next five seconds. "I think some discipline might be in order."

Kay tipped her head back and gave a wild shout of laughter as he kicked the door shut behind them.

About the author:

Dominique Adair is the pen name of award-winning novelist, J.C. Wilder. She lives just outside of Columbus, Ohio, where she skulks around town plotting her next book and contemplating where to hide the bodies (from her books of course—everyone knows that you can't *really* hide a body as they always pop up at the worst times).

Dominique Adair welcomes mail from readers. You can write to her c/o Ellora's Cave Publishing at P.O. Box 787, Hudson, Ohio 44236-0787.

Also by DOMINIQUE ADAIR:

- Blood Law: Xanthra Chronicles 1
- Last Kiss
- Tied With a Bow – with Jennifer Dunne & Madeline Oh

Why an electronic book?

We live in the Information Age—an exciting time in the history of human civilization in which technology rules supreme and continues to progress in leaps and bounds every minute of every hour of every day. For a multitude of reasons, more and more avid literary fans are opting to purchase e-books instead of paperbacks. The question to those not yet initiated to the world of electronic reading is simply: *why?*

1. *Price.* An electronic title at Ellora's Cave Publishing runs anywhere from 40-75% less than the cover price of the <u>exact same title</u> in paperback format. Why? Cold mathematics. It is less expensive to publish an e-book than it is to publish a paperback, so the savings are passed along to the consumer.

2. *Space.* Running out of room to house your paperback books? That is one worry you will never have with electronic novels. For a low one-time cost, you can purchase a handheld computer designed specifically for e-reading purposes. Many e-readers are larger than the average handheld, giving you plenty of screen room. Better yet, hundreds of titles can be stored within your new library—a single microchip. (Please note that Ellora's Cave does not endorse any specific brands. You can check our website at www.ellorascave.com for customer recommendations we make available to new consumers.)

3. *Mobility.* Because your new library now consists of only a microchip, your entire cache of books can be taken with you wherever you go.

4. *Personal preferences are accounted for.* Are the words you are currently reading too small? Too large? Too...ANNOYING? Paperback books cannot be modified according to personal preferences, but e-books can.

5. *Innovation.* The way you read a book is not the only advancement the Information Age has gifted the literary community with. There is also the factor of what you can read. Ellora's Cave Publishing will be introducing a new line of interactive titles that are available in e-book format only.

6. *Instant gratification.* Is it the middle of the night and all the bookstores are closed? Are you tired of waiting days—sometimes weeks—for online and offline bookstores to ship the novels you bought? Ellora's Cave Publishing sells instantaneous downloads 24 hours a day, 7 days a week, 365 days a year. Our e-book delivery system is 100% automated, meaning your order is filled as soon as you pay for it.

Those are a few of the top reasons why electronic novels are displacing paperbacks for many an avid reader. As always, Ellora's Cave Publishing welcomes your questions and comments. We invite you to email us at service@ellorascave.com or write to us directly at: P.O. Box 787, Hudson, Ohio 44236-0787.

Printed in the United States
25757LVS00002B/55-390

9 781843 606543